Mother

Book One

by Angelina Maffeo
First published September 2018
Second Edition 2020

Cover design by
Angelina Maffeo

Copyright 2018

ISBN 978-1-7327517-3-6

Before you start...

Thank you to all the writers and artists whose music often inspired the writing. I believe you created and performed with the intention of sharing your message, emotions, and talent with the world. If the readers don't know who the music came from, it's damn time they learned. They should stop posting photos of their lunch and acquaint themselves with real music and the warnings and messages you gave us through your music. Mother does work in mysterious ways.

Thank you to the real Shepherdess, Lizzy, who tended to all the beasties so I had the time to write and her endless insight, inspiration and dedication to reading every chapter.

Thank you to the real Violet, for her knowledge on series and fiction. Who told me a coupla times, as only a Virgo can, "Mother I'd tell you if you should stop, trust me. Keep writing!"

Mother was penned to express
my enduring gratitude to
the *Mother Goddess*
for always catching me before
my ass hit the pavement.

For Laurel

Thank you for all the insight from the other side of the veil and your Purple Kamikaze recipe. I miss you every day.

PRELUDE

Mabon Equinox 2018:

**Saturday September 23,
at precisely 2:54 am GMT,**

**4.5 billion emails are sent
containing the following information:**

You either believe and understand the
information within or you don't. Those
that don't will die. Those of you who
still retain the ability for rational
analysis and strategic reasoning, may
find this data useful.

Greed, ambivalence, stupidity, financial
manipulation of the world markets, the
technological crafting of a world wide
cultural of self-absorbed Sheepel, the
More is More mentality, the Hooray for me
and fuck everyone else mind set, these
put down deep roots in humankind in the
1980's. Like all insidicus viruses they
have replicated exponentially creating a
global pandemic.

For the last two hundred and fifty years,
since the birth of the industrial

revolution, humans have ravaged and polluted the earth's waters, air and land. You have annihilated billions of creatures in your incessant hunger for more, oblivious or indifferent to each creature's role in the delicate balance of this planet. You have compromised the infrastructure of the earth's crust with your unrelenting consumption of oil, natural gas and the most precious of gifts... water. Blinded by your ego and greed YOU have forgotten the simple truth: the Earth is a living breathing entity. The Ancients revered her as Mother Earth.

The SHTF is not going to happen... the Shit has already hit the fan. The earth's atmosphere is a FINITE space. The human race has put six pounds of shit in a one pound bag and the seams have begun to split. The glaciers like dominoes have already begun to tumble. There is nothing you can do but to stand skyclad and ride out the Mother of all storms.

Millions upon millions of humans will soon die. If you wish to live, put your hand back in your pocket. Stop expecting to be saved or rescued. You must save Her to save yourselves. The power brokers care only for themselves. Within 18 months the Global Machine will begin to fail. In the ensuing chaos of global wide panic, famine, increasing tectonic shifts, volcanic eruptions and yes, 100,000 year floods, the sheepel, consumed by their fear, will become like rabid dogs. These natural catastrophic events will increase in frequency, size and duration in the coming weeks. Mother Earth is fighting for her life. Know that She is a formidable enemy.

Read the signs. Plant your feet firmly on the earth. Assess what skills you don't have and learn them...NOW.

This will be the only transmission of this data. Use your internet while you still have it. If you are meant to survive, you will understand all that has and hasn't been said here.

Mother

chapter 1
BAD MOON A-RISIN'

"The winds of change are coming
You'll see the end come all too soon
Run the waters overflowing"

10:54 pm EDT, September 22,
Culpeper, Virginia

The ring of a cell phone echoed off the oak paneled walls of the Culpeper, Virginia mansion. A slightly annoyed male voice asked, "What is it, David?"

The voice of a man accustomed to getting his own way answered. "Sorry to disturb you so late, you need to read the text I just sent you. It's an email that came in ten minutes ago."

Now more curious than annoyed he snapped, "I'll call you back when I've read it."

11:06 pm EDT, September 22,
New York, New York

In Manhattan David's pacing is interrupted by the return call. "Where the hell did this come from and who's seen it?"

"As of yet we don't know who sent it. I have people working on it now. Evidently the whole world has or is or will be seeing it. It's trending on every form of social media. Houston, Washington and California have already contacted me. They have people on it too."

His annoyance with David's answer is more than a little apparent in his tone, "*'Within eighteen months'* is too precise to be a fluke. FIND THE FUCKING LEAK! I need to call D.C and Montana. Let me know when you have anything." The call ends.

David's irritation at the congressman's tone and his own dark thoughts are interrupted by Ozzie. "Sir, this isn't making any sense. We've tracked it to the Pine Island Glacier in Antarctica. The signal is bouncing off a satellite that shows the source as the glacier but that's utterly impossible. Word is everyone is coming up with a different location. France says it came from Stonehenge. Germany says the French are idiots; it clearly originates from the Sphinx. Russia doesn't want to divulge their information. China is claiming it's from Carrowkeel in Ireland. Ireland says No, it's Easter Island. London says Sedona, Arizona, Japan says Chichen Itza, Mexico. It's impossible to trace."

Ozzie's answer exacerbates David's dark mood. "Ozzie, don't give me impossible! I pay you to do the impossible. Find out who sent this and from where. Now!"

3:35 am GMT, September 23

Servers around the world overload and begin to crash from the unprecedented traffic.

3:54 am GMT, September 23

Globally landlines and cell companies overload. They too begin to crash.

Eastern Seaboard of the United States

The Autumn Equinox heralds the end of the harvest season for farmers in the northern states. The pace of daily life begins to slow. In contrast North Carolina farmers double down. The autumn and winter crops set to ground in the dog days of August are just starting to jump. Peas, sugar snaps, green beans, cabbage and broccoli step up the pace in their race with old Jack. As the summer heat begins to back off, the peppers and eggplants double their production as if to show their gratitude for the milder days and cooler nights. The bees are still gathering nectar to store for the winter. The root crops snuggle deeper into the earth, knowing it will protect them from the icy fingers of November's frost. In a week or two farmers will need to hell the Yukon Gold, Russet and sweet potatoes. Helling potatoes is an old southern term. Freeing the tubers from North Carolina's stubborn red clay often feels like you're digging to Hell.

The manor house on Dancing Goats Farm is a large Italianate Gothic beauty. Constructed in 1888 of hand made bricks, it stands on a bit over a thousand acres. Dancing Goats Farm is a self-sustaining, earth honoring, sanctuary. It's one among the nearly half a billion homesteads large and small that have sprung up in the last two decades. Their inception precipitated by their owners desire for chemical free food, a mandate to end the poisoning of the earth, the goal of a reduced carbon footprint, the need to provide for their family's spiritual well being and the longing to help heal Mother Earth.

5:26 am EDT, September 23,
Dancing Goats Farm
Moon Mountain, North Carolina

In the kitchen of the manor house the owner of Dancing Goats Farm poured boiling water into her French press. While she waits for the coffee to mature, she spoons out breakfast for her thirteen year old long haired red tabby, who is presently lounging on the island counter.

Tony's bright green eyes follow her every move. Satisfied with his portion he rises lazily, stretching as he makes his way to his bowl. The front door, at the far end of the house is open, welcoming the cool early morning breeze. Miss Penelope-Pit-Stop standing on the threshold can be heard impatiently demanding her breakfast. The woman knows there will be no peace unless all the feline tyrants are fed. Out the kitchen through the dining room, down the twenty foot long atrium, under the free flying staircase, into the central hall and out the front door, she finds Penelope dancing in front of her empty dish complaining loudly for the delay. Petite Miss Penelope, self proclaimed Huntress of the farm spends her days killing rodents and chasing squirrels to their death. One of her pre-dawn victims lies flattened in the road just beyond the edge of the path, it's tail fluttering in the breeze. Between bites Penelope glances at the dead squirrel. Another balancing on a branch across the way catches her eye. She offers a piercing yeooow to the squirrel as if to say "let that be a lesson to you" then resumes her breakfast.

On her way back to the kitchen the woman stops to feed Cleopatra, aka Madame Pouffe, who has draped herself elegantly across a stair tread midway up the stairs. Arriving back in the kitchen the woman finds Tony staring at his empty bowl waiting for his 'second breakfast'.

"When did you become a Hobbit cat?"
Ignoring her impertinent question he taps
his bowl with his white mittened paw.

5:32 am EDT, September 23

Felines appeased, mug of coffee in
hand, the woman settles in at her
computer to scan the local and
international news. While deleting the
extraneous crap emails her server
delivered to her inbox she pauses at an
email Sender: Mother, subject: Mother.
The hair on the back of her neck rises.

5:40 am EDT, September 23

Upstairs the woman knocks on a
bedroom door. "Violet, Coffee's on, in
the kitchen in three."

A groggy voice asks, "What the hell
time is it?"

"Almost six. I just got a profoundly
enlightening and disturbing email from
Mother. It's time to kick it into high
gear." Down the hall she knocks on
another door

"Lizzy up baby, Mother says the shit
has hit the fan."

In the front hall the woman pauses
at the yet open front door. The dawn sky
is aglow. Soft golden rays illuminate the
tree tops. The breeze is sweetly scented

from the pots of jasmine on either side of the double doors. She savors the moments beauty and peace a few seconds before closing the door. She heads for the kitchen, a copy of Mother's email clenched in her hand.

**5:46 am EDT, September 23,
Duck Hollow Farm,
Seymore, Connecticut**

Alexandra shoved her pit bull, Dahlia, aside and climbed out of bed. The sounds of Morgana chasing a mouse through the downstairs rooms drifts up the stairs. Alexandra shouts "You know the rule... No puke, poop or frigging dead bodies before I've had my coffee." Through the bathroom window she can hear the ducks and chickens waking. Down stairs as she starts her coffee her phone chimes. It's a text from her Auntie Gianna. "911 Check your email NOW! Sender and subject: Mother. Then call me."

**5:48 am EDT, September 23,
Boston, Massachusetts**

"Sadie wanta grab breakfast?"

"Not today hon, my ass is dragging. Double shifts are getting harder the older I get. A hot shower and eight hours sleep are all I want." Sadie's phone beeps in the bowels of her over stuffed bag. The sound is muffled by her Red Sox hoodie. Fifteen minutes later she stumbles through her front door.

"I am beat!" Sitting on the couch to remove her shoes she leaned back, one shoe off she thinks *I need to rest my eyes just for a minute.* Still snugly wrapped in her bag her phone begins to ring but she is now fast asleep. Her email is one of the 5 million never to be opened.

5:51 am EDT, September 23,
Dancing Goats Farm,
Moon Mountain, North Carolina

"Lizzy, you go to the office and get the texts and emails sent, then start on the calls. The phone tree is in the drawer in the SHTF folder. Have Theo let the Tribe know there is a mandatory meeting in the Hall at 11:00 sharp. Violet I need you to help Simon verify the inventory of the pantries and cellars. See what you can get done before the meeting. I want to be able to send the trucks and the gathering team out by 12:45. If you think you'll need more help grab Amber. Lizzy the only calls I'll take are Alexandra, Nikki, Rob or Sadie. If you start to get over run have Theo get you help to deal with them. I need Theo in his office going over the legal crap. You, he, whichever, can tell people we'll have more for them after the meeting. Hopefully by noon we'll have more information and a plan... yes one with more than one part. Shit, Sean won't be up for three hours but send him a text that say 'There is a pink rhinoceros running down Melrose' then find me when he calls. Questions?"

Only slightly less groggy, supporting her head with both hands, Violet squints at her mother, "Just a request mother... please make more coffee. Lots more coffee."

"Sorry my sweet Violet but you are the one who chose to be born on the equinox. You can take today's timing up with Mother. Speaking of hangovers... make sure we replace the booze from last night's revelries on the inventory shopping list."

Lizzy, less hung over says, "I have a question... why a pink rhinoceros?"

"One night I asked Sean what he was waiting for. '*Do you need a pink rhinoceros running through traffic on the 405 before you get the fuck out of California?*' So yes Lizzy, please word the text just that way."

While the woman starts another pot of coffee her phone rings "Auntie Gianna what the fuck!"

5:59 am EDT, September 23,
North of Cumberland Gap, Kentucky

Fern Slacum padded barefoot across

18

the worn plank floor of her cabin. She
paused to add a few sticks of kindling to
the coals in the cast iron cook stove
then grabbed her shawl from the hook and
stepped out the door. She inhales deeply.
The crisp mountain air fills her lungs as
a flock of wild geese passes overhead.
Their honking echoes through the holler
below. A ghostly mist hangs over the
creek yet untouched by the morning rays.
The mountain's beauty helps to dispel the
uneasy feelings from last night's dream.
She can hear the young'uns rising. She
gathers an arm load of wood and goes
inside. Her son-in-law is sitting at the
table lacing up his boots as her daughter
trims slices from yesterday's baked ham.
Fern dropped the wood in the box next to
the stove and began to break eggs in a
bowl.

Her grandkids, Okey and Betony pound
down the stairs "Mornin mamaw".

Without looking up from her task
Fern says, "Y'all gather the eggs and be
mindful of them dibbies fat Ruby hatched
out yesterday. Gonna be a hard winter.
They be might tasty when the larder gets
low come March."

As she dropped the ham in the
skillet, Rachel frowned at her mother.
"Ma, you sleep okay?"

As she beat the flour into the eggs
Fern said, "The sleepin' was fine it's

the dreaming has me worrisome. I'm feered somethin' powerful bad is on the wind. In my dream I was down at the crick and saw a raven sittin' in that old willow tree. He called to me "Mind your kin, harvest home, fold into the mountain." The sky went dark and rain fell hard an' fast. The crick over ran the banks. Lookin' back as I ran... looked as if all the people of world was washin down the crick. Ravens bein' spirit messengers it's best to listen." She waved her spatula at her son-in-law "Duncan you best drive over an tell Hamish to gather the clan here today." Before he could answer, Betony burst through the door egg basket in hand with Okey in tow. Fern smiled at the child's exuberance. "Y'all sit, the flannel cakes are comin' off the griddle now." Duncan glanced at his wife. The look on Rachel's face said, *She ain't never been wrong*.

12:00 pm GMT, September 23

World governments release statements calling the email a hoax. They advise the public to delete the email. Behind closed doors every country is scrambling to find the culprit and the location.

2:30 pm GMT, September 23,

Of the 4.5 billion emails 2,745,000,000 have been dutifully deleted as instructed by their government. 250 million are still being analyzed, 5

20

million have yet to be opened. 3.5 million have been read and the message understood.

10:45 am EDT, September 23,
Devil's Fork Gap
Smokey Mountains, Tennessee

In a remote mountain compound near Devil's Fork, Frank Lee was listening to the chatter on his HAM radio while checking his ammunition inventory. His wife Pauline was in their basement store room unpacking twenty new cases of canned food. They'd been online last night when the Mother email came in at 11:00 pm. Frank had instantly contacted the other three couples they'd built the compound with. Frank set up a four way call between Dan Hill and his wife Tracy in Chattanooga, Tennessee, Rory Bicks and his girlfriend Cindy Wall in Galax, Virginia, Billy Dalton and his wife Betty Lou in Spartanburg, South Carolina and themselves. Once they were all connected Frank started right in...

"First order of business is I say we jump to Code Orange preppin' status. I mean we have no frigging idea where this is comin' from but the threat is pretty clear. Y'all agree?"

Dan and Tracy agreed. "Yeah we're good with that."

Rory added "I think that's the

21

safest. We can always back it down to yellow when we get more information."

Billy's sure it isn't enough "The safest is to go to Code RED. We just don't know how big this is. Y'all can treat this as orange if y'all want but me an' Betty Lou are stickin' with red. We're gonna pack the truck tonight. In the morning we'll grab the guns, ammo, and BOBs, and head up. See y'all in the mornin Frank."

10:50 am EDT,

Eleven hours later the buzzer sounded in the office indicating the security gate had been opened. Checking the monitor, Frank saw Billy's pickup pulling into the garage. His inventory will have to wait. Frank called Pauline on the intercom, "Billy and Betty Lou are here. Goin' down to help unload."

Pauline brushed a curl from her eye. "Okay just finishin' up. I'll be right there." Four minutes later Pauline entered the garage as Frank and Billy were removing the camouflage tarp from the truck bed. She spots Betty Lou standing out of the way, looking a bit frazzled. "Hey girl rough trip? Y'all look like ya need another cup of coffee. Let's leave this to the boys. I have a bundt cake in the oven that should just about be ready." Pauline put a comforting arm around her friend's shoulder and led her to the stairs.

Frank and Billy got the supplies stored then carry the BOBs up to Billy and Betty Lou's room. The smell of warm bundt cake dripping with thick white icing lured the men to the kitchen... away from the office with the ham radio and computer screens.

2:54 pm GMT, September 23

The emails mysterious vanish. The emails, copies of the emails, screen dumps of the emails in fact all digital images of the emails vanish. Gone without a trace as if they were never there. A few thousand hard copies scattered across the globe are all that remain of the cryptic warning.

11:04 am EDT, September 23,
Devil's Fork Gap
Smokey Mountains, Tennessee,

Frank, Pauline, Billy and Betty Lou were seated around the kitchen table enjoying coffee and bundt cake when Billy started in on his wife. "Betty Lou, y'all need to learn how to bake as good as Pauline here. Frank, ya got yourself a good little wife."

Pauline hated the way Billy bullied Betty Lou and jumped to her defense. "Billy, it's no big thing. It's just a mix out of a box. I have tasted Betty

Lou's peach pie and it's heavenly."

Shaking his fork at Pauline he said,
"Ya but I don't like pie! I like cake and
she don't.."

They all jump when Frank's and
Billy's phones both rang at once. What
ever the texts said it caused both men to
leap up and race to the office.

Annoyed with Billy's hurtful
remarks, Pauline patted Betty's hand.
"I'll clean this up, y'all go lie down
for a bit. I always feel better after a
little cat nap myself."

Grateful for her friend's kindness
Betty said, "Are you sure? I would really
like to put my head down for a bit. Billy
had me runnin' all night. Packing the
truck, closing down the house and settin'
all kinds of crazy booby traps for
possible intruders. Then the whole ride
up he just kept drilling me on that
stupid protocol manual the boys wrote.
Every time I messed up he yelled at me.
He said I was the weak link in our
defense. The way he was drivin' you'd
think they'd dropped a bomb on the White
House instead of some silly old email. If
you really don't mind I think I will lie
down for a bit."

As Pauline was drying the last
coffee cup Frank and Billy burst into the
kitchen. Billy looked around the room.

24

"Where's Betty Lou gone now?"

Pauline raised an eyebrow and said, "She was feelin' poorly so I sent her to lie down for a bit."

Billy kicked the leg of a chair. "Damn her! If she wasn't my wife... That woman has no idea how serious this is."

Frank knew his wife had her fighting face on. He scowled at Billy. "Never mind that, let the woman sleep. It's not as if there's somethin' she should be doing right now. Pauline, the email just disappeared! It's gone from everywhere. People were starin' right at it one second an the next it was gone. Rory said he was tryin' to find out what happened and the whole web crashed again."

His wife forgotten for the moment, Billy slammed his palm cn the table. "Frank, I told y'all last night it was a code red situation. Didn't I? I was right too. This proves it."

Frank rolled his eyes at Billy's outburst. "Pauline, we talked it over with Rory and Dan. We all agree to go to code red. Dan and Tracy are headin up in the next hour as soon as they close their place up. Rory has to wait for Cindy to get home from work. They should be leavin' Virginia about 6:00 pm."

Now in full on prepper mode, Billy

said a bit too loud, "Y'all, we need a supply run. Can't have too much food. We better make a run before the stores empty out."

Pauline wanted to tell him to stop yelling so Betty Lou could rest. She knew this would only make him start in on the woman again so she tried another tactic. "Billy, me and Frank went down to our store early this mornin. We got twenty cases of food out'a the back room. All that's really left is the stuff on the shelves. Maybe y'all should go open the store for a few hours. We are the only place a body can buy food in these parts."

Still talking to loud Billy eyed Pauline. "Pauline, y'all not thinkin' right. Me or Frank has to stay by the radio and track what's happenin' out there. Frank, y'all man the communications. I'll take first watch in the tower."

Pauline tossed the dish towel on the counter and turned to her husband. "Frank do y'all *really* think that's necessary?" Frank shruged his shoulders to his wife's question. "Fine y'all play Rambo I'm goin down the hill to open the store. We have people countin' on us. At least until the food runs out." She gave Billy a dirty look on her way out. Billy missed the look and had no idea how close he's come to Pauline shooting him.

The castle-like great Hall was built after Gianna purchased the property a decade ago. It was built like a Medieval castle. The walls were constructed of blocks of rough cut granite. Six, eight foot tall arched Gothic windows lined the fifty foot long southern wall. Two rows of six Medieval style chandeliers were suspended from the vaulted ceiling to illuminate 2500 square foot room. On the west wall were a set of massive arched carved doors. The inner and outer panels were reinforced with steel plate. A smaller door at the east end of the room led to the eight hundred square foot space occupied by the kitchen, dry goods pantry, walk-in cooler, the butler's pantry with access to the root and wine cellars and the cheese cave below. The Hall was furnished with vintage and antique sideboards, hutches, tables and chairs, all of which predate the 1950's. The north wall was dominated by a fireplace, tall enough to stand in and deep enough to roast pig in. The black walnut mantel with its gargoyle corbels was carved by two of the farm's resident wood carvers. Along the wall on either side of the fireplace were cupboards that store enough wood to heat the Hall for two weeks. The ceiling was made of oak panels and beams with an outer layer of steel. The roof was covered with black slate. Inside three rows of concrete columns supported the immense weight.

The murmur of a dozen conversations could be heard from the forty full-time residents of Dancing Goats Farm gathered for the meeting. Gianna, followed by Violet, Lizzy, Theo and Nick, entered through the kitchen door. As the others took their seats at the table, Gianna narrowed her eyes and scanned the faces of her Tribe. "Okay let's settle down. Yes, we saw the that the email has vanished. That's why we're late. The big question on your minds is what do I believe this is? I believe, Mother works in mysterious ways. I believe it is a universal *and* personal directive. To our Tribe it means it's time to close ranks and fold into the farm. If I was a hard core prepper type I'd say we're at code orange." Colorful expletives from the group echo around the Hall.

Gianna shook her head. "Got that out of your systems? Good. Let me remind you... there is no panicking on this farm. As far as I can see, *WE* have no reason to panic. You need to understand at the moment attempting to communicate via phone or internet is pointless. If you have any contacts you feel you need to make, stop by the office after the meeting. Theo has a list you can be added to. As the lines clear he will send the messages for you. What I'm saying is STAY

OFF YOUR DAMN CELL PHONES! We are not involved in the chaos. I would like it if you would all turn them off. Just use radios today. You each know what your responsibilities are. Take care of them. For most of you it will be just another day on the farm.

Truck drivers and gatherers, go about your day until 12:30 then report to the Theo in the office.

Managers, review you inventories. Get the numbers and a list of any out-land supplies needed to Theo by 12:30. Missing the deadline is not an option. I don't want to send out again until I have a feel for the social climate out there.

Nick has informed me the reserve security people will be moving in full time.

Housekeeping, do a walk through and make sure the barracks are aired and stocked with fresh linens.

Food service, stock the barrack pantry and fridge. They should be trickling in over the next twenty four. Check with Simon for what he has set aside for over there.

JonJon where are you?"

A tall lanky eighteen year old stood. He was one of the resident communication and tech geeks. "Yes ma'am."

"You and Sammy will be alternating shifts until Theo says otherwise. Work out the schedule between yourselves and Theo."

Until further notice the gate to the Q will be closed. Let's reduce all unnecessary activity between the Q and the farm. Use the east portal if you have business out there.

Last but not least as your people arrive, those that have already been vetted will be brought through. The others will be temporarily held in the Q. You'll be notified when they get here. Security will process them as quickly as possible. Do not irritate Nick or his staff with calls inquiring if your people have arrived. Remember they are here to help protect you. You want them to have your back - so don't annoy the shit out of Nick or the men. It'll only piss them off.

I'm sure some of you still have some questions... if they don't pertain to the running of the farm, I don't fucking want to hear them right now. Let's rock and roll people, we have a farm to run!"

4:00 pm GMT, September 23

World governments release statements

30

declaring the vanishing of the email as proof that the email was simply a hoax. The public is congratulated for not being duped by people who have too much time on their hands. Meanwhile hackers, government analysts and corporate tech wizards continue their frantic search for the sender and the location. They can find no evidence of malware left behind. More perplexing, they can find no evidence that the email ever existed.

**11:30 pm GMT, September 23,
Blog posted Online,
Location Unknown**

By now five billion people have all but forgotten the so called *'hoax email'* and its message.

While most of the world has slipped back into complacency:

Kilauea consumes another 5000 acres of the Big Island.

The airport in **Bali** is being covered with six inches of volcanic ash.

The **National Hurricane Center** is watching hurricane Rafael as well as the two tropical depressions, soon to be named Sara and Tony, as they spin themselves into hurricanes.

500 people are missing in **India** lost in a mud slide.

Wild fires are burning thousands of acres in **New South Wales**.

Five days of torrential rain has caused extensive flooding throughout the **UK**.

A 6.5 earthquake rocked **Mexico**.

Extreme drought continues to tighten its grip on **Southern California, Arizona, and Texas**. The heat related death toll for the three states stands at 203.

There are 15 new verified cases of flesh-eating bacteria along the Gulf Coast of **Alabama**.

The new **Aggy report** out blames the summers' heat and drought for the 40% reduction of this year's hay and corn yields...

Willful ignorance **is a dangerous game**.

**8:00 pm EDT, September 23,
Miami, Florida**

The National Hurricane Center issues an advisory: Hurricane Rafael has been upgraded to a category 2 hurricane. It is located three hundred miles south of Texas, moving northwesterly at 23 mph.

**9:00 pm MDT, September 23,
Western Investments LP HQ**

Southeast of Bozeman, Montana

At a secluded ranch in southern Montana the world's most powerful men begin to arrive from around the globe. A highly trained private security force of two hundred patrol the 300-acre estate, the title to which is buried beneath a dozen layers of shell companies, numbered offshore accounts, and rests in a vault in Switzerland. The 10,000 square foot stone fortress is completely self-contained. Buried ten feet beneath it is a 10,000 square foot elegantly furnished bunker. In the center of the great Hall stands a fifteen foot long table, made from a seamless slice cut from the heart of a two thousand-year-old redwood giant. It was carried there by a mule team in 1865, when Montana was just a territory. The table is set for twelve: the twelve most powerful and ruthless men on the planet. They view the world as their personal game of Monopoly, as their predecessors did. One sentence is the reason for this hastily called emergency meeting... **"Within 18 months the Global Machine will begin to fail"**.

chapter 2
IT'S THE END OF THE WORLD

"But the Tribe's Doing fine"

**11:30 pm EDT, September 23,
Boston, Massachusetts**

Sadie dialed her mother's cell, the
call went right to voice mail. "Hi mamma.
Thank The Goddess I have tonight off. I
still can't fucking believe I slept
through one of the biggest events in the
history of the world! I didn't even get
to see the email! I made a shitload of
calls after we talked. Call me back if
you're still up love you." She put her
phone down and looked around her once
lovely apartment... thinking 'What a
frigging mess'. She navigates through the
boxes and piles of her belongings to get
to the door. Her order of steamed
dumplings has arrived. Curled up on the
couch with her dumplings and chop sticks.
Not for the first time today, she
questioned the move. 'Is it too soon? If
I wait, will it be too late? Why didn't I
move home sooner? The truck is already
paid for, I could cancel it. But if I
wait, what if I can't get a truck then?'
Annoyed with her self doubt she shouts
"Well asshole no truck would mean you'd

have to leave your stuff! But I really really love my stuff." That settled it. She grabbed the tape gun and began to seal another box. Thirty minutes into her packing frenzy her mother rang her back. "Hey momma any news?"

"Everything is running fine here. Have you made up your mind yet?"

"Yes I'm coming home. I got a truck for Tuesday. I've lined up some friends to help me load. Friends who think I'm bat shit crazy to take this seriously."

Relieved Gianna says, "Crazy isn't always a bad thing. It's better to be thought of as crazy and be wrong then to be thought sane and end up floating your car up the Charles river. I don't want you to drive straight through if you are coming alone."

Sighing Sadie says, "So far I'm coming alone and yes I'm planning to drive straight through. Don't give me that twelve hours is too long crap. You do it and I'm twenty five years younger than you."

Gianna knows when to pick her battles with this daughter who is so much like her. "Fine I'm so happy you coming I'm not going to argue with you. Have to tell you the Tribe has given you a new name... Rip as in Rip Van Winkle."

"Very fucking funny! Tell them I'm going to slap the first person who calls me that. One big dilemma in the packing department: my lemon Tree is heavy with unripe fruit. How do I pack it?"
"Wrap the top with cheese cloth. Make a box the size of the pot so it doesn't tip, then fill it in with naked popcorn."

"Mom, that's a fuck of a lot of popcorn!"

"Yes it is but when we unpack it we can feed the popcorn to the chickens and goats and the tree travels safely with no harm to the planet."

Around a mouthful of dumpling she asks, "Any word on where it came from or where the fuck it went?"

"My dear you know Mother gives and Mother takes. On that note *your* mother needs sleep badly. I'll text you through the day tomorrow. Love you."

12:00 am EDT, September 24, Miami, Florida

The **National Hurricane Center** issues an advisory: Rafael has been up graded to a category 3 hurricane. It's doubled in size and increased it's speed to 25 mph. It's still moving in a north westerly direction. There is speculation it may be a category 4 when it makes landfall

36

somewhere between **Galveston and New Orleans**.

12:00 am MDT, September 23,
Western Investments LP HQ
Southeast of Bozeman, Montana

Excusing themselves, the congressman and David step out onto the terrace for a cigar. Looking out over the manicured landscape illuminated by solar flood lights. David addressed the real reason they had left the group. "I'm not seeing the leak having come from one of us. I've spoken with everyone tonight. They're commitment is unwavering."

The congressman settled back in his chair. "David, I have to agree with you. After twenty years in congress, where lying is an art form, I can spot a liar in my sleep. It's not one of us. Which means we've been hacked. My connection in Homeland says they haven't a fucking clue. Neither does the CIA."

David took a seat and said, "According to our partners in there nor does any other country. They're all just chasing their God damn tails. Not even Julian has been able to figure out where it came from. I'm sure he wishes the programmer worked for him. I think he's jealous they didn't give it to him to publish."

The congressman digested what they

had learned while he smoked his cigar. "See that you keep a firm grip on his leash. We only need him for a few more months, then we can have him removed. You're sure he still has no idea who you are?" David nodded his assurance as the congressman stood signaling the end of their conversation. "Good. Let's keep it that way. We're too close to fuck up now. Let's double our security on every aspect of the project. All communications are to be encrypted. All calls are only to be made from secure lines." Leaving their cigars in the ashtray the pair of conspirators rejoined the group.

2:35 am EDT, September 24,
Devil's Fork Gap
Smokey Mountains, Tennessee

Dan rolled down and locked the bay door as Rory turned off his engine. "Hey Rory, good to see you, man. How was the drive?"

Rory ran his fingers through his longish hair and exhaled. "If you don't count the four and a half hour delay in getting on the road, not bad. When did you get here? You didn't have to wait up for us."

"Who could sleep? Tracy and I got here in the afternoon. Let me give you a hand with the load. Hey Cindy, the girls are all up in the kitchen."

Cindy liked Dan. She smiled while tugging at the seat of her jeans. "Hey Dan, I am so glad to be out of that seat. My butt went to sleep fifty miles back. Rory babe toss me my bag. I'll meet you up stairs. I need to get out of these jeans."

Handing Cindy her bag Rory asked, "Dan, where's Billy at?"

Dan rolled his eyes. "Frank said he's been sitting guard in the blind since about noon. We tried to get him to come down for dinner but Billy said not unless Frank took watch. Frank said "Screw that, Pauline's made pot roast."

"Frank's right about that, Pauline makes a mean pot roast. Why does Billy keep calling that old deer blind the 'watch tower'? I mean what's wrong with calling it what it is?"

Dan shrugged. "Maybe he thinks it'll make him a better shot if he gives it a fancy name."

Rory let out a hoot. "Don't let him hear you say that."

Dan eyed the heap of bins and boxes in the truck bed. "Rory, how about we leave the load till morning. Let's see if we can lure Billy down with a piece of Pauline's bundt cake."

Rory shook his head in agreement. "Sounds good. Wasn't looking forward to this tonight. This'll go a lot faster after a good nights sleep. Anyway I wanna hear what ya found out since I got on the road. The radio just kept repeating the same crap all the way here."

"Not much fact. There's a crapper full of theories floating around but no real hard facts. Preppers know the hoax story is bull but that's about it. I really don't think the government has a damn clue."

"Do they ever? Mores the point, would they tell us if they did?"

On the way up the stairs Rory said, "Pauline's pot roast and her bundt cake... that proves it Billy is crazy!"

1:10 am MDT, September 24,
Western Investments LP HQ
Southeast of Bozeman, Montana

Six of the twelve men prepared to depart the ranch, confident in the knowledge that whomever sent the email was powerless to interfere with their plans. It was simply a matter of time before the culprit was located and contained. Their quest was nearly accomplished. They had agreed to a six month acceleration in their timetable. The negotiations for their last acquisitions were nearly completed.

Within 12 months the Global Machine would begin to fail.

Thirty years of molding, pushing, controlling, stealthily manipulating and at times if needed destroying the world markets, the economies of whole countries and their unwashed, insipid and wholly expendable masses, had brought the prize within their reach. Nothing and no one would stop them. The men and women who sold them their integrity... some their very souls to achieve their soon to be irrelevant current political latitudes, would be swept from the game like the chess pieces they were. The ever grasping nouveau riche clawing their way to what they believe was the top of the food chain would learn the cruel lessons that come from reaching above their station.

Over brandies Ammar raised his glass in a toast. "My friends, the world is our oyster."

Raising his glass in return the congressman replied "Fuck the oysters, we poisoned them! All we want are the pearls!" A round of laughter oozing pure evil echoed off the walls.

Their end game was elegant in its diabolical simplicity: Four Triumvirates strategically positioned around the globe. In their hands alone would rest all the power in the world. These twelve intend to rule the world and everyone in it.

David made one more toast to end the evening; they raised their glasses in unison: "To us, gentlemen! There is no one in the world who can stop us now."

Like Julius Caesar, their arrogance would be the implement of their demise.

3:30 am EDT, September 24,
Devil's Fork Gap
Smokey Mountains, Tennessee

As Dan made his way toward the kitchen, he congratulated himself on having insisted they install these solar powered LED eyeball lights along the baseboards. He thought, 'A man wants to sneak off for a midnight snack he doesn't want to wake the whole house by turning on the lights, an he damn sure doesn't want to trip and break his neck in the dark.' Dan couldn't seem to fall asleep. He was all riled up like a kid the night before his first camping trip. Looking down the hall he wondered why the lights in the control room were still on. He stuck his head around the door jamb, and saw Billy sitting at the desk staring at the monitors. "Billy, what the hell are you still doing up? Ya gotta get some shut eye man."

Billy jumped at sound of Dan's voice. Momentarily frightened and then embarrassed he snapped, "Somebody has to keep track of what's happening. Who's gonna watch the security monitors? Didn't hear anybody else volunteer."

Dan tried to calm him. "Christ! What do ya think... armed terrorists or Democrats are gonna come creeping up the drive of this secluded mountain compound to capture us tonight? Us? Like we have information they want? We don't even know what *this* is. We got nothin'. How the hell would they even know we're here? For that matter why would they even know who we are?"

Dan's words had the opposite effect. Billy twirled the chair around to face Dan. Using his fist and the arms of the chair to punctuate each point he all but yelled, *"Dan Democrats are terrorists!* And... it's because we *don't* have any credible intel on this, that we gotta stay alert. And maybe we don't have intel but we do have two years worth of food, supplies and a shit load of guns and ammo. Did y'all think of that? An y'all know they been trackin' everyone on the preppin' groups for years. So ya, we're all on a list in the basement of the FBI!"

"Christ Billy keep it down your gonna wake everybody. Just saying it's a little early in the event to be this paranoid. If shit does come down you'll already be burnt out."

"Not *if* Dan, *when* shit comes down. Seems like I'm the only one truly committed here."

This pissed Dan off. "Ya know what-Screw you, Billy! If we're not all truly committed why the hell did we each sink $20,000 into this place? Tracy and I put in way more when you count the fact that this place was her dad's. I'm just saying y'all need to pace yourself. The time is coming when we all got to be at the top of our game. How about ya take a break? Come on, let's see what's in the fridge."

Realizing he *was* really hungry Billy relented. "All right, but I'm sayin' NOT comfortable leavin' the command post un-manned."

Continuing on to the kitchen, Dan thought *'Command Post?' who the hell are you commanding at 3:00 o'clock in the morning?*

4:00 am EDT, September 24, Miami, Florida

The **National Hurricane Center** issues an advisory: Rafael is still a category 3 hurricane with sustained winds of 128 mph. Its forward speed is 28 mph. They expect it to become a category 4 within the next hour. It could become a category 5 by the time it makes landfall near Galveston around 9:30 pm right at high tide. Wide spread mandatory evacuations have begun across the entire Gulf coast.

5:45 am EDT, September 24,
North of Cumberland Gap, Kentucky

Fern Slacum's extended family were all hard at work. Mindin' their kin an harvestin' home and preparing to fold into the mountain. Three hogs were being butchered. Last night fires were stoked in the smoke houses. Yesterday's fish already hung in the earthy hickory smoke.

The last of the apples had been picked. Some were wrapped in newsprint to store in baskets in the root cellars. Some were peeled and sliced to be put up for apple pie. Pints of applesauce and apple butter found their place on pantry shelves next to this summer's peaches and wild berry jams.

Come sun-up there would be a whole new list of chores. The younger men will be splitting truck loads of wood so as every family could keep warm through the cold months. Fern had given the order; huge pine trees were felled so they lay across the roads. Now there was but one way in and out of their tiny mountain community. That too would be closed when Fern said make it so. The last of the grapes not good enough for the wine bottled earlier this month, would be spread out in wide flat baskets to dry today in the sun. Water would be hauled to fill the cisterns. In bad times past, evil minded folk had fouled the crick up stream leavin' them with no fresh water for months.

Deer would be hunted two at a time so as to leave enough time to smoke and stew the meat without some spoiling. The root crops: carrots, turnips, and sweet potatoes would be pulled from the ground the day after today. Some to be added to the stews, some canned, and some carrots will spend the autumn in boxes of moist sand in the root cellars.

Rachel and her cousin Esther were on their way down the mountain in Duncan's old Ford pickup. They carry a list for every house. They need twenty pound bags of rice, flour, salt and sugar. Twenty of each means two per household. Some want cans of lard for making pies and Duncan's favorite, apple stack cake. Jugs of molasses, tins of baking powder and boxes of baking soda round out the lists. If a household didn't have the ready money to pay for their needs others in the clan chipped in by way of mindin' their kin. Ester's younger brother, Ansel, was following behind the women. He had a list of his own to fill for the men folk, too, they needed his truck to help to carry the supplies back up the mountain.

Unlike Fern, Rachel had gone to high school in town. After graduation she worked at the library for five years. That's where she met her husband. Seeing as Rachel knew so many townsfolk Fern asked her to talk around to see what was being said. It's not that Fern doubted the crow. Truth being, she trusted the crow more than she trusted the townsfolk, but it'd be good to know what was happening off mountain that might come round and bite her family and the mountain.

6:05 am EDT, September 24,
Dancing Goats Farm
Moon Mountain, North Carolina

Gianna entered the kitchen in search a second cup of coffee. "Morning, Violet."

"Morning mamma, did you see this cat 3 hurricane in the Gulf?"

Pouring a cup Gianna nodded. "Yes, I've been watching it since Saturday. Naming a hurricane after an Archangel kinda piques my interest. Did notice they misspelled his name but that's probably irrelevant. What the hell were they thinking? Raphael is known for stirring the waters. Oh, then there was the time he opened the desert and buried a demon there. If he's not too busy I can think of a few that want burying. The best little bit of today's *angelic trivia* is he had the job of delivering Sara to her destination!"

Violet furrowed her brow. "Sara

47

who?"

Taking a sip Gianna said, "Not really important, what is important is that at this moment there is a tropical storm about to turn into a hurricane named Sara out in the Atlantic!"

"Oh this can't be good. Who the hell picks these names?"

"At one point they named them after the saint who's day they formed on. Now the World Meteorological Organization headquarters in Geneva does. Wonder if they know someone involved in the process works for Mother? Do they even know they work for mother? I have a feeling the waters he's spinning this time, aren't coming to heal people."

Lizzy wandered in still half asleep "Who named who? What's spinning?"

Violet glanced over her shoulder. The sight of Lizzy trying to wrangle her mass of long chestnut hair into a hair tie reminded her to search through the covers for the one she'd lost in her sleep. At the moment her equally long mane was nothing short of a wild tangle. "Naming hurricanes. We're discussing who thought naming one Rafael was a good idea. Raphael the Archangel who spins the waters. This is a monster. It's already almost the size of Katrina. It's frigging huge."

Gianna added, "The forward speed is 28 miles per hour. I'm going to predict it tops out at thirty. What's you feeling on category, Vy?"

Passing Lizzy a cup Violet said, "This is going to a 5. It'll drop after it hits land but it will reach 5 before it does."

Frowning Gianna said, "What I can't see is where it's going after it makes landfall? I'm fairly certain the Gulf coast is toast or rather soup. Little bit edgy about Raphael's association with Sara... Lets hope if he hooks east he stays south of the state line. This is going to screw with gas and oil prices. Speaking of water you know I've been so frigging busy the last forty eight hours I haven't even looked at the Bergs. The whole Thwaites glacier could have slipped into the ocean and I'll have missed it!"

Lizzy settled on a stool with her coffee. "I think we'd have heard if a glacier that huge fell into the ocean. It's the size of Florida. There'd be a really big swish."

Violet laughed. Gianna said, "That swish could inundate the base of the Pine Island glacier. That could be the catalyst that causes it to slip into the ocean. If that happens we're looking at a rapid sea rise of at least six feet."

Lizzy asked, "What's that going to do to Greenland? six feet could cause the Peterman glacier to let go. That would be at least another 4 feet of rise!"

Gianna shook her head. "If that happens it will get bloody insane out there bloody fast. Best case billions will be left homeless. Worst case they're all fucked."

Lizzy savored the first sip of her coffee. "Playing catch up here... This means what to us?"

Gianna looked at both women. Heading out the door she said, "It means we need to get our asses out of the kitchen and get to work! Hey, when Theo shows his pretty face tell him I want to talk to him. I'll be in the Q."

Q is code for the farm's Quarantine Zone. The Q is an optical illusion. A three dimensional Trompe-l'œil. Ten acres designed to deceive the eyes of the out-landers. It appears to be a small homestead. White picket fenced farm house with an old concrete block barn, a goat shed, a chicken coop, a potting shed, an outhouse, one small hay field and a garden with a few fruit trees scattered about. Behind the farmhouse, the wall protecting the inner farm is camouflaged by a grove of trees with a thicket of wild blackberries. Visitors to the Q farmhouse never learn there is more. Maybe one in a hundred do. A stockade fence and gate separates Q Farm from the road it appears to be made of pine planks... it's not.

Like props on a movie lot the buildings are not what they seem. The barn's hay loft houses a small arsenal and twenty bunks for the vanguard. The hay door provides a 180 degree birds-eye view of both directions of the road for reconnaissance or a sniper's nest. The hay hood is fitted with a rappelling line. The stalls and tack room hold three WWII jeeps, a decommissioned retrofitted Army Humvee, two SUVs, Pepe, two live horses (for show) and Audrey. The back wall hung with an array of everyday farm implements is hinged. It swings out and up... it's the actual gate into Dancing Goats Farm. The outhouse is literally a *brick shit house*. A trap door hides an emergency access tunnel that leads under the wall into the guard tower inside the farm. There is a second emergency tunnel in the floor of the barn. The antique looking barn walls aren't. They're new and reinforced with steel.

Gianna entered the Q through the east portal. She walked around a stand of intentionally overgrown blueberry bushes toward the back door of the farmhouse. Inside some of her 'boys', as she likes calling them, are seated around the old pine plank table. They're dressed in

raggedy ass jeans, leather vests, arm
less flannel shirts, some wear black tee
shirts with scary images and words on
them. Every foot is clad in heavy biker
or military boots. A few heads are shaved
sporting bandannas. The rest wear their
hair longish. One even has a braid down
to the crack of his ass. Which is good
because sometimes it's out. Beards,
stashes, earrings and a whole lotta
tatts. They looked like the meanest,
scariest bikers on the planet.

A pair of hogs are parked outside
the barn next to a candy apple red 62
Impala looking like it hasn't seen a
mechanic or a hose in a decade. As is
most everything in the Q the boys and the
Impala are not as they seem. Under the
Impala's hood is a pristine, finely tuned
V8 with a four barrel Hemi.

You wouldn't know it from the looks
of them but every member of the farm's
security company is a retired combat
veteran. Most are Marines. Gianna is fond
of saying, *"My boys have wicked mad
skills"*. It's a gross understatement. The
sight of them lounging around the
property with half empty Tequila bottles
send most strangers running. If they but
knew the bottles held sweet tea... brewed
from the tea plants grown in one of the
farm's seven greenhouses. The boys,
though they come from different branches
of the service, work together like a well
oiled machine. The ninety man company,

composed of thirty van guard and sixty regulars, is under the command of Captain Nick Lorenzini.

At the moment a dozen of them have maps of the farm and surrounding areas spread across the table. They're assessing potential weak spots and breach scenarios. Gianna greeted the men, "Good morning, gentlemen." Smiling at Nick she asks, "Captain, where am I vulnerable?"

Nick answered her highly suggestive yet seemingly innocent question, with a grin boarding on wicked. "Morning ma'am. An air assault is our only threat. At daybreak I sent a squad out. If they are spotted by anyone they'll pass for hunters. They're orders are to recon for trespassers in the buffer zone and inspect the perimeter for signs of damage from animals or assholes. As you know, we drive it every day but I sent them on foot to catch anything new or anything we might have missed." Nick was interrupted by Cassandra entering the room.

Gianna was instantly pissed. "What the fuck is that goat doing in the house... *again*? Carmichael how many times do I have to tell *YOU* not to bring that goat in the house?"

A wiry 30 something man shrugged his shoulders and ran his fingers through his ginger hair before answering. "Ma'am you know I have PTSD syndrome. That Cassandra

53

girl is my service animal."

Gianna leaned menacingly across the table. *"You're going to have GFUYA syndrome if I find her in here again!"*

Carmichael scratched his head. "Ma'am, what's GFUYA syndrome?"

Nick shook his head trying to stifle a laugh. "Gianna's Foot Up Your Ass Syndrome you fucking idiot."

Momentarily amused she says, "And that's why Nick is the boss of all of you. Communication is never an issues with us."

Standing in the corner out of her view, Reno slid his hand over the lower half of his face to hide the grin that *will* need to be explained if either of Gianna or Nick catches it. Which he would rather not do. Everyone has heard how well these two communicate. Quiet and/or agreement are not always a factor in their conversations.

Turning her attention back to Carmichael she continued. Pointing at him she says, "You- Go- get that goat out of the house."

The men watch in silence as Carmichael leads the goat out by her collar. Out on the veranda they can hear Cassandra's obstreperous protests over being booted out. Carmichael pushes his luck, as he so often does with Gianna, "Ma'am she so sad she's crying. Can you hear her?"

Several of the men cringe knowing he's gone too far again. They wait for the yelling. "*You're* going to be crying if I hear one more word out of you about that damn goat! Now get your sorry ass back in this seat. NOW!" The screen door slammed and Carmichael slid into his seat sans the goat. Gianna wasn't through with him. "And when we're finished here, I'm checking the floors. If I find that goat pissed in here again, you'll be on your knees having group therapy with a scrub brush *all* day. Understood?" He just nodded. Turning her attention back to the Captain she said, "Nicholas, when you're done here I'd like a few words with you."

Carmichael was a bone of contention between them. Nick's voice was perfectly neutral but the gleam in his eyes said I warned you. "We're done here. DJ, you and Lee are on the front gate. The rest of you get in the barn. I want every piece of equipment gone over. I want no surprises when we need them."

The men gone, Nick turned his attention to back to Gianna. The look on her face warned him the subject of Carmichael's behavior was closed. Changing the direction she asked, "Is Tiny out with the patrol?"

"Tiny's downstairs handling intake. A handful of the Tribe's families have arrived."

To irritate him for the Carmichael look she said, "Nick, I know you told me you have Tiny process the incoming because he's so organized but I'm not fooled. You have him do it cause, who'd dare lie to a six foot four black man who's built like a frigging linebacker. I'm sure they think he'll snap them like a twig if they do. If they but knew he's a big teddy bear."

Smiling he asked, "Are you objecting?"

She shrugged. "Hell no. You know intimidation works for me."

She had her silver hair wound up in haphazard knot. Silky whips had escaped and feathered across her high cheek bones. He liked it better when she wore it down. "I'm sure you didn't come here to check on Tiny. Are you going to tell me or do I have to guess?"

Her green eyes held a glint sexual taunting. "The question that brought me here was, is there anything you think we need more of?" She took a breath and let it out slowly. "I think things might start getting ugly out there sooner than

56

later."

Nick matched her taunt with a look of his own. "Woman, I believe you know my feelings on the subject... *There's no such thing as too much firepower.*"

She narrowed her eyes, grinning she said, "Really? At the Equinox bonfire last night, I seem to remember you saying '*There's no such thing as too much firepower or fried eggplant.*'" She took a step closer. "You know I've got your eggplant covered babe." She paused for another breath. Nick's eyes slid down to watch the crystal resting between her breasts rise and fall. Still grinning. She said, "As for your firepower, I was wondering if would $15,000 help ease your... mind? Cause if you're not comfortable with what we have then, I'm *really* not comfortable."

Fighting to keep his grin from erupting into a laugh he said, "Yea, I think fifteen grand would make us both feel much more comfortable. I'd want to increase our firepower today... before things get out of hand."

Gianna turned toward the door knowing if she stared into those green eyes a second longer she would not be able to contain her laughter and she would lose this round. On her way out the door she said, "Yes please, the sooner you're back inside the walls the safer

I'll feel. Come by the house for the cash in fifteen?" As she cleared the bottom step she could hear him laughing.

When she got to the break in the hedge that led to the portal she found Cassandra chomping away at the blueberry blind. "What are you doing now? Get your sassy ass back inside the farm." Goat in hand she stepped through the portal. Once on the other side Cassandra bolted for the rose bushes lining the walkway to the front porch of the manor house. As Gianna reached the walkway Cassandra stopped chewing. Pink rose petals sticking out each side of her mouth she tilted her head to the side and looked up expectantly.

Still smiling from her win, Gianna reached down and gave the goat a hug. "You're not in trouble baby girl. It's autumn, and the bushes need to be cut back soon anyway. Knock yourself out."

In the basement Gianna rotated the dials on the large antique safe. She swung the door open and smiled. Inside are stacks of cash, a box of antique jewelry, one bag each of gold and silver coins, a metal box Nick kept there and her most important papers. She didn't know where Nick bought his toys and didn't want or need to. As she counted out the fifteen grand she added an extra ten thousand for Nick's shopping spree, thinking as she did, *You gotta love the*

North Carolina lottery. She'd taken a
lump-sum payment of $500 million...
that's how Dancing Goat Farm came to be.
As she closed the safe she whispered
"Thank you, Mother."

chapter 3
DON'+ COME AROUND HERE NO MORE

"Hell No, they're not getting my food!"

8:00 am EDT, September 24,
Dancing Goats Farm
Moon Mountain, North Carolina

Through the office window Theo could see Gianna getting into one of the go-carts. He snatched his phone off the desk. "Morning, Violet said you were looking for me. I'm in the office. Hold-up I'll be right out."

Gianna smiled watching him circumnavigate a wayward lamb. Like Lizzy, Theo is one of her acquired children. "Hop in, you can ride over to the Hall with me. Did you figure out where we sit legally in all the permutations of the laws as they are and could become?"

"We're sort of good as things are now. A few of Nick's toys are in the dark gray area. All right some are out right illegal. Martial Law is a whole other ball of wax. It would depend on too many

60

factors for me to make an educated guess. But reading the laws that are now on the books, the government could swoop in and take all of our supplies if they choose to."

Gianna nearly drove into at tree. "Soooo you're telling me that because I'm not one of those worthless, lazy fucks waiting around for someone else to save me, the United States government will reward my foresight and diligence by robbing me? Hell No! Fuck no! No fucking way will I stand by and let that happen! *Fine*, we just went to stealth mode. Inform the Tribe, evening curfew will be enforced starting tonight at 9:00 pm. Let them know there is a mandatory meeting today at noon. You can go over the restrictions with them while they eat. They need to know all going and coming traffic, is now restricted. Have the Hades crew report to the kitchen at 10:00 pm. We'll work through the night. Tell them after the meeting so they can rest up if they need to. Tell Amber we only need her or Tyler. Same goes for you and Brian. This is only a precautionary move. I want to be ahead of the curve if shit goes downhill fast. We can work over the next few nights. I'll tell Stephen to start installing the camouflage nets today. I don't want the village to be outed by some government drone."

"Blackout mode on lighting? What about Nick? Do you want him to increase the guards?"

"Nick isn't here. He went shopping for a few new toys, which may or may not be legal. Okay I'm sure they won't be. I'll take care of Nick when he gets back. Which should be late afternoon. I'm sure he's already handled the guard. Yes, let's go dark... not sure it's necessary at this stage but let's get them used to it. Do you know when Lizzy's and Violet's Vardos will be finished?"

"I think Lizzy said she was planning on moving back today maybe tomorrow. Do you want to excuse her for tonight? I'll make up a shift schedule for the Hades crew."

"Perfect. Any other areas we need to discuss?"

"Sammy and JonJon have their hands full sifting through the internet chatter. They fell three hours behind yesterday from the sheer volume. Last night I assigned Kevin and Carlos to shifts in the Shack to pick up the slack. We now have four on per shift. We don't want to find out about an event eight hours after it happens. There's so much bullshit out there to wade through. As of yet no one has any hard facts, just an insane amount of theories. 'Anonymous' is the flavor of the moment. Talked to Adrian late last night. He said it's not them. He should be here by noon. He asked for a plus one. I said yes with the understanding that once in, there'd be no leaving. He said she understood. She has no idea where he's bringing her and no wish to leave any time soon. She's been a busy girl lately so she's a little 'hot' right now. We'll use her in data sifting for now but she's not getting access to the Communication Shack until I'm comfortable with her."

"Good. I see you have everything in order and running smoothly as always. My plate is over full today. You take care of getting Adrian and the girl settled in. Where are you housing them?"

"In Python Cottage with the rest of the tech wizards. They'll take the last bedroom. No more Geeks through the gates, Mom!"

"Okay! Let's have dinner at my place around seven-ish. I want to catch up with Adrian and get a look at the girl. You and Brian, Adrian and the Girl, me and yes Nick will want come too. You can take the cart back. I have to go over things with Simon before we start moving supplies."

The sign hanging over the kitchen entrance read 'Alice's Restaurant'. It was one of dozens of signs scattered around the farm, paying homage to twentieth century Americana. "Morning Simon. Honey, Theo tells me we could be

seriously vulnerable under Martial Law.
I'm putting the Hades plan into effect
tonight. I understand you are reworking
your menus and staff due to the increase
in population but I would rather be safe
than sorry."

"Yea, been watching the news this
morning, I think you're on the money. I
was gonna suggest it to you this
afternoon. Increased plates means
increased staff. I don't want any fuck-
ups but shit happens. What they don't
know can't bite us in the ass later. I
was just sitting here making a list of
what to take from each room."

"It's tricky knowing how much to
leave for show and tell. Goddess willing
this will have been a wasted effort. The
Airy-Fairies are who I'm most concerned
with. Yes, they are a vital component of
the farm. I simply don't know how they
would do under government interrogation
if it came to that. They might break, or
more likely be flipped with the 'for the
greater good' line of bullshit. I'm not
willing to risk the contents of our
storehouses on their ability to keep
their mouths shut. Theo is making a
schedule for the Hades crew. They can
alternate days until the bulk has been
moved. I know it will be more work for
you to rotate the supplies. Curfew is
going into effect tonight so we won't
have to be quite so surreptitious while
we work."

"Ya, that sounds good. What time tonight?"

"We'll be here at 10:00 pm. If there isn't anything else we need to cover I'll leave you to it. I've got an ugly list to complete. Oh one more thing - please send over dinner for six around 7:00 pm."

"Anything special?"

"No. What ever you're serving tonight is fine. Thank you for being on the same page. It makes it so much easier."

"Hey this is my home too. I want to protect what we have here as much as you do. Besides if we have no food I'm out of a job."

8:30 am EDT, September 24,
Devil's Fork Gap
Smokey Mountains, Tennessee

Pauline set a basket of fresh baked biscuits on the table. "Tracy, will y'all get them away from that computer before these get cold."

Before Tracy could respond, Frank came through the door. "Pauline, don't go getten' yourself in a fit. We're here. Gravy smells extra good this mornin'."

Pauline eyed the four men dressed in

matching fatigues as they took their seat. "*What* are y'all dressed up for? Were we invaded while I was cookin' breakfast? Betty Lou, do want coffee or tea? You sleep good? Y'all look like ya did."

"Tea please Pauline. I do feel so much better this mornin'. I was thinkin' maybe I'd ride over to the store with y'all. If ya feel like some company today."

Billy, not using his inside voice said, "What all are ya thinkin' Betty Lou? Pauline's not leavin'. Fact is none of us are goin' anywhere till we know what the hell is goin' on."

Pauline was on him in a flash. "Billy Dalton, I will not be told I can not leave my own house. I have an obligation to my customers. I don't know what you men have been listenin' to in there but the news out here said nothin' about bein' invaded and shelterin' in place!"

Billy opened his mouth and Frank shook his head no. Pauline continued to set the men straight. "The biggest story this mornin' is about this hurricane Raf-a-el. They just upgraded it to a category 3. They're sayin' it's so big it's gonna effect the whole Gulf coast. They said it's as big as Katrina. There was talk of the widespread devastation it might cause. They showed miles an miles of traffic. People been stranded on the roads since last night. Rory, would y'all like some more gravy? Here let me get it. There all those people are, stuck in their cars with a hundred mile an hour wind headedin' straight for them. Now *there's* something to be worried about. There were solders dressed up like you four, goin' from car to car passin' out bottled water and sandwiches.

Cindy honey, would y'all like one of these sweet-rolls? I got the recipe from my mamma's 80 year old neighbor, Miss Bobby. Now Miss Bobby said she got it from her grandmother. Bet those people sittin' in their cars wish they had some warm sweet-rolls and coffee. Even if they get to a shelter they may not have a house to come back to. The reporter said it could be as bad as the 1900 hurricane. That one killed thousands of people. A man from the power company was interviewed about how they were sendin' trucks to stand by because they just knew Raf-a-el was gonna take down all the power lines. Can you imagine tryin' to survive with no electricity for weeks with that mess to clean up?

Now those people have somethin' to worry about. Here y'all are, high an dry, no hurricane about to blow this house down an y'all are makin' this big fuss over an email! I am part of this group because I do believe *End Days* are comin'... it's just not comin' today! Now soon as I clean up in here, I'm goin' down and open my store. Betty Lou, I would love the company. Cindy, you and Tracy are welcome to come too."

Trying not to laugh Cindy said, "Pauline, you made breakfast, the least I can do is clean up. I think I'll stay here. I have a book I want to finish afterwards."

Tracy nodded at Cindy's suggestion. "Yes, thank you Pauline this was so sweet of you. I think I'll stay and help Cindy clean up. You and Betty Lou scat now, you have customers waiting."

Pauline folded her apron and said, "Well if you ladies insist we'll just be runnin' along. Frank, I have my phone if y'all need me. You boys have a good day playin' soldier." On her way out the door she shot Billy at nasty look.

A welcomed silence fell over the kitchen. The three men looked at Frank. He held both palms out in a gesture of surrender. "I have never figured out how that woman can talk a blue streak like that and *still* eat a meal. But clearly she's not starvin'." The last referring to Pauline's round figure. "I say we all hit the computer and TV to check out this hurricane."

9:00 am EDT, September 24,

Miami, Florida

The **National Hurricane Center** issues an advisory: Hurricane Rafael has been upgraded to a category 4 hurricane, with winds of 155 mph, moving northwesterly at 29 mph. The eye is expected to make landfall just east of Galveston, TX around 9:30 pm.

**9:30 pm EDT, September 24,
Dancing Goats Farm,
Moon Mountain, North Carolina**

"Odens Eyes! I am fucking beat! It's *exhausting* being me. Good to see Adrian again though. Very pleased to have him as part of the Tribe. That Ferret girl... is very cool. I like her tatts and piercings. I think she'll fit in nicely. Theo, are you on the shift tonight or is Brian?"

"I am, *why?*"

"Because I'm making myself a double espresso and want to know if you would like one?"

"Yes ma'am"

"I think I hear someone at the front door - would you get it? It's probably Nick coming back. He's helping tonight but he had something to deal with after dinner."

"Since when do you lock your doors?"

"It's not locked, I just want to know who's coming in." The men entered the room as Gianna finished pouring the espressos. She handed Nick his. Smiling she asked, "Was your shopping trip fruitful dear? I didn't want to discuss your *possible* purchase of illegal guns over dinner with Ferret there."

Nick grinned as he took the cup from her. "Indeed it was. Found everything I was looking for and a few extras." His smile implied he'd had fun with the extra ten she'd given him.

Theo rolled his eyes at the thought of more illegal weapons to deal with.

Nick took one of the counter stools. "Now we can *both* feel better. I didn't want to ask during dinner, your text said we've gone to stealth mode. Has something happen I don't know about?"

Gianna sipped her espresso then shook her head no. "Theo and I discussed the government's ability to confiscate whatever they want. *This* does not make me a happy woman. I've been telling people for decades to get their shit together. They didn't listen, so fuck them. The government's not taking my stuff to feed their irresponsible asses. They're not getting my stuff! Consequently we're going to ground. Stephen already started getting the nets up. Starting tomorrow the animals will only be permitted to forage in the woods. Starting tonight we'll begin moving the bulk of the stores to Hades. It's a *preemptive precautionary* action. Your favorite Nicholas."

"It's a sound move, I *do love preemptive precautionary actions*. We all hate when you're not happy. You have a tendency to make us all unhappy too. Gia, turn on the TV? I want to see what the hurricane is doing. From what they're saying on the truck radio it sounds pretty bad. I want to keep track of where they think it will go next."

Gianna reached for the remote and turned the set on. The devastation on the screen sent shivers down Gianna's spine. Raphael had spun the waters across Texas, Louisiana and Mississippi. Alabama and all of the west coast of Florida were flooded. Almost a thousand miles wide. All three were thinking, *Holy Fucking Shit Please don't come to North Carolina.* It had just made landfall as a category 5 running right over Galveston. Houston was flooding. There were already massive power outages in Texas and Louisiana. 25 million would be without power before the night was over. Nick turned off the TV and the somber trio headed for Alice's Restaurant.

Tonight's half of the Hades crew was waiting for them when they arrived. At

71

the sight of her niece Gianna smiled. "Amber baby, haven't seen much of you in the past few days."

Amber gave Gianna a quick hug. "Hey Auntie. You know me just been lounging by the pool drinking margaritas and reading a romance novel."

Theo feigned shock and elbowed her. "*Stop lying* girl, I see you busting your ass in the greenhouses!"

Gianna asked Simon, "What's first?"

"Nick, will you double check that the doors are locked? I made a list of each item and where it goes in Hades. Two can wait at that end and empty the carts. Amber and Dawn, why don't you take a copy and work in Hades."

Amber narrowed her eyes. "Simon, I won't forget *you're* the one who sent me to work in hell!"

Simon sniped back, "Don't give me any shit or I'll lock you down there. Nick and Theo can alternate pulling the carts through the tunnel. Gianna and I will load the carts at this end so I know the right stuff goes."

Hades was a series of concrete underground bunkers. Its existence is known only to the Hades crew. Access to the hundred foot connecting tunnel was

through a false panel in back of the dry
goods pantry.

At the moment Hades bunkers held:
80,000 pounds of assorted rice
45,000 pounds of assorted wheat berries
40,000 pounds of assorted beans
8,000 pounds of raw sugar
70 - 100 gallon vats of raw honey
10,000 gallons of olive oil
12,000 pounds of assorted salts
800 pounds of leavening agents
10,000 pounds of baking soda
900 pounds of shortening
900 quarts of fruit
900 quarts of vegetables
1500 quarts of red sauce
7,000 pounds of peanut butter
5,000 pounds of nuts
900 quarts of assorted meats

The 15,000 pounds of smoked pork, beef
and sausage are stored in a separate
bunker, as are thousands of pounds of
sundries. The 20,000 MREs are stored
under the barracks. The manor house and
the farmhouse in the Q have stocked
pantries and a root cellars.

There are thirty-five housing units
on the farm. Each equipped with its own
storage bunker. Residents were encouraged
to preserve the food grown on the farm to
stock their root cellars. Dancing Goats
Farm was Apocalypse ready.

The crew, weary but pleased with how

much they had accomplished, left for
their beds at 3:00 am. The women pause
for a moment to smile at the beauty of
the Harvest Moon hanging low in the sky.

The Hades crew fell asleep unaware
that the Rafael's eye had stalled over
Galveston for two hours. At midnight it
hooked east, leaving behind devastation
not seen there since the storm of 1900.
The eye passed over Baton Rouge then
dipped back into the Gulf at Biloxi.
There it replenished itself over the warm
coastal water.

Out in the Atlantic, Tropical Storm
Sara had become a Category 1 hurricane.
Increasing in speed she has set her
sights on Charleston, South Carolina.

Thousands of miles south of
Hurricane Sara, an ominous crack echoed
across a frozen landscape.

6:00 am EDT, September 25,
Culpeper, Virginia,

The congressman watched the news
while he drank his morning coffee on his
way to DC. As he watched he thought, 'How
nice of Mother Nature to have lent a
hand.' This disaster fit perfectly into
their plan of chaos and disruption.

6:08 am EDT,

With help from her friends, Sadie

had managed to get her packing done, pick up and load the truck a day early. Monday night she crossed the George Washington Bridge at 11:00 pm. She cruised through DC just after 3:00 am. That's when things went a tad wrong. At 4:00 am she'd pulled over in a gas station in some place called Culpeper, Va. The station wasn't open yet so she took a cat nap.

A little before 6:00 am, she gassed up the truck, washed her face and grabbed a coffee. The nice guy at the counter gave her directions. *Yeah!* she thought, *it's not far now.* As she crossed the parking lot, a black limo with a flat tire thumped into the station. It came to a stop five feet in front of her. The rear window slid down. The man inside was staring at her. She met his eyes and the hair on the back of her neck stood up. *Evil*, she thought. *I'm looking into the eyes of pure evil.* She hurried to her truck. As she pulled out she could see him in her side mirror still staring after her. Aloud she said, "*You,* mother fucker, need to die." It was not until she crossed the North Carolina state line, did she feel the sense of foreboding leave her.

She offered a small prayer. "Sweet Mother Goddess, protect me on the last leg of this journey. And if you're not too busy would you please kill that evil asshole?"

Cindy was making her way to the kitchen to prepare breakfast. Yesterday, she and Tracy had talked and thought it wasn't fair for Pauline to do all the cooking. When the other girls got back they sat down and made a cooking and clean-up schedule. Cindy was thinking about what she would put in her omelet this morning, as she passed the *command center*, as Billy called it, she saw Billy face down on the desk. She thought 'That can't be very comfortable. While she made coffee she wondered if he was just asleep or maybe he was dead.' While the coffee brewed she got the cream from the fridge and a mug from the hook. Cindy had a firm rule about checking on potentially dead people... never before she's had her coffee. To some it might seem strange to have a rule about checking on people who might be dead. She'd learned the hard way that finding a dead person before you've had your coffee could really put a damper on the enjoyment of that first cup. Cindy'd worked first shift in a nursing home for several years, where lots of old people died in their sleep. If Billy was dead he'd just have to wait till after her coffee to be discovered. Besides, Billy was such a raving asshole he might have to wait until she had a second cup. As she was warming to the idea of the Billy being dead, Billy stumbled through the door. *Damn!*

9:35 am EDT, September 25,
Wall Street
New York, New York

By the opening bell it was instantly
clear this would not be a good day for
any company located south of the Mason
Dixon line... or the pecple who held
their stock. Before the opening bell, the
downward trend was apparent in the London
and Hong Kong markets. London knew first
hand how costly flooding could be. They
were at present dealing with
unprecedented flooding all across the UK.

10:25 am EDT, September 25,
Dancing Goats Farm,
Moon Mountain, North Carolina

Sadie rolled to a stop at the gate
of Q Farm. She leaned out the window and
waved to Carmichael standing in the hay
door. He waved back and spoke into his
radio. The gate swung open and she rolled
through. Charlie motioned for her to just
turn it off. She slid out and began to
work the kinks out of her muscles.
Carmichael wrapped her in a bear hug.
"It's about time you got here."

She punched him in the arm "I'm a
day early! I told mom I would be here
tomorrow."

Grinning he said, "Come on I'll walk

77

you through the portal. Charlie'll see
the truck is put in the Barn. We'll bring
it in later. The gates are closed. We're
in lock down. You wanna grab anything
from the truck now?"

She patted the bag hanging from her
shoulder. "Na, this one is good till
later. Let's go find mom and my sisters."

When Carmichael opened the portal
they saw Violet racing a go-cart toward
them. Amber was hanging out the side
waving like a mad woman. Carmichael
laughed as he closed the portal and went
back to his post. He loved all the
sister/cousins but Sadie was his
favorite.

12:00 pm EDT, September 25,
Devil's Fork Gap
Smokey Mountains, Tennessee

After breakfast the rest of the
camp's residents split, hauled, and
stacked wood, while Billy got some much
needed sleep.

Cindy had made baked mac and cheese
for lunch and tomato sandwiches, from the
last of Tracy and Dan's crop. Big knobby
German Johnsons sliced thick. "Betty Lou,
would you get the sweet tea out of the
refrigerator? Then I think we're ready
for lunch."

As the others filed up the stairs

78

for lunch, Billy met them at the top. Dan asked, "Hey Billy, how'd ya sleep?"

Billy, still not fully awake, scratched his head. "Good, real good. What'ch y'all been doin'? Anything new goin' on out there?"

Cindy stuck her head out of the kitchen. "Not right now Billy. You all get washed up. Foods on the table."

Dan passed his plate to Cindy. "What ya missed Billy was a killer hurricane rippin' across the southern half of the country. And an afternoon of ass bustin' work. We had a meeting after breakfast and assessed our non-food supplies. If that monster had come north it could trap us here with no power for who knows how long. Not likely we'd be high on the restore list. What if we had no power for two or three weeks? Now we have enough wood under cover to keep the wood stoves stoked for at least that long. The stacks out back could get wet if we got rain. Need to cover them later."

Passing Billy a plate Rory said, "We split two cords and stacked them in the garage. We had to move a few things around but it fits. In between stacking the girls gathered a mountain of kindling. That's all broken down and stored in the that wooden packing crate under the back stairs. Covered over the crate with one of the brown tarps. While the rest of us were doing that Frank felled two dead trees. A red oak an' a hickory. He got the oak cut and we got most of it stacked."

Between bites Frank said, "I got about half way through the hickory. That's real hard wood it really dulled the chain. After lunch I'll change the chain. We should be able to finish stackin' it in a coupla' hours."

Billy shrugged his shoulders. "Damn, can't believe I slept so long. Sorry 'bout not bein' there to help. So what's the hurricane done?

Dan said, "It swung east after it took out Galveston and cut a path of destruction from there to Tallahassee. Hurricane winds as high north as Montgomery. Right now it's moving' towards Jacksonville."

Pauline was unusually quiet for her extremely chatty self. Cindy asked "Pauline, you okay?"

"Yes, I'm just frettin' about my kin in South Carolina. They're sayin' this Sara hurricane could blow right through the low country. It's not as big as Raf-a-el but if it stalls like the one in 2015 it could be real bad flooding."

Betty Lou went to the fridge for more sweet-tea. "The report said it could

get bigger if it meets up with Rafael. I
don't know what all that email was about
but I'm sure glad it caused us to retreat
up here."

Around a mouthful of tomato sandwich
Billy said, "Before we get back to the
wood we should top off three of the
vehicles tanks. A coupla' the girls can
take the other truck and gas it up and
refill the gas cans."

Frank nodded. "Good idea, Billy.
Pauline, I think our tank might be the
lowest, from all the trips to the store.
Maybe Betty Lou can go with ya. Y'all can
check on the store while you're out. What
do ya think Billy, from now on we only
travel in pairs?" Billy had a mouth full
of mac and cheese, and nodded yes. Frank
had learned years ago the best way to get
Billy to do anything was to make him
think it was his idea. They'd been
friends since grade school. That's how
Billy and Betty Lou ended up as part of
their group. Billy could be an asshole a
lot of the time, but every team needed at
least one crazy bastard to scare off
intruders. Billy was their crazy bastard.

5:48 pm GMT, September 25,
Blog Posted Online,
Location Unknown

West Antarctica The sub-glacial
volcano under the Pine Island Glacier
rumbles. The vibrations causes last

81

nights crack in the Thwaites ice shelf to widen. Twenty miles away in the Amundsen Sea the Thwaites Iceberg Tongue breaks free of its footing sending a small tsunami rushing back toward Pine Island Bay. The impact on the ice shelf causes another ten foot widening of the crack. The stream of melt water flowing from under the Pine Island Glacier increases in volume by 60%.

7:46 am HST,

Hawaii, Hawaii The Big Island is rocked by a 7.6 earthquake. Kilauea erupts sending plumes of ash and lava 15,000 feet in the air. The Governor declares a state of emergency for the island.

5:48 pm GMT,

The **United Kingdom** A 3.9 earthquake rocks the South of England. Damage is reported from Wales to London.

8:00 pm EDT,September 25,
Dancing Goats Farm,
Moon Mountain, North Carolina

The back wall of the barn swung up and Sadie's rental truck rolled through. Twenty minutes later the empty truck exited the front gate, on its way to the drop-off location. The red Impala followed behind. The second half of the Hades crew is busy diligently dispersing

the Farms' supplies between the five
secret Hades bunkers.

**9:48 pm EDT, September 25,
Culpeper, Virginia**

The congressman leaned back and
closed his eyes, his neck throbbed. It
had been a seriously arduous day. The
thump thump thump of the limo's tires on
the ribbed pavement remind him of the
this morning's encounter with the woman
at the gas station.

He had seen her through the window
as the car had rolled to a stop. A
thoroughly alien emotion had washed over
him: Fear, unabashed Fear. An emotion so
foreign to him he didn't recognize it at
first. When he'd rolled down the window
and met her gaze his fear grew and yet he
could not look away. He'd thought about
his reaction on and off all day. He could
not remember her face, just her eyes and
the silver star she wore on a chain
around her neck. He thought it was a Star
of David at first.

An hour later when he was nearly
killed, he saw the same star, on the
shirt of a woman standing on the corner
where the accident happened. It had five
points, not six. The woman stared at him,
as the first one had. Then she walked
away... almost as if she'd been waiting
for the accident to happen and now that
it had, she moved on.

He'd spent hours in the hospital being tested and prodded. Meetings had been postponed. He had a mild concussion. They sent him away with an order for bed rest. He'd gone to his office instead. Now he was regretting that decision. His head was pounding. Yes indeed, it had been an extremely arduous and unsettling day.

chapter 4
gimme shelter

"Mother's storms come to take
There's no shelter in Her wake"

4:00 am EDT, September 26,
Miami, Florida

The **National Hurricane Center** begins
to issue advisories every half hour.
Hurricane Sara has been upgraded to a
category 3 with wind speeds of 118 mph.
It is expected to make landfall around
11:00 pm tonight at Charleston, South
Carolina.

During the early morning hours the
eye of Hurricane Rafael had passed over
Tallahassee. The capital of **Florida** now
lies in shambles. As Rafael squatted over
Tallahassee, three inches of rain per
hour fell on Atlanta. At Tallahassee the
hurricane veered slightly north. While
stalled over Valdosta **Georgia** it was
downgraded to a cat 2. The size is now
only six hundred miles across. The outer
edge of the storm is creating record
breaking storm surges from **Brunswick to
North Charleston.** The southern states

east of Dallas have become one huge swamp. FEMA is figuratively and literally swamped. Their resources are spread across **Texas, Louisiana, Mississippi, Alabama, Florida, Georgia, South Carolina and Hawaii**. Sara has yet to make landfall.

5:00 am EDT, September 26, Blog Posted Online, Location Unknown

At 2:00 am PDT, **Burbank, California** A 3.4 earthquake shook the residents from their beds. At the corner of Wilshire and Le Brea a twenty-four foot high geyser rose from the bowels of the La Brea Tar Pits.

Dallas, TX the emergency shelters are full. Refugees from Hurricane Rafael are still pouring into Dallas by the hundreds. The northbound lanes of Interstate highways 35, 45, 49, 55, 59, 65, 75, and 95 are moving at a crawl, as thousands of people flee north seeking refuge. Gas stations are running dry along the highways. Cars that have run out of gas further restrict the flow of traffic. Violent road rage has become the norm. Each state has called out their National Guard to aid local and state police in maintaining order. 95% of all commerce in the disaster zone has ground to a halt.

Through out the **Southeast** the death

toll is in the hundreds and climbing. **Food store** shelves empty as fast as they are filled. Shopkeepers are dealing with irate people who want food for their families. A rash of tornadoes broke out in central **Florida**. Hundreds of people are continuing to evacuate down the peninsula away from the hurricane. In central Florida there are no more rooms to be had at any price, so they keep driving south. Towns and cities north of the storm are frantically searching for places to house the thousands of refugees.

Thousands of flights have been canceled **across the US**. Thousands more are being rerouted. Airports across the country are filled with angry and frightened travelers. Tempers are short and fights have broken out. Airports are forced to double their security personnel.

Behind closed doors in **D.C.** congressmen and senators argue over disaster funds for their states. There just isn't enough money to go around.

For all branches of the **Military**, orders to deploy are canceled. The troops are deployed stateside to the disaster zones instead. In the confusion no one remembers to cancel the orders for the troops returning home.

5:00 am EDT, September 26,

Dancing Goats Farm,
Moon Mountain, North Carolina

Gianna woke and made her way to her kitchen. The house was quiet with the girls gone. The renovations to their Vardos completed ahead of schedule, they had moved back in yesterday. Sadie's cottage in the Gypsy Camp was packed with the furniture and boxes from her moving truck. Rather than tackle the mess on her first night home, she had opted to spend the night with her sister, Violet. Not that they got much sleep; Violet, Sadie and Lizzy were part of last night's Hades crew.

As she sipped her coffee she asked Tony "Shall we turn on the computer and see what fresh hell there is today?" In reply he rubbed his forehead on hers and then tapped his bowl. "I don't think this is a sincere show of affection. You just want a bowl of fresh goat's milk." As she poured Tony's milk she watched the horrifying images of the unfolding disaster. "Tony this is so bad. Do you know how lucky you are to live here?" He assumes this is a rhetorical question and continues lapping up his milk. She was reaching over the counter to get her cigarettes out of the drawer but Tony's in the way and won't budge an inch. "Hey, get out of the way hairball." She managed to get a hold of the cigarettes but couldn't seem to locate the lighter.

While she was searching Nick walked in behind her. He stood there a good ten seconds, enjoying the view before he said, "Morning." Realizing what she'd been reaching for he said, "Gia Stop, I have your fire right here." He lit her cigarette and Djarum Black for himself. Smiling as he did because he was sure she had no idea her reaching had caused her nightgown to ride up, giving him a greatly appreciated view all the way up her thighs to the curve of her ass.

She took a drag and exhaled. "Thank you, coffee? What's up handsome?" She always teased him over how handsome he was and how all the women smiled whenever he was near.

Nick Lorenzini; 64, 6'4", black hair with more than a touch of silver, green eyes, chiseled features, tall, dark and handsome. Though the dark had more to do with his temperament than his Italian ancestry. Nicky Lorenzini was on the top of *all* the single women's lists and a few who weren't single. When people asked about the nature of their relationship Gianna told them he was her partner and co-creator of the farm. What she didn't tell them was how much she enjoyed the opticals of her wickedly handsome partner. She and Nick had a deep friendship built on years of mutual respect and need. She... had issues of trust. He... had done one too many Tours. She needed someone she could count on for the safety of her family and Tribe. He needed a place to be what he had become.

They'd met ten years ago just after she'd won the money and was hunting for the property. A drunk had stopped her in a hotel parking lot. He wouldn't take no for an answer. Then he stupidly grabbed her by the arm. Nick stepped in and flipped him on his ass. She looked up at Nick and said, "Thank you, but I could have handled this myself. I'm not a man, so I don't have a problem kneeing one in the balls." He smiled then she said, "C'mon, good lookin' let me buy you a drink for you efforts." They talked for hours, as if they'd known each other for years. They closed the hotel bar, them ended up in an all night diner. Nick loved her vision. By breakfast he had committed to helping her build it. Nick was with her when she found the property. Gianna had found her sanctuary, Nick had found a place where being really fucking scary wouldn't be a problem.

Nick took the coffee she offered and a stool. Reluctantly he pushed the image of her naked ass from his mind. "Gia it's going to get pretty fucking ugly... fast. What's going out there is seriously bad making it strategically more complicated to keep this place both safe and hidden. It's not going to get better any time soon. Watching this makes me think we should have found a place in Idaho. We're relatively insulated here but if it goes the way I think it will, *They will find us.* We could have dozens refugees outside the Q's gates begging for food and a place to stay in a matter of days."

"I know you're right. I don't think Mother is anywhere near finished. The hordes are going to move north. We don't have a lot of ground between us and them, but don't you think they'll go toward the urban areas? It's what they know. Short of a Kevlar dome over the whole farm - what else do we need to do?"

"Yes they'll go to the cities in the beginning. However the way they're overrunning the areas just north of the storm, I'd say we're about twelve hours max away from Martial Law. At first it may be confined to the affected states. The reality is the government doesn't have a plan for this. They are so fucking far from being equipped to handle this volume of refugees it will quickly spiral out of control. When they realize they're about to lose control, that's when Martial Law will go into effect."

Gianna shook her head. "I know you're right. They don't even have an evacuation plan for a nuclear attack. In fact they have a law forbidding the federal government from creating a nuclear evacuation plan. How fucked up is that? It's all left to the states. When your state is trashed, I guess your simply fucked."

"Even if they had a half assed plan, neither the state governments nor the federal government have enough food stockpiled to feed this many people for months. If they did, we wouldn't have thousands of homeless Vets starving in the streets. It's September - you can't grow in the north and the southeast is trashed. When it comes to appropriating civilian supplies, we may fool them with the Q for a while. When they do find the farm, and they will, I'm confident that Hades bunkers are safe.

Not everything is. I spent last night thinking about what wasn't. We need another bunker for animals. I think we should put up greenhouse over it. Maybe out in the Gypsy Camp. If they take everything, or what they think is everything, we can rebuild as long as we have pairs. And I won't have to hear you bitch. That's always a plus."

"Okay smart ass, how do we keep it hidden while we build it? We could do it by hand but that may take longer than we have. So we need a prefab but how do we get it in without everyone knowing?"

"A semi-finished storage container. A pair actually, that we can connect. We'll buy them then park them off site. We'll bring them in after curfew. We can use the service road to come around to the back of the camp."

"Where is the closest place to buy them?"

"In Raleigh."

"Good; close enough to be easy but not so close they'll know where it's going. Can we send some of the boys today? What do we need, two pickups and two long bed trailers, right? So let's send them now. Who do you want to send?"

"Charlie, Lee, Gabe and..."

"And I think you should let Tiny out of the fucking basement. Send Tiny. Who's gonna fuck with Tiny?"

"   OK! Tiny can go. Woman don't nag me before I've finished my coffee. They'll take the two Dodge rams and the two hay trailers. Card or cash?"

"I'll give them cash but I'd rather they put it on the card if they can. Not sure how much money we're going to be able to get out of the banks after this week. Oh, make sure they have their carry permits on them this time. No fuck ups! Let me get the cash. Be right back." As he watched her walk down the hall, he thought about the image that had greeted him earlier.

Gianna returned with the credit card and the cash. "This should do it. Think

I'll make a Costco run today. Who knows, they may start moving stock to where the people are."

Nick frowned at the idea. "I'm going with you. I don't want you out there without me."

She leaned across the counter. "*No* you're not. Don't make that face at me. I don't want both of us off the farm at the same time any more." He tried to object but she wouldn't let him. "Nick, if one of us doesn't come back from a run, one of us has to be here to keep things going." The thought of her not returning caused a tightening in his chest. He knew she was right, but he still didn't want her out there without him to protect her. She saw the tightening in his jaw and smiled knowing she had won. "Besides sweet cheeks, you had your shopping trip yesterday. I'll take Violet, Sadie and Amber. Think I'll let Carmichael ride shot gun."

His fist hit the counter. "No! Are you fucking crazy?" He realized instantly his reaction was over the top, but he was pissed she'd be out there without him.

"If you're going to be a rude asshole I'm not speaking to you. As long as you or I are there to keep hold of his leash Carmichael's fine. Seriously Nick, he needs this outing as an emotional cushion. *You know* he doesn't do well with

94

cages. This place could get a little psychologically confining for him after awhile. He needs a fun road trip. He'll be fine. You get Tiny and the boys on the road. I need to round up the girls." She slid off the stool and left him fuming.

"Woman where are you going?"

"Upstairs to change that is unless you think I should go shopping in my nightgown."

The thought of her outside the walls in that silk thing without him snapped his control. "NO!" He slammed the door on his way out.

While she dressed Gianna called Violet and Sadie at the Gypsy Camp then Amber. "Hey honey are you up for a Costco run?

"Shit yes! Give me fifteen minutes to go over today's list with Dawn. Auntie, do we want to take the white cargo van? We've been using it to move stuff faster, it's here at 'Summerland'."

"Yes, I'll have Nick send one of the boys for it. He's moving other vehicles through the gate right now. Meet us in the Q."

He was gone when she returned to the kitchen. She hadn't heard his rude exit. She called him. "Nick, I need my Dark

Lady and the white cargo van moved out to
the Q. The van is over at the Summerland
greenhouse. I don't know where my truck
is."

He still had his pissed at her voice
on. "We'll get the van. The truck is
parked in front of the barn. Lee and
Charlie used it to do a 20 mile recon
last night."

6:30 am EDT,

Gianna met the women at the Q gate.
"Violet and Sadie take the van. Amber,
you're with me. I want a word with the
boys before they leave. Carmichael you're
in the truck with me."

"Are you sure ma'am? The girls might
need me in the van."

"No! You ride in the truck with me
because *you*, like 'Alan Shore', cannot be
trusted!"

Gianna walked up as Nick was giving
the men their orders. She came in at the
tail end. "...low profile. You're looking
to buy these for your cabin in the
mountains down near Ashville. Charlie,
you work the deal. Try to pay with the
card. Tiny holds the cash. They may
already be hit by victims of the storm.
If your choices are limited, call me."
Nick turned to Gianna. "Ma'am, did you
have something you wanted to say?"

"No Nicholas, I believe you've said it all. Travel safe boys, come back to us in one piece."

Charlie stepped forward. "Ma'am would you tell Lee no Tom Petty on this trip, please. Last night all he would play out on recon was Tom Petty songs. I'm kinda Petty-ied out."

Gianna shrugged her shoulders "Well... frankly, I don't see how a body could be *Petty-ied* out. *'Don't come around here no more'*, seems like a damn good recon mantra to me, but it's a long ride, so Lee, no Tom Petty today."

"No problem Ma'am. Today seems more like a Rolling Stones day."

This last did not make Charlie any happier. Charlie was a born and bred Texan. As far as he was concerned there was County music and the rest was just a whole lot of noise. "Tiny you ride with Lee. I'll drive the second truck with Gabe."

Gianna turned and left without even a 'see you later' to Nick for his outburst in the kitchen. Carmichael was still standing next to the black truck. "Ma'am we have no intel on how the civilian population is taking this. I really think..."

Gianna swung around and eyeballed him with a look that any Marine Drill Sergeant would be proud to call his own. She punctuated each word with her index finger in his chest. "You're out of my sight... you're out of your fucking mind! Marine, get your ass in that truck!"

Nick watched the interaction and thought, *'Oh he'll be just fine'*. Watching her pull through the gate he wished he'd sent two of the vanguard with her.

Down the road Gianna glanced in the rear view mirror. Carmichael was contently tapping out a drum solo, the song to which only he could hear. He was not offended by her disciplining him. He liked when she reeled him in. Even better, that she knew he couldn't always reel himself in. She cares about him. It makes him feel safe. After Iraq, he didn't think he'd ever own that emotion again. As they cruised down the road *'Gimme Shelter'* rocked on in his head.

7:10 am EDT, September 26,
Devil's Fork Gap
Smokey Mountains, Tennessee

Frank took the graveyard shift thinking it would be the time when there would be the least amount of traffic, and his shift would end just in time for breakfast! He was right about the breakfast, he was way off on the traffic. He'd spent most of the night talking to

HAM operators across the southeast. At the moment he was filling the guys in on what he had heard.

"Reports out'a Charlotte said that South Carolinians started showing up in the afternoon but a big wave of evacuees hit there 'bout 1:00 am. My buddy in Chattanooga said they started seein' the first wave of evacuees 'round 3:00 am. Emergency shelters and motels straight across from Chattanooga to Fayetteville are booked. Parking lots are filled with the big trucks that drove north to get around the storm. Some don't know what to do with their loads cause they were headed to locations south of the storm. Others had to pull over to keep from bein' over their road hours. Then there are the ones who can't find gas. This will tell you how stupid the people running things are... the frigging SPR office is in New Orleans, now under ten feet of water! The four emergency fuel storage sites, two in Texas and two in Louisiana, are also under water. Round 6:00 am residents in the areas bein' overrun by evacuees were linein' up at the pumps toppin' off their tanks and fillin' cans. Remember what happened after Harvey in 2017? This is gonna be much worse.

Dan shook his head. "Wish we'd stored two hundred gallons instead of just a hundred."

"The news says they have no idea how long it will take for the water to recede. They say millions will be homeless. There's a rumor outta' Washington that everyone bein' held by immigration is gonna' be sent back."

Billy interjected, "That'll save The government a few billion!"

"I need to talk to Pauline an' see what she thinks but I'm leanin' toward emptyin' out the store today and boardin' it up."

Rory added his two cents. "As for the gas, I think if we all start rationing today we'll be okay for a good long while. We should see if we can get the propane tank topped off today. Frank what's still in the store?" Their conversation was interrupted by a call to breakfast.

5:16 am PDT, September 26, Hollywood, California

A 5.8 earthquake rattled **Hollywood. Universal City** sustained extensive structural damage. In Topanga Canyon boulders rocked loose crushing homes and cars. The water level in the Hollywood Reservoir dropped two feet...

7:30 am EDT, September 26, Miami, Florida

100

The **National Hurricane Center** issues an advisory Hurricane Sara is holding at category 3, wind speeds have increased to 128 mph. It's still expected to make landfall around 11:00 pm tonight at **Charleston, South Carolina.** Mandatory evacuations of Charleston, **North Charleston, Mt. Pleasant,** and the islands has begun. Voluntary evacuation zone is for everything east of interstate 95 and to the west of downtown Charleston. Now a Tropical storm, Rafael's rain bands are drenching all of South Carolina. Rafael entered the Atlantic just south of Savannah ten minutes ago. It is expected to merge with Sara over the next few hours.

**9:00 am EDT, September 26,
Devil's Fork Gap
Smokey Mountains, Tennessee**

Frank, not wanting to provoke Pauline into one of her diatribes over breakfast, warned the other men to keep the conversation lite while they ate. After breakfast the four couples gathered in the living room to discuss current events and what actions they should take. Frank looked at his wife. "It's gettin' pretty bad out there. People are fleein' the storm areas. Gas is short and will get shorter. Food deliveries are sittin' in big trucks in parking lots. Soon there's gonna' be serious food shortages too. Pauline, I think it's time to close the store and board it up."

Pauline frowned. Dan jumped in before she could protest. "We don't know how people will react in this. It's best we hunker-down inside the compound. This situation is why we built this place. If the store is not protected they will break in."

Rory offered his plan. "I say we go down in two trucks and take empty boxes and bins with us. Frank said he has the plywood stored in the back room. We can work on securing the doors and windows while the rest of you pack up everything and load the trucks. We do this in daylight so folks know the place is empty and will spread the word. 'No point breaking in there.' See what I'm saying Pauline? Billy will stay here to watch the place."

Pauline sighed. She was a practical woman. "I suppose y'all are right. Well, let's get to it."

Twenty minutes later they pulled up to the store. Pauline waved at the two people standing around in front of the store. "Hey Martha, Stan, how are y'all doin'?"

"We're fine, just hoping you would open and here you are."

Before Pauline blew the cover story he'd made up Frank said, "Hey folks there's not much left, but y'all are welcome to come in an buy what's on the shelves." He held the door and followed them in. While Pauline bustled around turning on lights and unlocking the back door for Rory and Dan, Frank kept the shoppers engaged. "What with all the trouble down south deliveries to our suppliers have been delayed. We're here to close up the store today. A few friends came to help. Pauline wants us to stay with her kin in Virginia. Thinkin' it might be a good idea."

Martha and Stan stocked up on can goods, batteries and a bottle of lamp oil. As Pauline was ringing up the order two more customers came in. More trickled in over the next hour. There were only two boxes of merchandise left on the shelves when they locked the door.

11:30 am EDT,

Frank put the new padlock on the door while the others got in the trucks. As they were pulling out a dirty banged up Suburban pulled in. The back was loaded with camping gear and duffle bags. A rough looking man rolled down the window. "We was told there was a store here. This don't look open. Do you know of any other?"

Frank didn't like the looks of these guys. That Texas accent said he wasn't local. "There was a store here but they couldn't get deliveries cause of all that's happenin' down south so they emptied out what was left and closed it up. You just missed them."

Dan whispered "The guy in the back is eyeing the shelving stickin' out of the tarp."

Frank continued. "They had sold out'a the food, but he sold me some shelving for my garage. Think he said he was headed to Kingsport."

The guy in the back seat of the Suburban hit the driver in the back of his head. "There ain't nothin' here. GO! let's get the fuck down the road." They pulled a U-turn and peeled out heading north towards Kingsport.

Rory punched Dan in the shoulder. "Dan you may have just saved our lives. Good lookin' out. Thank God we brought those tarps. What do y'all think they were lookin' for?"

Dan said, "Guess pretty much anything they could get their hands on. Judging by the gear in the back I'd say shelter is high on their list. Camping in late September might be fine in Texas but they're gonna freeze their balls off up here in these mountains."

Frank exhaled loudly. "It's only been twenty-four hours, they're already makin' it up here. What's the next twenty-four gonna bring? They get up here and find this ain't no place for livin' ruff in October, they'll be bangin' on doors beggin' for people to take'em in. Shit we gotta get back an' lock the place down."

Frank got out and walked around to the passenger side of the other truck. "Pauline, you get in with me. Let Dan drive his truck. If those assholes are waitin' down the road I want to have at least one of us men in each truck."

Dan and Rory got out too. "Frank, I'll ride shotgun with Dan. Let the girls ride with you. You follow behind us." Tracy climbed in the back with Cindy and Betty Lou. Before getting in Dan's truck, Rory removed the 12 gauge from under the seat. He was now literally *Ridin'* Shotgun.

chapter 5

THE EVE OF DESTRUCTION

"Be aware,
Mother's on a tier,
Her destruction's Everywhere"

12:30 pm EDT, September 26,
Dancing Goats Farm
Moon Mountain, North Carolina

Theo and Lizzy arrived at Alice's Restaurant as the truck and van were backing up to the door. Gianna jumped out of the truck. "Hey you two, good timing. Let's get the stuff out of the freezer first." The cargo van was retrofitted with an 8 cubic foot DC powered chest freezer.

Simon stuck his head out the door. "What the fuck are you bringing me all this shit for?"

Gianna smiled. "Don't get your knickers in a twist. Most of this is for the girls and me."

Shaking his head no he asked, "And what did this trip cost you? Did you manage to stay under two grand?"

Amber handed him a box. "Fuck no! Try one and a half times that."

Taking the box he said, "Who the fuck spends five thousand dollars at the grocery store?"

Gianna followed him inside carrying another box. She set it on the counter and pulled out two bottles, one Jameson Black and one Jameson Reserve. "So I should take these back?"

Grinning he took them from her. "Don't be a Fucking Idict."

Theo was rummaging through the box he carried in, looking for anything he might like to claim. "Oh, Sean called. He said the rhino ran through Burbank and then was spotted again in Hollywood early this morning. He's on the road. He'll call again when he gets to Phoenix. He has me texting any traffic issues ahead of him. I'm recommending he take 27 north at El Paso. He can pick up 40 east in Albuquerque. It will be a fuck of a lot longer - but that's what he gets for not listening to you earlier."

Amber noticed Theo's rummaging. "Ah, *Theo*... that's not *really* helping!"

"Amber this *really* isn't *my* job." On the way out the door he added, "I'm taking these."

Violet looked at her cousin "What - did he just take?"

"A thing of Mixed Nuts."

Sadie chimed in, "Well, *that's* appropriate."

From outside the door... "I can still hear you *Sadie*."

Sadie sniped back, "Well, quit eavesdropping and get back to your *real* job *Theo*."

From farther down the walk, "Remember *Sadie*, I do the scheduling."

Neither one could ever let the other have the last word... *willingly*.

2:00 pm EDT, September 26,
Devil's Fork Gap
Smokey Mountain, Tennessee

Frank found his wife in the kitchen. "We got the shelves put together in the store room. There's space now for all of the stuff we brought back from the store. I can't believe we missed those four cases last time. Dan said he slipped them out the back door. He didn't want the people comin' in the store to buy them. What's all this?"

There are canning supplies spread out on the counter and table. Pauline was stirring a huge pot that smelled like beef stew. Cindy said, "We girls thought about the meat in the freezer and how we could lose it if the power went out. So we made up a bunch of it into this stew to can. It's a lot easier to heat a ready-made meal than to cook one from scratch on the wood stove."

Frank grinned at their quick thinking. "That's real smart of y'all."

Rory yelled from the living room. "Holy Shit! - Everyone get in here quick!"

The President was on the TV announcing that he had just declared Martial Law in Texas, Louisiana, Mississippi, Alabama, Florida and Georgia for the 'safety' of all American citizens.

Billy began pacing back and forth smacking his fist into his palm. "I knew it when I woke up this mornin'. Then when y'all came back an told me about those Texans I knew it for sure!"

Dan said, "Calm down Billy, you're scaring the girls. What did you know?"

Billy threw his arms up. "I knew this was the day the shit would hit the fan!"

Dan stood and put his hand on Billy's shoulder. "Listen man, it's not happenin' here in Tennessee. Maybe it's a good thing. If the government doesn't get people under control we could end up with more like those guys we ran into today."

Despite Dan's words Billy kept escalating. "Listen Dan, we all gotta be on full red alert. *Everybody's got to carry - at all times.* We gotta have one person in the command room and one in the tower - at all times." Then Billy ran out of the room.

Frank ran after him. "Hey Billy wait up. Where y'all going?

Billy yelled back, "Gonna make sure the bars are across the gates."

Cindy stood up. "Well, I have no intention of cooking with a gun on my hip while I'm working a pressure canner! I'm going to check the stew."

Rory stood too. "Billy's crazy but he's not entirely wrong. We do need to be more vigilant. Those assholes today would have pulled a gun on us, maybe even shot us, if they thought we had anything they might want. A minute can make a big difference right now. If we had left a minute earlier we would have been gone before they got there. If they had been a minute earlier they would have seen Frank locking the door and today would have played out a whole lot differently than it did. I don't think anybody needs to wear a gun in the kitchen, but having one close at hand say in a drawer just in case - seems like a good idea to me. Y'all just think about it. I'm going to check on what's being said online. And Ladies, that stew is smelling mighty good."

2:15 pm EDT, September 26,
Dancing Goats Farm,
Moon Mountain, North Carolina

Nick found Gianna standing on her back porch staring out over the farm deep in contemplation. He knew that expression. She had a mind like a steel trap. Beneath that Earth Mother persona was a brilliant strategist. She had a talent for viewing a situation and extrapolating all possible outcomes. It was one of the things they had in common. He could almost hear the gears turning. He stepped up behind her. Her perfume filled his head. He loved the way she smelled. "I take it you've heard."

She turned and smiled up at him. "That's one of the things I love most about you, Nicholas. Whenever there's a difficult situation I turn and you're always there by my side. You nailed it this morning. You said within twelve hours to Martial Law and it's been nine. kitchen or office?"

111

He opened the door for her and said, "The kitchen has always been our war room. The men are about twenty miles out from the Q. Given the changes today and what they've encountered out there, I'm having them come straight here.

There were no problems getting there. They found what we wanted and the guy took the card. By the time they were finished securing the loads, a dozen buyers had shown up. Most of them wanted the units we'd bought, which of course were the last two. It was a bit rough getting out of there. Tiny got out and cleared a path to the gate as only Tiny can. Refugees were already pouring off 95. Traffic on the way back was a bitch. They stopped for gas in Winston-Salem. They waited for almost an hour."

"Can we have Charlie stop at the bank? I think the max cash on that card is $800. Tell him to get as much as he can." Nick texted Charlie as he listened. "Once they're back let's send Violet on a cash run to the other three banks. Send two guard and Carmichael with her. Inside she can make thousand dollar withdrawals."

Nick looked up and shook his head. "*No*, not Carmichael, I saw how well he was behaving before you even left, and it wasn't *fine*. I'll send Lee. Fuel is already an issue. I've sent Freddy and

Becky out towards Mt. Airy with gas cans. They have twenty of them tarped in the bed. They're stopping at every station, filling one or two cans each stop. We have four hundred gallons in reserve, not including the two 65 gallon barrels in the barn, and four more out behind Summerland. We'll use what they bring back to keep the barrels and the vehicles topped off. I'd rather we buy as long as we can, keeping the reserve for when there is no more. I'll send a different team out each day till that happens. Roy is out now doing his weekly check on the fuel blinds."

The eight Fuel Blinds look like ramshackled hunting blinds. The difference being, buried underneath them are fifty gallon fuel drums. Roy checks for damage and stirs the tanks weekly.

"What is our total number of gallons at this moment?"

"The barrels aren't quite full so let's say 50 gallons per barrel- that's 400 plus the reserve. So we're sitting at 800 gallons not counting the vehicles."

"Okay I'd like to see us have at least another 200 gallons in barrels. That would give us a gallon a day for two years once we can't get any more. Do we have enough barrels for that?"

"We have at least six we can use for

gas. After your *little* Costco run
yesterday I'm sure we have more food put
back than FEMA. We also have the ability
to produce more, which others may not be
able to do for long. Food generally does
not fall under my purview. However, the
gross lack of available food out there
can and will present security issues
here. The less attention we draw at the Q
the better. I'm restricting access. No
one except you, me and the Guard.
Everyone else needs permission from one
of us." Gianna shook her head in
agreement.

The company reserves have ALL
checked in. The last thirty came in at
noon. Tonight, we will be running field
exercises out east of Hundred Acre Wood.
We will continue to recon twice a day,
changing up the times every day. This
morning I assigned Stephen all of the
reserves who had checked in. I talked to
him on my way here. He said they had most
of the nets up. Can we get the Mad
Scientist to send up his drone this
afternoon? I want to know what's still
exposed."

"Ahhh ya, I'll ride over to 'Studio
City' and talk to him when we're finished
here. After he sends up his 'birds', I'll
have Glen put a copy of the footage on a
thumb drive for you. I need to check with
Jerry anyway. I want the numbers on what
he has bottled. Some of it should be sent
to Hades."

"Right, neither of us want's to go into the apocalypse without enough booze. After I see the footage I may want to add more nets. I want to go to, what is it you call it, oh right cammie mode?

"Fine. Anyone who has a problem with it can either stay inside or they can bunk with Hansel and Gretel."

Nick laughed. "At some point, they may need a bigger house. Carl and his family got back, about an hour after you left. He looked pretty frigging road weary. He drove straight through from Maine. He said unless something urgent came up, he'd talk to you in the morning. Think all he wanted was a shower and a bed."

"That's good. Glad they made it back safely. The rule of thumb when going into an apocalypse is... it's best to have ones *Fixer* in-house.

Nick fanned shock. "Gianna, I thought *I* was your *'Fixer'*"

Gianna grinned wickedly. "You my sweet, are not my *Fixer*. You are my *Facilitator* and my *sledge hammer*. You and Carl are very different. Why would I use my sledge hammer when a screw driver between the ribs will do?" A very sexy smile spread across his face. She changed the subject knowing he was trying to make her laugh. "Nick, I don't think we have anyone out there other than Sean. If he hauls ass to Albuquerque he might get ahead of the mob."

"Gia, I think that's wishful thinking on your part. I can't see him not getting caught up in that mess."

"Nicholas, you better hope he doesn't Cause *you'll* be the one to go and get him out of it!"

"Has Adrian found anything useful?"

"They're working on finding all the information on what the government is doing as they do it. They're looking for chatter on anyone who might try to strike at the country while we're up to our asses in alligators! There's a report somewhere in this mess on other Natural Disasters happening around the globe. Look in that pile in front of you."

Nick interrupted her. "Hold on, just got a text from Becky. She says they're being followed by a truckload of redneck assholes. They keep passing them and then slowing down." Nick called DJ. "Becky's got trouble on her 6. She's 5 klicks north. Runnem' down and hold 'em till I get there." Nick was halfway to the east portal before the conversation was done.

Through the binoculars DJ spied them about a mile ahead. "The bastard in the truck just slammed on his brakes. He's skidded sideways blocking the road. Freddy's trying to stop. Shit! I think he bumped them. One of the guys standing in the truck bed almost fell out. One has a rifle. Looks like one of them is motioning Becky and Freddy out of their truck."

The driver said, "DJ, you can shut up now, I can see them, they're fifteen feet in front of us!"

The black pickup rolled to a stop. There were three men standing in the bed of an old Ford. The one with a shotgun resting in the crook of his arm, turned and waved the black truck off. Ignoring him, DJ stepped out of the truck. "Boys, I think maybe there's been a slight misunderstanding..."

The one with the shotgun sneered. "The only misunderstanding here is you not understanding me wavin' you off."

DJ smiled knowing he had the upper hand. "No, that's where you're wrong, country boy... that truck over there is ours... as in we own the pink slip."

The men in the ratty pickup were suddenly distracted by the rumble of the Harley rolling to a stop alongside the black truck. Nick got off the bike and walked over to DJ. Nick looked from the country boys over to DJ and back to the country boys.

In a low menacing voice Nick said, "You have ten seconds to get out of here. After that you're dead."

The word dead was still hanging in the air, as six members of the vanguard rose up out of the black truck bed. Without uttering a sound three of the men in the Ford jackrabbit into the woods. The asshole with the gun took five seconds too long to make up his mind. From behind, Freddy yanked him over the side of the pickup. DJ caught the rifle in mid air. Nick walked around the back of the pickup. The man was flat on his back with Becky's boot on his throat. Nick yanked him to his feet by the front of his shirt. Nick looked him in the eye for 20 seconds. Disgusted with what he saw there, Nick shoved the man backwards into the waiting hands of the vanguard.

"This asshole learned nothing from this little encounter. Think we'll have to kill him." Nick walked back to his bike. As he passed DJ he said, "Text the Lady. Tell her I'll be home in time for tea." Then he roared off.

DJ was shaking his head and laughing as he pulled out his phone. He knew Nick wanted the Lady to know the situation was contained. However the image of Nick sipping tea on the veranda was just too incongruous for words.

The men hog tied, blindfolded, and tossed country boy face down in their truck bed. They push his pickup off the road into a drainage ditch and headed home. On the way the man could hear them joking about the incident.

"Hey, did you hear the sound when the pickup went into the ditch?"

"Yea, that was the sound of the front axle snapping."

"Fuck, that's too bad..."

"What does it matter? It's not like he's ever going to drive it again."

"Think he knows there's no coming back from this ride?"

"Do we care? The Boss may kill him. An order is an order."

The man tried to roll on his side and was forced down by a boot on the small of his back. The owner of the boot said "Where do you think *you're* going, fuckwad?"

The black truck rolled into the barn. Antonio turned off the engine.

Nick was already there. "Put him in the box. We'll move him to Hansel and Gretel's after curfew. Wash the truck and wipe down the bike. Becky, find Roy and get the fuel put up."

Nick headed back to the farm to give Gianna the incident report.

Two of the men lifted country boy out of the truck and drop him in a hole in the barn floor and closed the lid.

4:00 pm EDT, September 26,
Planet Earth Blog Online,
Location Unknown

In the Atlantic off South Carolina Rafael and Sara have merged into a cat 4 hurricane. The projected course will take the eye over Fort Sumpter and up the Ashley and Cooper Rivers. The mandatory evacuation area is now everything east of I-95. Parts of the interstate are beginning to flood. Twelve inches of rain have fallen in the eastern half of South Carolina in the last thirteen hours. The Low Country is becoming one huge wetland.

Hawaii continues to be shaken by smaller aftershocks. Lava flows from Kilauea are hampering the earthquake rescue efforts.

California is still assessing the damage from this morning's earthquakes. The death toll stands at 58 with hundreds still missing.

Greenland's Helheim glacier claved

another 10 billion ton iceberg last night. Half mile high shards of ice are breaking off of the iceberg and shattering as they hit the water. This is creating hundreds of smaller ice floats.

In Antarctica scientists are closely monitoring both the widening crack in the Thwaites Glacier ice sheet and the path the Thwaites Iceberg Tongue is taking. Since breaking free it has drifted 400 miles west.

Japan's Mount Shinmmoedake is erupting. Scientists are watching Mount Sakurajima closely after having discovered earlier this year that the two volcanoes are connect by an ancient subterranean lava flow. The Mount Shinmmoedake eruption brings the total to eight major volcanoes that are now actively erupting around the Ring of Fire.

Russia is reporting 'issues' with it's nuclear power plant in Obininsk, located 110 km south west of Moscow. A thousand acre peat bog fire is burning in Siberia and spreading unchecked.

The Ebola outbreak in the Democratic Republic of the Congo is escalating. A thousand new cases were reported this week.

The World Health Organization warns that antibiotics currently in development will not work on the growing number of drug resistant infections.

The White House has informed NATO it has begun to pull all of its troops out, sighting a greater need for them at home.

In Africa fourteen countries report an escalation of fighting and drought. South Africa has run out of water.

4:30 pm EDT, September 26,
Devil's Fork Gap
Smokey Mountains, Tennessee

Billy whispered into his radio. "Dan, come in."

Frank came into the room as Dan answered. "What's up Billy? Why are you whispering?"

"Dan there's a truck out in fronta' the gate. Two guys got out an' are snoopin' around."

Frank leaned over and switched on the monitor for the front gate camera. "Sure as shit there are two guys screwing with the gate trying to get it open." He took the radio from Dan. "Billy, y'all just sit tight. Let's see what all they do." Frank and Dan watch as the intruders try to pick the lock. Having no luck they circle around to the back side of the compound.

Rubbing his hands together, Dan said. "This is gonna be good."

Billy asks, "I don't see 'em any more. Y'all got eyes on 'em?"

"Yes. They're goin' round the side."

Frank and Dan watched as the two intruders disappeared.

Dan grabbed the radio. "Billy, It Worked! Both of them at one time!"

Billy can hear Frank hooting in the background. "Can the camera see 'em in the hole? I think I best stay put. Don't know if anybody's still in the truck."

"You stay put. Frank and I are going out the back to see what we have. Make sure no one sneaks up behind us. Rory will take over in here."

Not sure if the guys in their trap are armed, Frank and Dan get close enough to hear what they are saying, but not close enough to get shot... hopefully.

"What the hell happened?"

"It's a fuckin' trap! Those bastards!"

"What bastards?"

"The ones who set the trap you

123

asshole! If you weren't my brother I'd have left you back in Georgia. We gotta' get out of here and find a empty house to stay in."

"You said this was empty. Why would they lock it up if they was home?"

"To keep people like us out, asshole!"

Without moving forward Frank yelled. "That's right, assholes such as y'all. This is our home an y'all tried to break in. As I see it I have every right to shoot you. Thinkin' y'all need to set there for a while an think on that."

Walking away Frank and Dan could hear the two of them begging to be set free.

Inside Frank yelled to Rory , "Tell Billy to come down. We have two prisoners." Dan and the girls were already in the living room.

"Hey Billy, You can come down now. We have to have a meeting about what to do with them."

Billy burst into the living room. "What the hell happened? I told y'all we needed to be on red alert. Ya shoulda' shot them. Why didn't' ya?"

Rory look at him in disbelief.

"Billy, we can't just go shooting people. We need to call the Sheriff. They were trying to break into our house. That's a crime. They'll be arrested. Does everyone agree?"

Not waiting for their answers, Cindy stepped into the kitchen and dialed 911 "Yes we need a deputy out here. We just caught two men trying to break into our house. No, they're outside in a hole. It's a trap we built, they fell in. Yes, that's the address. Thank you." Back in the living room she cut Billy off in mid rant. "This is ridiculous we're not killers. There is a deputy on the way." Everyone but Billy was secretly relieved.

6:30 pm EDT, September 26, New York, New York

The congressman raised the window between him and the driver then pulled out his phone. "David, You're going to love this. Washington is a shit storm! Everyone is screaming for money. There's none to give them. I was tempted to tell them in a few months it won't matter... no matter how much they got, just to shut them up. How is everyone holding up? Did anyone take a big hit in the market?"

"They're stable. In fact Ammar is quite pleased with the gas and oil loses in Texas and Louisiana. The value of his oil fields just skyrocketed. Jeb said he'd be fine; oil is only a fraction of his personal holdings. His ranch is fine. He's here in New York for a charity event so he didn't even get his feet wet. How's your head?"

"I'm fine. I think these hurricane disasters will work to our advantage in the long run. Still nothing on the email?"

"Not a thing. I have another call coming in I need to take. Great news."

8:00 pm EDT, September 26,
Planet Earth Blog Online,
Location Unknown

I-95 in South Carolina is closed due to flooding.

The Governor of **North Carolina** closed the southern border of the state. Refugees traveling north are restricted to I-95 to travel through to Virginia. Refugees can also take 77 into Charlotte to find assistance. The National Guard has been called out to enforce the restrictions.

Due to widespread looting Martial Law has been declared for **South Carolina**. Troops are being deployed there. A statewide curfew has gone into effect.

In Greenland a glacial earthquake of 4.8 caused cracks in the Helheim Glacier. An iceberg the size of Delaware claved

126

off.

The death toll in **California**
continued to rise when an unstable
apartment building collapsed. It stands
at 204.

A 6.5 earthquake has struck **Mexico City**.

There have been riots at both
California and Texas border crossings. 50
people have been arrested, 10 people
shot, 2 are dead.

In **Dallas** people attacked the FEMA
staff when they ran out of food and
water. Three FEMA members were
hospitalized. Tear gas was used to
disperse the crowd.

8:10 pm EDT, September 26,
Dancing Goats Farm,
Moon Mountain, North Carolina

Nick found Gianna sitting in the
kitchen with a very large glass of wine
and Adrian's latest print out of the news
on the net in her hand. She was listening
to Barry McGuire. 'This is foreboding'.
he thought. Nick tried to lighten her
mood. "You know you have solar power
here, right? You don't have to get
smashed in the twilight with the lights
off to save electricity."

She glanced up at him. "Here babe

127

sit and read these. The top one is the one we were looking for when you ran out of here this afternoon. The other is the later report. Someone is posting these news bulletins on line."

When he was finished reading he tossed them on the table. "Fuck! When you put it like that... shit I need a beer." He got one out of the fridge. Sitting across from her he asked, "Gia I get *'The eve of destruction'* but what do we follow it up with?"

"The only thing we can Nicholas... a little Grace at Woodstock to feed your head."

chapter 6
DEATH OF THE AMERICAN PIE

"The ocean took the space,
The generations have no place,
It's time to face,
The Clock's gone twelve"

6:00 am EDT, September 27,
Dancing Goats Farm,
Moon Mountain, North Carolina

Violet found her mother with her elbows on the counter her face in her hands. "Mother are you ckay?"

Tilting her head Gianna asked. "Yes why?"

"Because you don't look okay."

Sitting up she frowned at her daughter. "Thank you. That's *just* what every 64 year old woman wants to hear *first thing* in the morning! What are you doing here? Wait a minute... what time is it?"

"It's six o' clock"

"In the morning? Shit, the world must have come to an end if you're voluntarily up at 6:00 am."

Violet sighed and rolled her eyes at her mother's sarcasm "I'm not up, I just haven't gone to bed yet. Why are you asleep sitting up?"

"I was waiting for my coffee. Nick and I were drinking last night... OK?"

"Go sit at the table before you fall off that stool. I'll bring your coffee."

Yawing Gianna slid off the stool, "I don't care what they say about you, you *are* a good child."

Violet set the mug down in front of her mother and picked up the empty wine and beer bottles. "What drove you two to drink?"

Gianna took a sip and smiled gratefully. "I didn't get to read Adrian's report in the afternoon because of the 'country boy' incident. Followed by the 'dog and pony show' for the Sheriff's deputy when he showed up asking if we'd seen the missing guy. Then I had to go to 'Studio City' to arrange the drone footage Nick asked for. Going there is almost like actually going to L.A. It always takes longer than you think it will. When I finally got home at 7:30, I read the afternoon report and the 6:00 pm one... Nick found me into my third glass of wine listening to '*Eve of Destruction*'. After he read them he needed a beer... well several beers as you can see. I have no idea what time I wandered up to bed or what time he left. I slept through my five o'clock alarm. Cleo woke me at five thirty-ish by sitting her big pouffe ass on my boobs."

"Oh yea, fat cat walking on your boobs will wake you up every time. Anyway, Nick came by the Gypsy Camp late last night. He was on his way back from Hansel & Gretel's. He was totally closed mouthed as to why he was there. He stopped by to talk about where to put the new bunker. He wants to get it in over the next few days. AND, there are security issues with our Gypsy Flair! Some of it showed up on the drone footage. He gave me two options. One, take it down, which is not an option or two, we need more nets. Do we have more nets or do we need to buy some?"

"That would be a Stephen question. Find out what we have. Check with Nick he may have said something about needing more. If we need more gc get them and get back home quickly. After yesterday I don't want you leaving without four of the guards. Turn that on honey."

Violet turned the TV on and headed out the door. Over her shoulder she said, "I'll be back in a few as soon as I talk to Stephen and Nick. Make a list of anything else you want. OH... will you tell Sadie I'll meet her here, if she shows up before I find her?"

The screen door closed behind Violet with a bang. Cleopatra jumped into Gianna's lap nearly up ending mug. "Shit, Cleo, watch out for my coffee. And stop twirling. Sit down! I'm *trying* to see what the fuck has happened to the world while we slept. Are you settled now? Just sit here and pretend you're a nice cat."

6:05 AM EDT,

Images of people rioting at food stores that were empty... The news chopper's film of the flooded areas with homes floating down streets showed how high the water was... 18 people had been shot for looting last night... the highways moving north were still clogged with bumper to bumper cars... in North Carolina it was still pretty calm... the army troops manning the roadblocks on the South Carolina side of the border were fucking frightening.

Hurricane Sara came and Charleston was gone. The islands on the north side of the hurricane were still under water. The the houses on the south side of the hurricane had been swept out to sea. The antique shops on King Street had water up to the top of the doorways. Palmetto palms were piled up like fancy toothpicks. The flooding in Columbia was worse than 2015. Sara had been downgraded to a Tropical Storm so the wind was less but she was heavy with moisture. She veered south and was now drowning Atlanta. Chattanooga was getting driving rain from her outer bands.

"Cleopatra, if I keep watching this I may need some Baileys in my coffee! Oh my stars, pretty girl, Georgia is taking an ass whooping. Much more of this and next spring there won't be any peach trees, never mind peach blossoms!"

7:00 am am EDT, September 27,
Planet Earth's Not Doing Well
Online Blog,
Location Unknown

Overnight the **Federal Government** has appropriated the Chesapeake Energy Arena from the city to use as a processing center for the refugees. When the doors opened at 7:00 am there were already 2000 cars, trucks and motor homes in the parking lot. When the arena was full, they began to funnel the refugees to the Cox Convention Center and then to the Renaissance Oklahoma City Convention Center Hotel, which they had also appropriated.

In **Memphis** they appropriated The Memphis Cook Convention Center.

In **Nashville** they appropriated the

Memorial Gymnasium, the Bridgestone Arena, and the Tennessee State Fairgrounds Sports Arena. The last being smaller, but the fairgrounds gave them room for FEMA and Red Cross tents and trailers.

In both **Tennessee and Oklahoma**, Martial Law had been enacted just prior to the appropriations.

Yesterday, in a preemptive move, the Governor of **North Carolina** made a proposal to Washington that resulted in the closing of the roads at the North Carolina southern border and the funneling of the traffic north and west. To sweeten the deal the Governor had volunteered the use of the Charlotte Convention Center and the Bojangles Coliseum, thereby protecting his residents from falling under Martial Law, at least for now.

7:10 am EDT, September 27,
Devil's Fork Gap
Smokey Mountains, Tennessee

The residents of the mountaintop compound were waking to a world that was profoundly different than the day before. They'd actually captured intruders. With the exception of Billy, they'd all realized they were not quite ready to kill in cold blood. They also realized the incident at the store yesterday was not a 'one off'. People who wanted what

134

they had were out there. More would more than likely come, and when they did, there might not be help from the Law.

The deputies had taken almost an hour to get there last night. Before the deputies took the men away, they cautioned Frank and the others that the force was spread thin but they were doing their best. They congratulated them on their setup and suggested they remain inside their compound for the foreseeable future.

The biggest shock would come when they learned that their state was now under Martial Law. To make matters worse, Tennessee along with Oklahoma had been designated as 'Holding States'. A place to stockpile thousands of homeless storm refugees.

Billy and Rory removed the crossbars on the compound's gate. "Billy, I'll drive the intruders' truck and you ride shotgun with Frank behind me."

"Good plan. If there's any trouble we can swing 'round and I'll blast them!"

"That's just what I was thinking Billy!" Rory lied. He was not looking forward to this trip, or the opportunity for Billy to *blast* anyone, but it had to be done. The deputy had said they would get someone to pick up the intruder's truck in the next few days. They couldn't say when. Dan had pointed out that the truck was blocking the gate. No one thought it was a good idea to leave it off to the side at the end of the drive, because it would most likely be looted and draw unwanted attention to the compound. The deputy radioed in and asked what the Sheriff wanted them to do. He said these were unusual circumstances and Frank could drive it down to the station in the morning. They'd pulled it into the compound for the night. Billy had insisted he keep an eye on things from his 'tower' for an hour or so after the deputies left. While he was gone, Dan, Rory, and Frank talked about how to best deal with Billy's 'trigger happy' attitude without antagonizing him. Frank knew him best and could sort of control Billy. Before they all went to bed, Dan and Rory had agreed to let Frank be the boss of Billy, while the rest of them would placate Billy when needed.

Dan closed and bolted the gates behind them. He found the girls in the living room. "They're off. It should take them about two hours. Frank wants to see if they can gas-up the truck before they head back. Rory wants to have a word with the Sheriff to find out what this Martial Law means for us. I'm gonna split more wood for a bit. What are you planning to do today?"

Tracy was glad her husband would be out from under foot. "Pauline wants to bake some bread and cakes to put in the freezer. Betty Lou is going to help her. Cindy and I are going to cook up some of the chicken in the freezer. Thought we'd put up some chicken and dumplings. While that's cooking, we're going to fry up some chicken for supper and maybe put some in the freezer too."

"Sounds like you girls have a full day planned. Call me on the radio if anyone comes around."

Dan tossed his jacket on the wood pile. The mountain air was crisp this morning but he'd be warm in a few minutes. Dan liked splitting wood. Too much sitting around made a man soft. You put in the labor and you got a beautiful stack of wood when you're done. It kept your mind busy so you wouldn't worry over shit you couldn't change. Dan thought he knew what Martial Law would mean to them and he didn't like it. After the others got back he would talk to them about burying several stashes of supplies around the property. They had learned about the processing centers from some of the Ham Radio guys. He wondered where the government was going to get food to feed all those people.

9:30 am EDT, September 27,
Dancing Goats Farm,
Moon Mountain, North Carolina

Six year old Angelena stood looking

down at her Great Aunt. "Hey Auntie, I found you!"

"Hey Angelena, I didn't know I was lost. Give me a hug, my tiny beauty queen."

"Auntie why are you sleeping on the ground in the butterfly garden?"

"Not sleeping my sweet. Just letting the earth heal me. Auntie has had a lot of stress the last few days. Lying here on the moss listening to the water trickle over the stones in the Koi pond makes me all better. Where's your mom, kitten fish?"

Amber rounded the holly bush. "I'm here Auntie. Give me your hand. Let me help you up. I went back to the camp and everyone is gone. I was looking for Sadie to watch Angelena while she unpacks. It's too hot in the greenhouse for Angelena today."

Gianna freed a few leaves caught in her hair. "Violet went to buy more nets, guess she went with her. Oh, before I forget, after yesterday's incident, I don't want anyone leaving without permission from me or Nick. And they are to take four of the guard with them. No exceptions."

"I get why you're worried, but Violet and Sadie packin'... there's a

pair that beats a full house *every* time.
I could almost feel sorry for anyone
comin' up against those two... but no...
fuckem' if they piss my cousins off, they
get what they get.

Tyler said to tell you he's sorry he
didn't get back to you this morning. He's
running a line for the new bunker behind
the camp. However the grid is in perfect
running order. He's tested everything
twice since Sunday. He has twenty five
backup parts for anything that could
break. He put up a parts shed in Studio
City last week and gave them each a key.
All five of them think nothing of waking
us in the middle of the night if they
need an electrical part for one of their
inventions. Now they have keys and it's
close by so he doesn't have to hear them
bitch about how far they have to go to
get what they need. I told him to tell
them. 'It's closer than Radio Shack!' So
there are two problems solved for you."

Gianna sighed. "Sorry that they keep
waking you honey. I'll have a talk with
them about personal space, and how not to
invade it. I know they can be a handful
at times but their collective IQ could
rival an MIT Think Tank. Their esoteric
knowledge and work experience is vast and
invaluable. Kinda like having Google in
our back yard."

Amber linked her arm through her
Aunt's as the walked. "It's all good now.

I need to get back to work. Can she stay with you?"

Gianna lifted a curl from Angelena's eyes. "Do you want to spend the day with me miss thing?"

Angelena put her hand on her hips and tilted her face to Gianna. "Auntie can I drive the go-cart again?"

Gianna mimicked the child's stance. "Well... since I'm the boss of this place I don't see how anyone could stop us."

Angelena put her tiny hand in her Aunt's. "It's good to be the queen, right Auntie?"

Gianna beamed at her golden curled great niece. "Yes my darling, It certainly is."

**10:30 am EDT, September 27,
United States of America
Blog Online,
Location Unknown**

Unlike the people in the holding states, the people of **North Carolina** are pretty fucking grateful for their governor this morning. Democrats and Republicans alike praised him for his fast thinking and quick action. Charlotte was a bit ill with him for being the city chosen to 'take one for the team'. However, during the governor's morning

140

press conference, he said in the days to
come North Carolina might have to
volunteer facilities in Greensboro or
Raleigh to aid our neighbors who had lost
so much, in their time of need. Knowing
they were not the only ones 'taking one
for the team', took the sting out of it
for many Charlotteans.

The governor had also brokered a
deal with FEMA to purchase food from
North Carolina companies. Campbell Soup,
Sanderson Farms, Bimbo Bakeries, Snyder's
Lance, and Seal The Seasons are among the
15 companies included in the deal. The
volume FEMA wants will require the
companies to hire more people to run
double shifts. This is not normally how
FEMA purchases products. These being
extraordinary times, FEMA had been given
a free hand to get the job done. All in
all, North Carolina is riding out the
storm just fine.

HUD was scrambling to find housing.
On the suggestion of a congressman from
Virginia, they were moving the refugees
to **Ohio, Indiana and Kansas**. The 'excuse
given' was to relieve the human logjam in
the states bordering the storm ravaged
region.

Uprooting millions of people is Not
an easy job. People don't yet realize
that for thousands of them there will be
no going home. Many refuse to go. They
are told they will be turned out of the

141

facility they are presently in. Faced with the option of fending for themselves, 90% of them are going where they are assigned.

Tropical Storm Sara has lost most of her bluster but not her moisture. She spent her last twelve hours stalled between **Jackson and Monroe Mississippi** dumping tens of thousands of gallons of rain into the **Mississippi River**, which had already overflowed its banks yesterday.

A word from and about
Mother Nature

Mother felt... if only... they had directed their resources away from acquiring fossil fuels and had instead, created a rain catchment system by which they could transport excessive rain to the drought stricken western half of the country... Then again, if they had stopped filling the atmosphere with shit from burning fossil fuels... they might not be in this mess. Southern Mississippi would not be becoming a swamp, whose size will be more than ten times greater than the 438,000 acre Okefenokee Swamp.

Mother... is cleaning house. Humans have nearly destroyed her magnificent translucent waters. Her oceans will get worse before they get better. But after decades, they will begin to heal themselves. Thousands might have to die before they come to understand the oceans and seas are now off limits to humans... a fitting punishment for the destroyers.

The youngest to survive the Earth Changes will grow old and die before humans can once more feel the kiss of the waves upon their feet. Maybe by then they will come to understand that to ride upon, to play within, and to explore the beauty of the oceans is a privilege not a right. The watery domains belong to the beings who live in them... NOT humans. Humans are only guests. All of Her creatures are sentient. All but humans understand this.

Water and Fire... the great purifiers. There will be no restraint in their application now. The oceans and rivers will rise up and eradicate the enclaves of their wicked invaders. 'Prescribed Burns' are what is called for. A need to scorch the earth, to root out the invasive species that has robbed others of their rightful place in Earth's scheme. All this will be done to revitalize Mother Earth, to nurture the restoration of her forests, prairies and rain forests.

The United States will not be the sole recipient of her wrath. It is simply first on the list; the home of some of the greatest offenders. The stewards of her tropical paradises, who have soiled and gutted her island jewels will forfeit their lands and their lives, as will the stewards who have plundered her mountains, deserts, meadows, valleys, grasslands, moors and sky. They need to be taught the Earth is part of Her. They can not own Her. They are but stewards who serve at Her pleasure.

Most humans are nothing more than ego-maniacal beasts, who, when confronted with these impending disasters, will rip one another to shreds. Some believe if they are the biggest and cruelest they will be the survivors. They are wrong. Dead wrong. Mother will eat them alive. Only those who are one with Mother will walk the earth in the end.

3:30 am HDT, September 27, O'ahu, Hawaii

Alone on a moonlit beach the KiloKilo softly sang an ancient song. Before her eyes the midnight sky opened. The fiery continence of 'She who shapes the sacred land', Tutū Pele hovered above her. The Goddess's message is simple and to the point: 'The Hawai'i Maoli must abandon the big island and come to O'ahu today.' Tutū Pele's image faded. An angry Kilauea erupting filled the sky. Then, it too faded.

When the night sky above her was once more filled with only stars, the woman rises and hurries off to find her

eldest son. Tutū Pele is taking back the
Big Island. He must warn their people.
The Hawai'i Maoli must leave there or
they will die.

chapter 7
SLIP SLIDIN' AWAY

"Just when you think...
I've got it in hand,
It slips away like grains of sand"

1:32 am EDT, September 27,
Devil's Fork Gap
Smokey Mountains, Tennessee

Frank, Rory and Billy were unusually quiet on their ride back. What they saw at the Sheriff's station and in town has deeply disturbed each of them in different ways. During the dozens of conversations they'd had, which led to the building of their compound, they'd imagined countless scenarios of what the SHTF would look like. None of them came close to the chaos they had witnessed this morning in Frog Pond.

They sat cooling their heels for forty-five minutes while the deputy figured out where the truck should go. She couldn't locate the suspects it belonged to. Finally the female deputy returned. She apologized and explained the delay. She couldn't locate the men

146

because they had been transferred to Chattanooga. The Army was taking custody of any storm refugees who were suspects. The men had been classified as looters. That placed them under the jurisdiction of the United States Army. Once the deputy had located them, it had taken her another fifteen minutes to speak to someone who could tell her what the Army wanted the department to do with the truck. A crisp voice instructed her to hold it in the Sheriff's impound lot then abruptly hung up on her. This created another dilemma which she needed the Sheriff to solve. Frog Pond's Sheriff's office doesn't have an impound lot. The Sheriff remedied the situation with a call to Chuck Walker. The truck would be picked up and stored at Chuck's salvage yard. The deputy gave them a copy of the police report and a receipt for the truck. Apologizing once again for the delay, she showed them to the door.

Frank and Billy sat in line for gas, while Rory went to the Stop & Save. The girls had requested they bring back fresh vegetables, milk and apples. The store was a frigging mad house. Most of the shelves were bare. Rory managed to get his hands on a bag of carrots and a head of iceberg that look like it had been used for football practice. People were pushing and shoving, grabbing for items. The door on the milk case was hanging at an angle, which was okay, since there were no dairy products left to sell. Two

147

burly men had come to blows over the last
frozen turkey. Rory saw a stock boy with
with his arms full of bagged apples as he
was coming through the swinging doors.
Rory snagged a bag off the top before the
shoppers mobbed the frightened teenager.
The checkout line was a fifteen minute
nightmare. The card readers had gone
down. An irate woman three people ahead
of Rory didn't have cash. She refused
step out of line while her son ran to
find his father. Those in line behind her
had to listen to the woman as she berated
the poor checker over how the people of
Tennessee lacked compassion for people
who had lost everything. What kind of
Christians lived here anyway? And the
indignity of having to send her son for
cash when she had plenty of money in the
bank. Rory was of the opinion that those
who made such statements usually didn't.

Outside, National Guardsmen were
stopping cars, asking people to show ID.
Locals were allowed to pass. Anyone
deemed to be a non-local was directed to
the parking lot of the old abandoned
elementary school. When Rory got back to
the truck he found a Guardsman talking to
Frank through the window. They were all
asked to show their IDs. Frank was OK but
Rory and Billy posed a problem with their
out of state licenses. Frank explained
they had just come from the Sheriff's
station and why. Rory could see Billy was
getting hot under the collar. His South
Carolina address put him at risk of being

classified as a refugee and being sent to the processing facilities in Nashville.

The Guardsman gave Frank a ticket allowing him to buy five gallons of gas, told him to stay inside his vehicle, and had him move forward to the pump. A guardsman stood ready to pump the gas while a pair of armed guardsmen stood by. Rory and Billy were made to stand to the side while another guardsman checked their story with the Sheriff's office. Rory offered a silent prayer that the deputy would be there to confirm that the two of them were part owners of the the property. Rory with his Virginia ID was in better shape than Billy. He'd most likely be told to go home to Virginia. If it went bad Billy would not go quietly.

Frank pulled to the side and waited to see how things played out. After ten minutes they were given back their ID's and told to go back to the compound with instructions to stay within the boundaries of their property until further notice. They drove past the elementary school on their way out of town. The parking lot was nearly full. A line of weary looking people snaked around the rows of vehicles waiting to talk to one of the three Army personnel seated at a long table. Rory counted eighteen armed soldiers. At the edge of town they passed a shitload of Humvees and Army transport trucks parked in an empty field. There were at least a hundred soldiers standing around. Most of them were armed.

Frank and Rory were disturbed and fucking irate over the morning's events. Conversely, Billy was scared silent, frightened by how close he had come to ending up at a processing facility. Rory was additionally pissed that they no longer flew under the government's radar. A small part of him was wishing they had shot the intruders and buried them in the woods. When they were allowed to leave the property again, only Frank, Pauline, Dan or Tracy would go into town. There was no point in risking being caught up in that shit storm again. They must rethink how they would deal with intruders from now on.

12:00 pm EDT, September 27,
The Real News for Planet Earth
Blog Online,
Location Unknown

   Moscow, Russia is struggling with its own mass evacuation problems. The 'issues' they'd been dealing with at the nuclear power plant in Obninsk had gone from being an issue to a critical situation. Anonymous sources said: Some officials have questioned the morality of the news blackout currently in place.

   "Shouldn't we warn the countries that could be affected if the core goes into meltdown?" They asked.

"This would be much worse than Chernobyl. Tens of thousands could be harmed or killed by the explosion and fallout. Moscow itself could become uninhabitable."

"Do we not owe the Russian people the right to save themselves?"

The answer came down from the Top... "No! It would only cause mass hysteria. They would die anyway, there is no plan for an evacuation of this size. It's better their last hours are not spent in panic."

Evidently the Top and his entourage then boarded a plane bound for a secret bunker on an island in the East Siberian Sea.

Beijing, China had just been struck by a 7.9 earthquake. Most communications were down. Reports from outside the city said the damage was catastrophic. The death toll could reach into the hundreds of thousands. The water level in the Miyum Reservoir had dropped by four feet. The shaking was felt as far away as the Sichuan Province.

1:45 am EDT, September 27,
Dancing Goats Farm
Moon Mountain, North Carolina

Sean had been on the road for a

151

little under 24 hours. At 12:10 am Theo sent him a text, telling him Martial Law had been invoked in Texas and Oklahoma. At that moment Sean was entering Las Cruces, New Mexico. Theo instructed him to go north to Albuquerque, tonight, if he could stay awake. He made it. After eighteen hours on the road Sean slept for almost five. "Oh My God, She's answers! How the fuck are you and what the Hell is going on? I'm in Albuquerque, by the way. Got here and slept like a bear."

"Thank the Goddess you're safe. Things have gotten rather shitty here in the good old US of A. Talk about timing, babe, you dodged a bullet last night. Theo didn't know what the government would do with people on the roads in Texas. A very good call it was too. Cause what they're doing is not good. Your trip just got a fuck of a lot longer though. You need to keep going north to Trinidad, Colorado. From there go east on Rt-160 to Dodge City, Kansas, and on to Wichita. Call next time you stop. It's about thirteen hours to Wichita from where you are."

"What is happening that I need to add another day to this trip?"

"Where do I start? The government has taken over large venues and is sending the refugees from the hurricanes and flooding to them. Word is, the Army has boots on the ground in at least ten states. We're going to bring you straight across to Louisville and then down to here. Travel safe but cover as many miles as you can in a stretch. I want you here before things get any freakier. How is your wife holding up?"

"By the time we got to Phoenix she was frantic. She'd been talking to her sister. Her sister said North Carolina wasn't safe. She made me take her to the airport. She flew to Connecticut to be with her family, so I'm traveling light. I can make less stops and cover more miles. I'll call you later. Arrivederci."

"Ciao."

**12:30 pm EDT, September 27,
Smokey Mountains, Tennessee**

After a much needed comfort-food lunch of tender southern fried chicken and mashed taters with gravy, the men told the girls they were going out to cut and split more wood. Betty Lou suggested it was a good way to work off their lunch. The guys real intention was to discuss what had happened in town in more detail without unnecessarily upsetting the girls. Choices had to be made on how they would handle things from now on. It was clear they need to manage their supplies more carefully. Servings needed to be a bit smaller. Less side dishes with each meal. There would be absolutely no wasting of food. They needed to watch

153

their gas consumption more closely. No more trips to town unless it was an emergency. They would have the girls fill every container they could find with water. The compound had a well but the pump was electric. They should put jugs in the bathroom for flushing. Billy said he would start to dig an outhouse. The septic might be an issue at some point. Dan and Rory liked that idea. Maybe it would burn off some of Billy's crazy energy. If nothing else it would keep him busy. Tomorrow, Dan would figure out a hand pump system in the event the power went out for a long period.

All agreed they would dig more pits around the outside of the wall. A few in the woods would be added after the house was more secure. Dan surprised himself when he heard his voice suggest they add spikes to the bottom of the pits.

They needed to figure out a way to reinforce the stockade fencing around the back. Billy suggested they cut fist size pine poles to attach on the inside across the seams. Bigger pine trunks could be used as braces. Rory thought Billy's gone into real survival mode. He liked the effect it was having on him.

Next they would move at least one truck out of the garage and fill the space with as much wood as they could find. Others might have the same idea. They didn't want neighbors poaching their

supply. Starting at the back of the
property they'd work their way in
harvesting wood as they came. The wooden
crate with the kindling would need to be
emptied and moved inside along with the
split wood stacked out back. Could be two
trucks would be moving outside.

That brought them to around to the
subject of neighbors. How to deal with
and respond to the folks who lived on
either side. The property backed up to
protected land so no problem there. Frank
and Pauline knew the neighbors because
they had been living at the compound full
time for almost two years.

Harvey and Barbra Goldberg were the
neighbors to the north. They had come up
here in the seventies, flower children
looking to live off the land. There had
been ten of them in the beginning. Over
the years the rest of the group drifted
away. One of them returned every once in
awhile to visit.

Pauline met them this past summer.
Barbra had called Pauline to say she had
extra produce and would they like some?
Pauline walked over and rang the bell.
The place looked like a fort that had
been built by Hobbits. The ten foot tall
wall the bell hung on was a patchwork of
salvaged metals. Many patches were
flattened automobile hoods welded
together. There were sections of
corrugated sheet metal in the mix. Wild

black berries grew thick around the base
of the wall. The gates made of the same
materials as the wall, hung on a massive
stone arch. To Pauline's surprise one
side swung out and up like a castle from
an old movie. All they needed was a
drawbridge. Inside there were gardens,
fruit trees, and a step-down greenhouse.
Behind the berm house she could see a
barn, several sheds, and a pen with
goats. Chickens and ducks roamed
everywhere. Barbra looked like the aging
hippie she was: mid calf colorful skirt,
and a homespun blouse. Her long silver
hair wound up in a haphazard bun. She
introduced Pauline to her friend Shelly,
a former member of Shangri La Farm.
Shelly's two grandchildren were playing
tug of war with an enormous long haired
white dog. Barbra offered Pauline a glass
of fresh lemon-aid. The women were
sitting on the patio waiting for Harvey
and Shelly's husband, Bud, to bring the
days harvest in from the gardens.

When she left Pauline was carrying a
bushel basket filled with greens,
peppers, tomatoes and several kinds of
squash. There were even a few peaches.
Pauline thought about them and the
Shangri La Farm all the way home. Harvey
told her next time she came to visit, she
should use the old path through the
woods. It was shorter by half than going
all the way around on the road. Harvey
said they used it to go between their
place and hers back when old Sam was

still alive. As Sam got on in years one
of them would go and check in on him
every few days, more often in the winter
months. Harvey and Barbra knew Sam's
daughter Tracy had tried to get him to
move in with her and her husband but Sam
wouldn't leave his home. It was Harvey
who had found the old man. Sam had passed
on peacefully in his sleep. They hadn't
used the trail in the last five years. It
might be a bit overgrown now but he was
sure she could still find it.

The neighbors to the south were a
group of 30-somethings. A pair of
brothers and a wife. Between them they
were short about ten teeth. It wasn't
clear if the woman belonged with one or
both of the brothers. They had a couple
of kids with them too. Frank had met them
one day when they waved him down. They
had a flat and had forgotten to put the
tire iron back in the truck. While one
brother changed the tire the other chewed
Franks ear getting around to asking if
Frank minded if they hunted in the back
of his woods. Frank though it would be
okay as long as they didn't shoot in the
direction of the house. Frank was not
sure if he could even remember their
names. In Frank's opinion they should
make contact with Harvey and Barbra. He
thought it best to steer clear of the
brothers. They all agreed and would
contact the hippies tomorrow, unless
Pauline had a phone number for them, in
which case they'd give them a call

tonight.

1:30 pm EDT, September 27,
Dancing Goats Farm,
Moon Mountain, North Carolina

Violet and Sadie return with the supplies but not with very pleasant attitudes. Some asshole put his hands on Sadie. She jacked him up against the side of a building before Freddy could close the six feet between himself and women. The asshole got even more rude and before Freddy could get between them, Violet offered to blow his balls off. After that Freddy made the sisters walk in the middle of the guard to prevent another incident. Nick had warned him make it a low profile quick in and out. These two were making it very hard to follow those orders. The sisters were pissy for the rest of the outing because they thought they didn't need a baby sitter.

When she found out how badly the outing had gone, Gianna was *really* pissed off with her daughters."What part of keep a low profile don't you two understand? I sent the guard with you to make that happen. Have you forgotten I had to charm my way around officer friendly just yesterday? I can not afford to have the fucking cops in here snooping around. FYI... Hansel & Gretel, have a *house guest!*"

Violet got defensive. "We didn't

158

know."

Gianna got loud. "Violet I shouldn't have to explain the need for not attracting attention to the farm. Now more than ever! Look, Ladies, I know everyone is a little wound up and on edge. I'm counting on *my* daughters to help me keep it to a low roar... please!"

Sadie spied Nick coming across the yard with *that* look on his face. "Okay mother we got it." She grabbed her sister by the arm. "We're leaving now we don't need to hear it from Nick, too." As they hurry away Gianna heard Sadie said, "Hey sissy, thanks for offering to shoot him in the balls for me."

An extremely angry Nick came to an abrupt halt and glared down at Gianna. Before he could start to bitch at her, Gianna put a finger to his lips to stop the tirade she knew was coming. "Take a breath darling, I already ripped them a new one. I'm sorry, they have my temper."

"But they don't have your restraint in public situations." Nick thought, 'Here you're anything but restrained.'

"Don't blame Freddy for this. This is all on my daughters. If it makes you feel any better, what they don't know yet, is that they're grounded until you say otherwise." This seemed to somewhat appease Nick. "But really Nick, you've known them for years. Are you really shocked, that Violet tried to shoot someone in the balls who assaulted her sister? Darling, there is a reason why I call Violet my Kraken. Underneath the veil of her Gypsy, healer persona, sleeps the spirit of a legendary giant cephalopod. What can I do to make you feel better?" Knowing he shouldn't answer that he turned an stalked off.

4:00 pm EDT, September 27,
More Real News of Planet Earth
Blog Online
Location Unknown

Los Angeles was still being shaken with aftershocks. The death toll was at 302. 2000 are still missing. The Red Cross was running short on blood. The 10 and the 405 have suffered structural damage which was hampering evacuations. There are cracks across two of the runways at LAX, causing further delays for airlines that are still dealing with passengers stranded due to Hurricanes Rafael and Sara.

Beijing, China, The death toll is at 658,429. They believe it may go as high as 3 million. Over 35,000 injured are waiting for medical care. The rescue efforts are being hampered by dozens of fires that have broken out across the city caused by natural gas mains whose shutoffs are buried under tons of rubble.

Saudi Arabia A Habcob 75 miles wide with winds of 55 mph brought Riyadh to a standstill today. The King Khalid International airport was closed for over five hours due to drifts of sand and damaged planes scattered across the runways.

Atlanta, Georgia The lupine is behaving true to form: making it bleed to lead... his attacks on the government's handling of these catastrophic events has incited riots in Chicago, San Diego, and DC. The National Guard is using teargas in an attempt to control the thousands blocking the streets. Hundreds have been arrested.

Antarctica Scientists tracking the Thwaites Glacier say it has begun to slide into Pine Island Bay. They have measured a forward movement of 3 feet in the last 24 hours. The melting of the glacier could cause a sea rise of at least 3 feet.

8:30 pm EDT, September 27, Charlotte, North Carolina

There are now 20 thousand refugees at the processing facilities in **Charlotte**. Only 3% of them have refused the housing 'offered' by HUD. Of that 600 (3%), 400 have refused because they have family they can stay with outside of North Carolina. These people are given a set of instructions they must follow:

161

They are given a voucher for a full
tank of gas to be filled at the Army
tanker in the parking lot.

They may only travel on Northbound
I-77. Once on I-77 they may not get off
the highway.

They have one hour and forty five
minutes from the time they redeem the gas
voucher, to reach the border check point.
They are given two numbers. One is an an
emergency phone number. The other is to
be given to the soldier at the border
check point on the Virginia state line.

If they have car trouble or a
medical emergency, they are to pull over,
call the emergency number and wait for
help to arrive.

If they do not reach the check point
within two hours of gassing up, an APB
will be issued on their license tags.

When they are found they will be
arrested.

The remaining 200 have not been told
their fate. They are to be taken by Army
transport to a holding facility at **Camp
Lejeune**. One person or family at a time,
they are surreptitiously removed from the
general population.

Four Good ol' boys from Alabama are

162

among the 200 who refused to go. Craig, Wyatt, Silas, and Axel between them have 33 years of prison time. Their collective resumes include armed robbery, assault, and rape. While the other three sleep, Axel watches the room. Those that had refused the governments 'offer' of relocation and do not have family who will take them in were sent to yet another 'waiting room'. Every fifteen minutes or so one of the soldiers comes in, tells someone or a group they have more questions for them or they need to go over the information on their registration form, and they leave with him. They had started with the blacks which suited Axel just fine. He'd been busy watching that sweet little brunette sitting in the corner with her family. Young and ripe for picking, maybe thirteen. He did like 'em young. A soldier boy speaking to her father disrupted Axel's view. Whatever the guy said, it made the little hottie and her family leave with him. Axel started looking around the room for a redhead that had caught his eye on the way in. She wasn't here. A lot of people wasn't here. Must have been 150 when they came in... now was maybe 100 here. People are leaving an' not coming back. Somethin's not right here.

In prison you get a sense for when shit's not right. Like when a beat-down is about to happen and you don't want to get caught up in it cause you'll lose

163

your yard privileges. You just know somethin's not right and you get your ass gone. Deep inside his reptilian brain something stirred. He could almost taste it on the tip of his tongue... something here wasn't right.

Axel jammed his elbow into Wyatt's back. They woke the other two then he explained what he knew to be happenin'. They needed to get out of here. Axel convinced the soldier outside the door that they had changed their minds and wanted to take the government's 'generous' offer. They were sent to get back in the processing line. They drifted back into the crowd. Silas found a way outside. They slipped out through a hole in the chain link fence. Craig was bitchin' about leaving his car. To shut him up Axel pointed out it had barely made it here and wouldn't have lasted much longer. They made their way through the Queen City keeping to the shadows. They had pressed into a doorway when they heard a truck rumbling up from behind. It was a big ass Army transport. The street lamp illuminated the back of the truck as it rolled by. For a second the redhead's tear-stained face came into view. Then it was gone. Axel's reptile brain unfurled its tail. That truck was goin' no place good.

They moved on through the night keeping low, looking for a car to boost. In the back of a strip mall they found what they were looking for. A young woman was crossing the unlit lot. While she is looking in her bag for her keys, Axel cupped her chin from behind and slit her throat. Wyatt grabbed the dead woman's purse and keys, then jumped in the driver's seat. As he pulled away, he tossed the bag to Axel. "Who-wee! we got a full tank a gas."

Axel searched the bag and tossed it out the window. "We have thirty bucks an' a fancy ass phone."

"Did y'all have to kill her?"

"Craig what chall whinin' about now? Son that's one less african pollutin' the gene pool. You get me boy? Silas, y'all know how to work this? Find us a map." Axel flipped the phone over the seat to Silas. He leaned deeper into the seat, relishing the cool night air on his face. Two hours later in Hendersonville they acquire a new ride from Great Westerns' parking lot. They dump the dead woman's' car in the parking lot at the Ashville Airport and continue north up I-29.

Just before midnight Wyatt pulled the stolen Cadillac off the road at the mouth of the Mountain Ccmpound's dirt driveway. Axel got out and walked ten feet up the drive. Retreating to the road he investigated the next property. There are several vehicles, three of which do not seem to be working in the front yard of a trailer. This trailer is not going to win any 'house beautiful' prizes. There is a dim light visible through the open windows. Drunken voices drift through the darkness... a man, a woman, and maybe another man. Axel returned to the car and signaled the others to follow him. As they reached the yard he held up three fingers then pointed to Wyatt and Silas. Turning to Craig he signaled him to stay.

It was over in sixty seconds. In one smooth well-learned motion, Axel slit the throat of the man who answered the door. Then tossed the body down the steps as Silas and Wyatt rush the man and the woman sitting on the stained couch. In a back room Axel found two children asleep in one bed. A flash of his knife and they were gone.

From the trailer door Silas tossed Craig the keys and nodded in the direction of the Cadillac. Craig parked the Caddy behind the junk cars. Inside he found the others going through the cupboards. Wyatt shouted he found a case of beer. The sons of Alabama kicked back and drank themselves to sleep.

chapter 8
FIRE & RAIN

"Look to the sky
For answers found
Hold on tight
Then stand your ground"

12:10 am EDT, September 28,
Devil's Fork Gap
Smokey Mountains, Tennessee

Hey Frank, you still up."

"Yup I'm here. Y'all gettin' tired or just lonesome?"

"A big Cadillac pulled up at the end of the drive few minutes ago. Think someone got out, but it's black as pitch out here. I couldn't be sure. It sat there about four minutes then drove off. Think it might have gone to the brothers' house next door. Couldn't really see for all the trees. Other than that it's quiet. Ya might want to check the monitors at the front and side."

"Doin' that now. I'll keep watch for a bit just in case somebody's out there.

You comin' in now?"

"Not yet. I wanna see if that Cadillac comes back. It's kinda a classy car for that lot next door."

"Maybe they're sellin' drugs. Been watchin' the news. It's startin' to look like Pauline's End Times out there. Shit, she hears me makin' fun like that she'll pitch another fit. She is ill with me. She went to bed in a huff. No sugar for me tonight."

"What the hell happened? She's generally so even tempered."

"Had to break the news about not leavin' the property. You know how she is about goin' to church on Sundays."

"Glad I was up here for that one."

"She was acting like I should just go out and fix all this shit so she can talk to God on Sunday. She's a sensible woman about most things except when it comes to God. I told her she could just as easy talk to him here but no, she wants to talk to him at his house! She thinks he listens better when she talks to him in church. She was so riled up I was makin' sure I was between her and the rifle."

Dan was laughing at his friends woman troubles. "Sounds like I picked the right night for watch."

"But seriously Dan, this shit is gettin' real bad out there. I talked a HAM guy over in Fayetteville tonight, his wife works at Camp Lejeun. She told him they have refugees locked up in there. The government offered them housing up north some place and they said no. Next thing they know, the Army packed them in a truck and locked them up at the base." "No shit! Are you sure about this? The Army taking people to a Marine base?"

"He said his wife is real friendly with one'a the women who's husband is guardin' them. Another HAM guy in Martinsville, Virginia said there's a military checkpoint at the state line. He had to go Mt. Airy and they made him show his ID and gave him a number to get back into Virginia. Said on his way back he was talkin' to some refugees from Mississippi while they were waitin' in line to get through. Seems everybody who said they would take the HUD housing has to pass through the checkpoint to go north. Once they get on 77 they can't get off till they get to Virginia." If they get off they'd be arrested."

Their conversation was interrupted when Cindy stuck her head in the room. "Hey Frank, can I hang out with you and Dan?"

"Sure Cindy grab a seat. Dan,

Cindy's with us so keep it clean! Rory gone to bed?"

"Yes, he was dead tired. Boys, I'm a Yankee living in Virginia I'm sure I swear worse than you all. Rory was out before his head hit the pillow. You guys put in an unbelievable amount of wood today. So what are we talking about?"

"Well Frank was telling me about Pauline's fit. Then we moved on to what's going on outside these walls."

"Hey Dan, why don't y'all come in now?"

"Be right in."

Cindy, Frank and Dan talked for an hour. Cindy filled them in on all the natural disasters happening around the world they'd missed while working outside all day. They made a list of more that they thought they should do to make their food go farther. Cindy offered her ideas on how to protect the compound better.

Around half past one they traipsed off to their beds. Same time a dark figure crept up the driveway, moved around the outside of the compound, then went back the way he came. Frank had forgotten to hit record on the surveillance cameras. There would be no footage of their prowler to review in the morning. Rory was so right... a minute can make a big difference now.

4:00 am EDT, September 28,
The Ugly News for Planet Earth
Blog Location Still Unknown

During the first hours of the new
day a fair amount of the world's
population surrendered to the dark side.

Civil war is erupting all across the
Dark Continent as well as the **Middle
East**.

As if on cue, different terrorist
groups around the globe have kicked up
their game. Major attacks in **France,
Germany** and **New York** collectively claimed
over a thousand lives. Smaller lone wolf
assaults dot the globe.

In **Chicago,** a congresswoman urged
the rioters to continue their civil
disobedience. They obliged by setting
fire to downtown Chicago.

New riots began in **Missouri** and
California. Bands of refugees not yet
confined to the processing areas began to
go into hiding. They are looting stores
that sell survival supplies and food.

More troops have been dispatched to
Oklahoma and now **Arkansas**. Martial Law
has gone into effect in Arkansas.

A spate of tornadoes danced a brutal

path through **tornado alley,** leaving a swath of destruction in their wake. FEMA's office in **DC** said they don't know when they can send help. The local FEMA offices are for now, on their own.

Colorado, Utah, and **Nevada** have taken a page from North Carolina's book and set plans into motion to close their borders.

The waters from the hurricanes show no sign of receding. Along the **Gulf coast,** looters are using small boats to scavenge in the submerged areas. So far the Coast Guard shot and killed 8, arrested 35 and confiscated 18 water crafts.

The looting was not confined to the United States. **Beijing** was experiencing an epidemic of civil unrest not seen since the fall of the Imperial City. Troops were being recalled from Subi Reef to help quell the violence and looting in their earthquake ravaged capitol.

Preppers throughout the **New England** states have begun a mass exodus to their bug-out locations. Survivalists nation-wide are locking down their compounds.

5:24 am EDT, September 28,
Dancing Goats Farm,
Moon Mountain, North Carolina

Violet burst into the kitchen.

Without a good morning she started ranting. "Mother, I don't know what the hell happened last night. It's as if someone threw a switch and people lost their mother fucking minds!"

Gianna eyed her eldest and hoped her entrance wasn't a portent of what the day would bring. "That is a very apt description my dear. It's now imperative that the Tribe functions as a cohesive organism. No petty bullshit will be tolerated. Calling a meeting of all the supervisors and department heads for 9:00 am."

No sooner had Violet's tirade ended, when Nick burst into the room, the expression on his face reflecting Violet's state of mind. Gianna looked at Nick and thought it's going to be one of *those* days.

He too jumped right in without a greeting. "The recon unit was attacked last night. Our men are okay; the same cannot be said for Dark Lady, she took a few bullets to the driver's side of the bed. No damage to the engine or tires. Two men broke through the gate and drove up behind Reno and tried to cut him off." Reno spent a year running hooch in Kentucky. He's got some of Gianna's 'wicked mad skills' behind the wheel. "He easily out-maneuvered them. The assholes opened fire. Our boys returned fire. They must have realized the fire power they were up against, cause they ran. The idiots tried to back out and lost control. Fucked up their truck which gave the guys a chance to catch up to them. Reno said he's sure they wounded both of them. I've posted men at every 1500' along the inside perimeter. From now on there will a sniper in the nest 24/7. Had to put Carmichael on first watch. He went rabid when he heard what they did to your truck. He was ranting that you loved Dark Lady and how upset you'd be. He tried to go after them. In the nest I can keep eyes on him. He might need a Gianna talking to. Think it'll help me, keeping him from going rogue."

Annoyed Gianna narrowed her eyes and asked, "And you didn't wake me *why*?"

Nick stepped closer to Gianna the muscles in his jaw tightened as he tried to control his irritation at her question. "It's my job, not yours, to keep this place safe. After what's happened and is happening, your job, of running the farm, just has gotten a fuck of a lot tougher. I need you rested in ace running form, not sleep deprived and annoying the shit out of me. It's not as if your being woken would have changed anything."

Gianna tried to step back but his hands encircled her biceps holding inches from chest. Her first instinct was to kick him but the heat and the scent of him was intoxicating.

Unaware of her reaction to his nearness Nick continued "You stick to *your* responsibilities and I'll handle *mine*. Security and your safety is my responsibility. I don't need you telling me how to do it." He took a breath and saw the heat in her eyes. He realized the effect he was having on her and his face softened. "Gia, we're a dynamic team, we don't fix what isn't broken." Reluctantly he let her go.

Violet watched Nick's outburst with amusement. "Well, aren't you the *bossy boots* this morning Nicky boy."

At the sound of her voice he stepped away from Gianna. He hadn't seen Violet when he came in. "Miss Violet, after yesterday's episode, You have no room to be calling me bossy." He raised an eyebrow and said, "She's *your* mother... you know how she gets... if I don't reel her in now she'll be out there on recon tonight."

Violet nodded in agreement. "So true Nick."

Gianna regained her composure and gave them both a nasty look. "You know what... Fuck the both of you. You've made your point Nicholas. Violet Ann don't you have some where to be?"

Nick and Violet share a grin. "Vy, I know I'm on the top of the shit list when she uses my full name."

"Keep it up Nicholas, and you'll be crying." Gianna was no match for him physically but... she was privy to his darkest secrets and knew how to use them, *if* ever she was of a mind to. A dangerous lady to piss off. Nick quit before their repartee slid from jokes to jabs as it often did with the two of them lately. On her way out Gianna added, "Please make sure both of you smart asses are at the meeting. I need to go over a few things with Theo before then. Vy, make sure all of Hades crew attends." She slammed the door behind her.

5:30 am EDT, September 28,
Cumberland Gap, Kentucky

Fern needed to send word 'time had come to close the road'. She'd been keepin' abreast of the happenins' off the mountain. When Rachel had gotten back from her supply run earlier in the week she had relayed what folks had been talkin' about. After Rachel finished the shopping she and Ester had stopped for lunch at Pattie's Place. Pattie's bein' the place a body could hear all the news from in town and on the mountain. Rachael thought what she'd heard at Pattie's was a bit strange. She failed to see how it would have any effect on life on the mountain. Still, she being a dutiful

176

daughter, told her mama when she got back. Fern added wood to the cook stove, knowing dark times was comin' soon.

The Tennessee Righteous flee from Tennessee to North Carolina

Within two hours of Tennessee falling under Martial Law, several groups fled into the mountains looking to cross the North Carolina state line. Tennessee being the place that spawned the KKK, some of these groups were of like mind. The "Tennessee Righteous" was one such group. Since entering North Carolina they had passed through Zionville and had worked their way into the Elk Knob State Park. A friend of the 'cause' had lent them a cabin there. The place wasn't much more than a shack. Hale and eighteen of the members had fled in a panic. Sixteen of the less well-known members, and one of the leaders, stayed behind to pack up caches of food, ammunition and such. The plan was to join Hale and the others at the cabin.

Things *did not* go as planned. The Tennessee Righteous was on an FBI watch-list. The FBI, having been given a heads-up on what the White House was planning for Tennessee, were already in Johnson City when the order for Martial Law came through. The instant they got word, agents headed to a farm owned by one of the group's leaders An hour later the FBI team was in place. The order was for the

177

agents to wait until after the members had loaded the trucks and moved out, before they pulled the convoy over. Five miles into what turned out to be a very short trip, the FBI changed their Righteous travel plans.

Fifteen members of the Tennessee Righteous were arrested. The Feds confiscated 5 vehicles, 1,550 pounds of food and medical supplies, 40,000 in cash and gold, and a 15' box truck loaded to the hilt with survival gear, guns, ammo, explosives, and a hundred pounds of assorted drugs. One of the members wives, Sally Anne, was trying to round up her kids and was delayed in joining the convoy. She did not get caught in the FBI's raid. Another of the wives riding in the convoy texted Sally Anne as the Feds brought the hammer down. Sally Anne hightailed it off the farm on a dirt road at the far side of the hay field. She drove north to Atkins, Virginia then south and down into North Carolina, just before the governor closed the northern border. It took her a hour to find the cabin because her GPS couldn't find Meat Camp Road.

Sally Anne caught up with the members who had escaped on the morning of the 27th. Hale, the group's leader, was bullshit to say the least, when she gave him the news of the raid. They'd left with little more than their go-bags. Counting on the convoy's arrival had screwed them royally. With less than $200 left between them, there was no way they could stay hidden here now. Their phones had been left at the farm to prevent them from being tracked. Sally Anne had a burner she'd bought to let her mama know she and the kids were safe but none of the numbers Hale needed were in it. New phones with the numbers of members and supporters programmed into them but not activated yet, were in the cache the FBI got. Hale speculated as to how long it would take before the FBI started rounding up every person at the other end of those numbers. He surmised they'd been kicking' doors in before Sally Anne had reached the camp. Sally Anne's husband, who'd been driving the box truck, had most of their personal cash. She spent some of the $300 she had on gas, and bought food with what was left. Her truck was mostly packed with stuff for her kids. She told Hale, she was keeping the food for her kids, but she would make up a big pot of chili for the men. What she had that would be helpful to the group was a tent, a cooler, a scoped hunting rifle, and her personal 38. She made it clear she wasn't parting with the 38 - it had belonged to her daddy.

The name and phone number of the friend who owned the place they were staying in was in a phone now in the possession of the FBI. It wouldn't take them long to pick him up. Once they ran the friend's tax records the FBI would

know about the cabin. Sooner than later
they'd be comin' up Meat Camp Road. When
that happened the Tennessee Righteous
would be dead meat. They needed to move.
Hale weighed his options: go back up into
the mountains closer to the Tennessee
line; or east, deeper into North
Carolina? East was more populated with
better chances to scavenge but could they
blend in? More cops too. Up in the
mountains they might find an empty place
but how deep into North Carolina would
the Feds search. There had to be a
federal warrant out for him by now. His
name and prints were all over the shit in
the trucks the FBI confiscated leaving
the farm. That settled it for him. They'd
go east and keep to the back roads.
They'd head for Holly Springs. Everyone
was tired and stressed. Sally hadn't
slept in 24 hours, but they needed to be
gone from here. They'd leave in the
morning by ten. They'd rest tonight.

Sally Anne only had a pot and four
bowls in the her truck. They found four
more bowls in the cabin. While the men
took turns eating Sally Anne's chili,
Hale search the real estate listings in
Holly Springs, on the burner phone. He
found a secluded ten acre lot with a
stream that would do nicely as a base
when they got there. Hale estimated two
hours to make the trip. After they ate
their meager meal Hale sent out two men
to search for license plates off vehicles
parked at camps around the state park.

Many would be closed up for the winter about now. They came back with four North Carolina plates. They switched them for their Tennessee tags. Cal had found a couple of old Army blankets in one of the trucks they stole the tags off.

As they packed the vehicles some of the men pulled Hale aside and told him they wanted to take Sally Anne's food to share among the group. Hale narrowed his eyes looking from man to man. An unpleasant grin creased his long thin face. "Our friend and brother, James Blaylock was arrested by the FBI while tryin' to bring us our supplies. He will do a long stretch for his brave actions. James Blaylock is about the meanest man alive - y'all know this to be true. Ya' also know James Blaylock loves his wife and kids. What the fuck do you suppose he's gonna do when he finds out you stupid bastards took food out'a their mouths? Has hunger made y'all soft in the head? Do y'all not remember he has four brothers just about as mean as him? The Blaylocks will run every last one of y'all to ground, an' gut ya like the pigs ya' are." Hale spat at their feet, turned and walked away. There was no more talk about Sally Anne's food.

They rolled into Holly Springs a little past noon. They spent the afternoon getting acquainted with the layout of the town and what it had to offer. While in town they'd liberated a

181

few more North Carolina plates off
tourists they'd come across. Hale and
Ethan went ahead and scouted the
property. At dusk, an econovan, four
pickups of varying ages, and a '67 Buick
Le Sabre rolled silently up the dirt
trail into the woods and set up camp.

**6:00 am EDT, September 29,
Washington, DC**

The congressman look at the caller
ID and motioned for the driver to roll up
the window as he answered the call.
"David, has anyone spoken to Ammar?"

"Yes, Charles spoke with him by SAT
phone last night. Communications there
are sketchy. The sandstorm damaged cell
towers. His jet was slightly damaged.
Repairs are underway. It should be
completed by tomorrow. Do you have things
under control there? I'm hearing rumors
all is not well in the big house."

"Congress, is a cluster-fuck right
now. So much so, I stayed in in town last
night. Genuine panic abounds. The
southern states are on their knees
begging for help. Many won't have a seat
much longer. The EPA thinks the water
won't retreat to where it was before the
storm. By 'suggesting' the refugees be
transported to other states I have
successfully and almost effortlessly
stripped them of their constituents.
Between the loss of land and population

182

they don't have a leg to stand on. I've already 'suggested' quietly that the ones who have been affected be removed or at least suspended from congress."

"Brilliant move. This will leave you with a smaller number to maneuver into position. It's all happening sooner then we intended. As long as you're there steering the rudder, I'm confident we'll stay on course."

"I've got another bit of good new for everyone. FEMA is fucked. I've just 'suggested' we look outside the government for help with relief efforts. I passed along a list of companies he might choose from. Fifteen of the twenty on the list are ours."

David laughed. "Do we own mother nature too? Or at the least she must be on our payroll somewhere. Let's talk tonight after we see what events transpire through the day."

**6:00 am EDT, September 29,
Holly Springs, North Carolina**

Hale rolled out of the back of his truck bed. The rest of the group were still asleep. He sat with his legs hanging off the tailgate lighting a Camel. He took a drag looking at the incongruous sight before him of dirty vehicles, kids toys and people rolled in blankets on the ground, he thought 'This

183

is a real ball of shit! They're gonna
wake up hungry. They'd finished off the
last of the cold chili before turning in
for the night. He'd given Sally Anne 50
bucks to pick up some food when they were
in town. Fifty doesn't go far feedin'
eighteen people. Sally Anne had food for
her and her kids for maybe a week. The
$50 would go farther if they had a way to
cook. Fuck, he wanted a cup of coffee. He
wasn't looking forward to a bologna
sandwich and a plastic cup of tepid
sweet-tea. They needed to take the car
into town and leave it there for getting
around. He'd find a place to park it
where it wouldn't be noticed when it sat
there overnight. He didn't want to keep
driving over the trail raising dust, it
might be noticed if they left new tracks.
It was only a mile walk to town. First
thing today was to scout around for an
abandoned house. They couldn't spend more
than a few nights on the ground.
Yesterday they'd passed a boy scout camp.
Tonight they'd see what tools and
supplies could be scavenged there.
Blankets would be nice. Sally Anne should
see what could be had for cheap at the
thrift shop. They might need to sell one
of the vehicles. 'He wondered how Cal
would feel about selling his truck.
Cal... where the fuck was Cal... or
Ethan? Shit, those two assholes must have
gone out scavenging.' Having no idea when
they'd left, Hale didn't know if he
should be worried they're not back yet.
Across the camp the kids were getting out

of the truck, looking for a place to pee.
Hale jumped off the tailgate and jogged
after them. The last thing he needed was
kids crying cause their privates were
covered in poison ivy blisters.

Hale and the kids return to camp to
a sight Hale needed even less than kids
poison-ivyied asses. Ethan and Cal had
returned... with... bullet wounds.
Ethan's was a through and through in his
left shoulder. Cal's was bad. He took one
in the leg and one in the back. He's lost
too much blood for it not to have hit one
of his organs. The look on Ethan's face
tells Hale he knows even if they take Cal
to a hospital, his brother's gonna die.
This is a fuck of a way to start the day.
They cover Cal with a blanket, it's
evident he's gone into shock. Fifteen
minutes later Cal was dead. Sally Anne
had the kids in her truck so their crying
didn't give away their location. Hale
told Bubba to get the camp shovel out
from behind the seat in his truck. They
can take turns digging. It's gonna be a
bitch with that tiny shovel. Hale does
what he can for Ethan's shoulder with the
limited supplies from the first-aid kit
under his seat.

Ethan told him, Cal couldn't sleep
and was determined to go find food. Ethan
per usual followed his older brother's
lead. They stole a truck down the road a
piece. A bit after that, they came up on
two guys in a sweet black pickup goin'

through a gate, then locking' it behind
them. Cal figured if they locked the gate
there must be something worth protecting.
Cal leaned the truck into the gate and
broke the chain. When he caught up with
the guys Cal stupidly tried to cut the
black truck off. The driver managed to
swerve around Cal and stopped. Not
thinking they might be armed, Ethan tried
to scare them by shooting up the side of
their truck; only they were armed... with
semi-automatic rifles. Ethan tried to
back them out, crashed and screwed up the
truck. It got them back on the road but
died after about a mile. Half carrying,
half dragging his brother, Ethan got lost
in the woods trying find the camp in the
dark, as Cal bled out. Hale started
swearing about the cops looking for them
now for a new set of crimes, AND they'd
lost their fucking rifles!

Ethan was sorry about the rifles but he
couldn't carry his brother and them with
his shoulder shot up. He didn't think the
guys had called the sheriff. He didn't
hear any sirens. From the road that place
looked like any old farm. But the deeper
they went down the track inside the gate,
the more it looked like a huge walled
compound. Hale said would think on that
later; now he was worried about his
people, who needed food and shelter.

6:00 am EST, September 29,
Hawaii, Hawaii

186

4700 miles west of Hale, the Kilo Kilo is worrying about her people. Not all on the Big Island heeded her warning. She hoped these few are enough, for them to start again. Then the sand beneath her sandal-less feet began to shudder. Tutū Pele's voice filled the night air as her molten rage filled the black eastern sky. Her people were screaming. The banyan trees swayed. Loosed Coconuts sailed through the village. Her son took her by the shoulders begging her to come inside. "Be calm my son, She who shapes the sacred land speaks not to us, but to the east." Knowing he was not comforted, she followed him inside.

The rupture of Kilauea knocked planes from the sky. The *Big Island* fractured from Silo to Kampala causing the land between them to slide into the ocean. Hawaii's Sleeping Beauty, Sauna Ea, answers her sister Kilauea's call. Wait, free at last surges down her slopes. Sauna Lao and Balalaika join their sisters in their fire dance. As each new partner joins in, another chunk of the Big Island vanishes beneath the waves. An inferno of lava fills the space between them. When they are done every trace of humans will have been eradicated from the place once known as The Big Island.

Tutū Pele's revenge is not over... She sends tsunamis in every direction except northeast. The Goddess spares the smaller Hawaiian islands as she had told the Kilo Kilo she would.

The first tsunami washes over Baja California reaching within 8 miles of its eastern coast. A 110' tall wave submerges the **California** coast from San Diego to Oxnard, reaching 15 miles inland in some places. **Catalina Island** will be just a sandbar after Tutū Pele's visit.

A smaller tsunami, only 80' tall, washes much of **San Francisco** and all of the Bay.

Monterey... well, there is no more Monterey.

The city south of where Monterey once stood will henceforth be known as **"Camel-*In*-The-Sea"**

chapter 9
THE PROPHET'S SONG

"Hear the words
the warning's clear
Your ambivalence
has brought you here"

9:45 am EST, September 29,
Dancing Goats Farm,
Moon Mountain, North Carolina

Nick and Gianna entered the Hall fifteen minutes late for the meeting. "Sorry sorry sorry everyone. I seem to be suddenly making a habit of being late for meetings. Please bear with me. I feel like a one-legged man in an ass kicking contest. Do we need to cover what made me late?"

From Sadie, "If you mean the latest bull from Washington, then no."

Violet says, "If you are referring to the fact that Antarctica just showed her ass... then no."

"Good. What does all of this mean to us? Nick, you first please."

"In the event you haven't heard, our recon team was attacked last night. They broke through the gate in the zone. No one was hurt except the Dark Lady. She took several bullets in the bed. She will be fine. Mikey has her in the shop as we speak.

You may have seen increased number of guards posted. They will be a permanent fixture until I deem it safe to stand down. Odds are that won't be for a very long time. Have your people be *hyper-vigilant*. Report anything not normal to me or the Sergeant ASAP.

There will be absolutely no leaving the farm. The only people outside these walls are the vanguard. Please make that clear. If anyone starts whining about needing to leave, explain to them the only way to leave here now is in a body bag. I am dead serious. I won't allow a person with the knowledge of the farm existence and what we have going on here to leave. As fucking scary as it sounds, *'We Are At War'*.

The government has stripped a third of it's citizens of their constitutional rights. One third of our citizens are either dead or will be soon with the impending sea rise. Half of the remaining third are frightened, homeless and/or dangerous. People, who only last week would have given you the shirt off their back, will now try to take what you have by any means necessary.

We are now going to use the Q for what it was designed for. The gates will be open to the outside from time to time. I want them to see the vanguard. They need to believe this place is overrun with nasty drunk bikers. They'll cross us off as a place to seek refuge. To that end, the women on the Hades team need to work out a schedule for who's in the Q and when.

Groups will be moving into the area looking for anything they can get their hands on. A view of life in 'biker village' Q will dissuade some of them. Others are more prepared to fight for what they want. I believe one such group is here now. Those two from last night are not locals. The vanguard has been compiling a database of photos of everyone in the town for the last four years. Our vehicles all have a video feed. These two are not in our database. If there are more of them, you can count on a return visit.

We're rolling in the forest today. Amber you've done a terrific job covering the greenhouses. The movable forest will provide the coverage we need to stay hidden. I did a walk through this morning. Really good work. If there are more evergreens you can pull out of the woods let's do it after we get the planters in place. If you need help, just let me know how many. We need as much tree camouflage as we can get.

Stephen, you've done a great job with the camouflage nets. All that's left is for you to get the hay bales and rolls out of the fields today. Same goes for you with the labor.

Last, we are in full blackout mode. The patrol will check each dwelling tonight for breaches. They'll let you know if you have any."

Gianna asked, "Stephen what do you need?"

"I'll take twenty if you can spare them. We should be able to get the hay up by supper."

"Amber, what do you need honey?"

"I'll take ten guys to move the trees. Anyone who knows how to properly work a fork lift would be good. Some of those Southern Magnolias are huge. Yes, we have some trees we can pull out of the Hundred Acre Wood. Nick, I'd like us to ride through the zone in the next day or so, whatever works for you. There are fir trees that are so thickly bunched they need to be thinned or they'll choke each other out. Dead firs don't provide much cover for the wall. In here they can be used to fill in. I could tag them and you could have your boys dig them up if you don't want me out there."

"Simon, you're next."

"I think I have everything under control. Going to pull back on the variety of options at a meal. We used to feed the leftovers to the hogs, but that was before. Violet and I have gone over the baking supplies. We're both satisfied. I'm happy with the transfers. Getting supplies won't be that big a deal. If I need anything I'll just send Amber."

"Fuck you, Simon!" He loves to bait her.

"Tyler, how do we stand."

"The new shed in Studio City is working out great. The new lines are run. The solar has been checked three times. The wind turbines all have their camouflage blades on. The winter ones are in the shop getting repainting where needed. The hydro-plant is making more than we can use. That will change as people start using their heat. The nets have reduced the sunlight to the panels but again we have more than we need right now. We're going to switch all the dryer vents to vent inside tomorrow. Simon and I are working on a way to have the kitchen fans vent into the Hall. We could be all tucked in and the smell of Simon's cooking could blow our cover."

"Great catch guys. Let me know when it's ready. Andy, anything you need?"

"The infirmary is fully stocked. I sterilized the clean-room today. We have one surgeon, one vet, two midwives and six with nursing training, and me. I think we're in great shape."

"Lizzy what's the livestock report?"

"The cattle, horses, and goats are perfectly happy in the woods. I'm leaving the barn open at night so they can graze if they want to, but not the goats. They make too much noise and their white coats don't blend with the night. The same goes for the sheep. But sheep need more pasture grazing time. Going to set up a movable pen with a camouflage cover. Simon, I know how you feel about freezing food but you may want to reconsider, things being what they are. Right now we have two dozen head of sheep. At least three boys are ready to harvest. I'd like to reduce the crazy English hogs by half. But that would mean running the smokehouse. Not sure how Nick feels about that..."

"How many are we talking about?"

"That would be eight."

Nick said, "Simon, can you make the

time to get them butchered and dressed now? Things are a bit dicey, but it would be better to do it sooner. We can also use the smokehouse in the Q as a cover for the smell, if it becomes an issue. I have at least five that are skilled at butchering. Maybe you could supervise them, to get it done your way."

"Ya, we can get started on that today. We can talk after the meeting."

"The chickens, ducks, turkeys and geese are all good but noisy. I'm putting the turkeys, geese and ducks in the barn at night since we went to blackout mode. Simon, we have an abundance of duck if you want to smoke some. And the bunnies are Amber's domain."

"Keep your mitts off my bunnies, Simon!"

"That just leaves the Water Wizard."

"Tested all four wells yesterday. All the cisterns have been flushed and refilled. The old water's been tested and cycled to the greenhouses and irrigation. Had a thought about the composting toilets even though it's not my area. What if we spread some of the waste outside the zone. People aren't gonna want to snoop around a place that smells like shit. What do you think Nick?"

Nick had trouble keeping a straight

face. "I'm going to keep that in mind if we get in a bind."

Gianna was pleased with everyone's report. "On that note, I think we're done. Thank you all for being so great at your jobs. Remember, if you need help, let Theo, Nick, or myself know."

After the meeting ended Theo pulled Nick aside. Nick knew it's bad from the look on Theo's face. When it was bad news Theo could get a bit wordy. "Don't sugar coat it just tell me what it is."

"Sean may be missing. I have not had contact with him since Dodge City at 11:45 am on the 28th. He called and said he was going to sleep for five or six hours and he would text me when he got back on the road. I should have gotten a text around 6 pm last night. I figured he forgot or had an issue with his phone. I've sent seven text and calls. It just goes to voice mail. Between sleep and 18 hours drive time he should be here... what time is it... okay it's 10:15 so."

Nick did the math and didn't like what he came up with. "He should be here in an hour. If he's had car trouble he could be delayed but he should have contacted us by now. Put Ferret on it. Have her sweep everyplace he could be between Dodge City and here." Nick looked over at Gianna talking with Amber. "Theo do not say anything to her yet. She has enough to deal with right now. Her knowing won't help us find him any faster, it'll only upset her sooner. Lets see what we turn up in the next few hours. I'll let you know when you can tell her." Theo shook his head and hurried off to get Ferret working on locating Sean.

Nick and Gianna rode over to the Q together. He was running possible scenarios in his head for Sean's delay when Gianna's niece called. "Oh my God Auntie you wouldn't believe how bad it's gotten. I tried to rent a truck and there were none within a hundred miles so I bought one. A 20' box truck. I woke up the other night and Mommy was standing in my room. She said "Get the fuck out of that bed and get your ass to my sister's house. You are so out of time." Then she vanished. It was one o'clock in the morning. She was so clear, I got up, made coffee, and started packing."

"When was this?"

"Three nights ago. I couldn't call you 'cause we had a crazy storm that took out cell towers and shit. I just crossed into Virginia. Some guy at the gas station told me the North Carolina border is closed. I'm fucking freaking out. My life is in this truck. What if they don't let me in?"

"Not to worry baby, Auntie can fix

this. Just come down 29 at Danielle take 58 west to 311. That will bring you to the border. I will meet you there. Call when you get to Lynchburg."

"Auntie how the *hell* are you going to get them to let me cross?"

"Guns and money baby... one or both works every time." Gianna hung up. By the way Nick was gripping the steering wheel of the cart, she can see he's not pleased with her conversation. This wasn't going to be pretty. She tried to defuse his rage. "Nicholas, that was a nice job you did with your report you gave to the staff. You handled the news of the attack well."

Nick started to pay attention to her conversation when Gia said she could 'fix this'. Now she was trying to placate him cause she knew he wouldn't like it. "STOP blowing smoke up my ass Gianna! Just give me the fucking details. Do you even remember we have an extraction team?... and you're not on it! I don't want you out there. I can't protect you when you're out running around the fucking countryside. You're not going out there without me. I think you should let me do my job!"

Gianna took a breath. Clearly there was no fixing this. "Not this one darling. I can be charming and persuasive in a manor you can't."

Nick knew what that meant and he didn't like *that* either. How the fuck could he keep her safe if she kept running off without him?

1:00 am EDT, September 29,
The Bad News on Planet Earth
It's Still a Blog Online
Not Telling You Where

Washington DC The president recalled all military personnel from around the world to return to the US. After a series of calls involving the UK, France, Russia, China, and the US, several Satellites mysteriously begin jamming all communications to and from Antarctica.

The US borders are now closed. Homeland Security has begun a mass expulsion of all non-US citizens. The official word is it's based on a 'Credible Threat'.

California has been placed under Martial Law. The US-Mexico border crossing in California was damaged by the tsunami. The Army Core of Engineers have blown it up. The Army has a shoot-to-kill order for anyone crossing the border into **California, Arizona, New Mexico or Texas.** Deportations to Mexico are being shuttled through Nogales, Arizona.

The president of **Mexico** doesn't have time to be pissed; he's too busy dealing with the damage and death from the tsunami, the earthquake, and a volcano that has erupted again in southern Mexico.

Canada is fine with the border closing. It will stop the flood of refugees from the hurricanes and the illegals running from ICE.

DC Quietly, cabinet members' are sending their families to their luxury bug out homes.

1:30 am EDT, September 29, Smokey Mountains, Tennessee

Axel opened the door of the trailer to get a better view of the place. "What a shit hole." They'd dumped the bodies around back while Craig had gone for the Caddy last night. Axel thumped down the steps and went around the back of the trailer. The tarp they had tossed over the bodies had partially blown off. The woman's head and one of the kids legs were sticking out. Axel reached for the edge of the tarp, the woman's empty eyes stared up at him. "Damn, you an ugly bitch and a shitty housewife too." He pulled the tarp over her then dropped a cinder block on it to keep it from blown' off again. Her head made a sickening sound like when you drop a ripe watermelon. Axel laughed when he heard it. "Guess we can't stay here too long y'all already startin' to stink." Back in

200

the trailer he went through the cabinets.

Wyatt was up. "What the fuck, didn't they feed the kids? I already looked. Just found this box of corn flakes. There's some canned beans in the one over the sink."

Axel found a half loaf of dollar store bread in the fridge. He checked it for mold, which was growing on several plastic bowls next to it. The bread looked okay to eat. He took two pieces and hit sleeping Silas in the head with the rest of the loaf.

"What the fuck, asshole?"

"Get up, we got to find another place. This shit hole stinks and that's before the bodies out back begin to rot. Slipped over to the neighbor's last night. It's tighter than a gnats ass. I want to see what else is down the road." Axel left for the car and passed Craig pissing on the side of the trailer. "Git in. We're leaving." Wyatt got in behind the wheel.

Silas jumped in as Wyatt was backing out. "Wyatt, ya almost broke my god damn leg."

As they passed by the mountain compound. Axel studied it in the daylight... *Ya a gnats ass.* The next place over an old man was checking his mailbox. Acxel yelled, "Stop." Wyatt hit the brakes. "Come on." Axel slid out of the car. "Pardon me sir. We got kinda lost last night and we're runnin' low on gas. Would you happen to have a gallon we could buy?"

At first glance, Harvey knows them for the dangerous dirt-bags they are. He patted his chest. Damn he was getting sloppy in his old age. His holster was empty. He'd taken his gun off for breakfast and left it on the sideboard. He knew he'd never get in and lock the gate before this piece of crap was on him. "I might have a gallon I can sell you..." as he pulled the bell rope. The clang startled the three coming up the driveway, too fast to be polite. "Just letting the little woman know we have company. Want to make sure she's decent." Wyatt, Craig and Silas went through the gate behind Harvey. Axel hung back, checking up and down the road for cars that might remember seeing the Caddy there.

Once inside the gate, Harvey stumbled, going down on all fours... in one smooth motion Barbra stepped out from behind the rose trellis as she let *lo' Jenny* rip... the first blast caught Craig in the throat. The second hit Silas in chest. She pumped two rounds into Wyatt's back as he fled through the gate. Axel dragged him toward the car. Worried the old woman was gonna come through the gate, he glanced through the car window saw the keys and drop Wyatt, dove through the passenger door, cranked the Caddy and stomped on the gas.

Next door, everyone had just sat down to lunch when they heard the unmistakable sound of a semi-automatic shotgun. The men grabbed their weapon of choice as they bolted down the stairs. Pauline hit the remote for the garage door from the top of the stairs. Frank started the truck as Billy and Dan open the gate.

Rory yelled, "I'll stay with the girls."

"Right, close the gate behind us." Dan jumped in shouting: "Go!"

Frank raced down the road skidding a bit on the curve and again as he turned into the drive. Dan got out first. Harvey had a bloody towel wrapped around one hand and dirt smudges on both knees. Dan looked over at Barbra in her flowing skirt, long hair blowing in the breeze with a shotgun resting casually in her arm and thought '*Annie Oakley as a hippie*'. What he said was, "You folks badly hurt?"

Frank stopped staring at the dead man he'd almost stepped on getting out of the truck... "We're y'all neighbors."

Harvey nodded to Dan "You're Sam's son-in-law Tracy's husband. Oh, this is nothing. I cut my palm when I hit the dirt. Barbra is a damn good shot but in the heat of the moment shit can happen. So I dove for cover a bit hard."

Barbra said, "You're Pauline's husband Frank. But we don't know this gentleman."

"I'm Billy ma'am. That must have been some pretty fancy shooting." They could hear the deputy's siren winding up the mountain road. Barb had called them when Harvey rang the warning bell.

Dan said, "We'll get out of the way now that we know you're okay. Guess you'll have some explaining to do when the deputy gets here."

Barb smiled. "Why don't you all come over for a drink after we're finished with the cops... that is, unless they arrest me."

Harvey laughed. "Don't listen to her, she's not getting arrested. Just come on back when they leave."

11:30 am EST, September 29,
Dancing Goats Farm
Moon Mountain, North Carolina

Gianna was pleased with the work on Dark Lady. Mikey is an artist at bodywork. The boys had the front gate open and were doing a superb job of looking like a disreputable bunch of reprobates. Nick was still *very not happy* with her going on this road trip. He refused to let her take Carmichael as one of her team. "Too many things could go wrong. You being out there without me is wrong! I don't want another of them to be Carmichael. You'll take two SUVs and one of the SAT phones. You'll take six men of my choosing. Don't even think about arguing with me woman."

Gianna gave him her best 'obedient little woman' smile. "Nicholas you know best. As you pointed out it *is* you job dear." On the way back her place she called Carl AKA the Fixer. "Hi honey, rested up from your family vacation?"

"Yes I am, thank you."

"Good, I need you. Now would be perfect."

"I'll be there in five." He always knew where she was when she called. It was just one of his spooky talents. Some might call his talents dark... very dark, but you can't have the light without the dark. In some circles the 'errands' he ran for her might be euphemism as 'wet work'. For her there was no moral dilemma in it. A girl's got to do what a girl's got to do. She did whatever it took to keep her family and her Tribe safe and

205

happy. To that end there was Carl.

When he arrived she explained the errand. He agreed with Nick on the number of vehicles and men. He recommended they take 10 grand for 'walking around money'. He wanted to leave *now*. He calculated three and a half hours, in a truck, to Danville. Normal time from the farm to 311, an hour and twenty. With Reno driving, they could shave twenty off that. SO, yea, NOW. They'd barely have an hour to secure the location, while Carl convinced who was ever on the check point, through money or death if he had to, to let Alexandra's truck into North Carolina. He left to talk to Nick about firepower and maybe a few toys. Gianna went to the money store in the basement, then hurried to the Q.

12:00 pm EDT, September 29, Holly Springs, North Carolina

Hale had left everyone at the camp except Bubba. Ethan needed to rest up and grieve for his brother. Cal and Ethan should not have gone out alone, but no fucker killed and wounded his men and walked away. He'd see they paid, later.

After the way the day had started Hale didn't expect it to be a fruitful rest of the day. However, things had turned around and were looking sunnier. He'd found a ramshackle house set back a good two hundred feet from the road

206

surrounded by overgrown woods. He and
Bubba had searched the property and
buildings. The old barn was still solid
enough to hide the vehicles in. The house
had four rooms upstairs and four down and
a kitchen. The screening on the back
porch hung in shreds. A few pieces of old
furniture dotted the rooms. Bubba had
spotted a rough made trestle table in the
barn and some chairs hanging from the
rafters. It needed a good cleaning but it
fit the bill nicely. Hale had them leave
the camp one vehicle at a time. He didn't
want to attract interest as to who'd been
staying in the woods with Cal's body in a
shallow grave. Sally Anne and the kids
had been sent to town with Bubba. He gave
her another 50 for food and to see what
she could find at the thrift shop for
their new home.

Bubba had just pulled in. A camp stove
was the find of the day along with few
kitchen odds and ends. Hale had texted
them that they'd found a box of dishes
and glassware in the barn along with an
old cast iron fry pan. Some of the men
had dragged the furniture out on the
front porch and beat the dust out of
them. There were fireplaces in a few of
the rooms. Others gathered fallen
deadwood to stack next to each one.
Tucker set snare traps at the edge of the
small pasture behind the house. Big John
had located a well with a hand pump under
a mass of overgrown brambles. It took
some work, but he got it pumping. He told

Sally Anne the water tasted good but they should boil it to be safe. While the kids played in the yard, Sally Anne set about cleaning up the kitchen. Everyone was grateful for a place to sleep.

In the barn Hale and two others clear off the work bench. They stack any items they collect that might be useful. Up in the loft Bubba was rootin' through a stack of boxes and crates that'd been stored there for decades. He'd found a hundred year old youth bed frame for the kids. The cedar chest stocked with quilts and blankets would make the nights bearable. At the very back of the pile, tucked under the eve, Bubba struck gold.

Bubba let out a rebel yell so loud, Hale was sure they heard it back in Tennessee. "Hale, Hitler himself musta' guided us here! Get your ass up here. Gold, I struck gold!"

Hale raced up the stairs believing Bubba had found a box of gold. At the top those hopes of gold coins were dashed... however what Bubba had in his hands was indeed as good as gold to the brothers of the Tennessee Righteous. In Bubba's hands was a genuine Nazi SS Officers Jacket. Hale all but fell to his knees in adoration. "Holy Shit!"

"There's this big old trunk stuck back up under all this shit. This was inside. Wait till y'all see what all's in

here. Got a stack a papers on top.
Letters and newspaper clippings about the
clan back in the day."

They dragged the trunk over to the
hay-door to better see what all Bubba'd
found. The men working in the barn below
join them, eager to find out what the
ruckus was. Had Bubba found one of Black
Beard's treasure chests, the Tennessee
Righteous wouldn't have been happier...
The farm had belonged to a member of the
KKK. The papers contained a dozen
articles on clan marches and trials
dating back to the 50's & 60's. There was
a letter his daughter had written him in
1982. It said she and her husband were
opposed to his racist beliefs. He would
never be allowed to poison her children's
minds with his hateful views. They found
a handwritten Will leaving the farm to
her brother, dated a year after the
letter. Several stacks, each containing
dozens of receipts held together with
paper clips, told the story of the man's
passion for Nazi memorabilia.

The contents of the trunk was all
that was left of his years of collecting.
Besides the jacket Bubba had been
holding, there were five more jackets and
six pairs of pants. Further investigating
produced a smaller wooden box filled with
officers' caps, belts, medals and several
swastika armbands. The woolen uniforms
were a tad moth-eaten but it didn't dim
the collective joy felt by the Tennessee

Righteous gathered before them.

12:00 pm EDT, September 29,
Devil's Fork Gap
Smokey Mountains, Tennessee

After having spoken with Harvey and Barbra, the Sheriff sent deputies to canvass the sparsely populated road. A deputy rang the buzzer at the gate and identified herself. "This is Deputy Sanford. I believe I spoke with you folks down at the sheriff's station the other day. Y'all brought in the looters' truck. I'd like to speak to y'all about y'alls neighbors the Goldbergs."

Pauline pressed the talk button in the kitchen. "Yes ma'am, we all'll be down directly." When they were assembled outside the gate, Deputy Sanford took their statements and personal information.

After Rory had give his info, he stepped aside and leaned against the gate, his arms defensively crossed, thinking, 'Fucking great! all they're missing is my shoe size.'

After she left, Billy'd gone to the tower hoping to spy some of the action going on at Shangri La Farm. No sooner had he settled in with his binoculars when the sheriff's car came racing down the road, lights flashing, siren blaring, then screeched to a halt next door. Over the next thirty minutes Billy was entertained by the parade of a variety of Law Enforcement vehicles lined up and down their quiet country road. An unmarked black SUV had just followed the coroners wagon on to the brothers' property.

Billy'd been giving blow by blow reports to the guys in the house. "Looks like the Feds just pulled in. The coroner's here too. Wonder who got killed. We got people from the Sheriffs Department, Tennessee Highway Patrol, our Volunteer Fire Department and now the FBI. Who in the hell are these people? Frank, y'all shoulda' done a better job of learnin' 'bout our neighbors. Oh, hold on, I think they're bringin' dogs..." Billy never let up on the talk button of his radio.

Inside all they could do was listen and hold their questions for when he finally shut up. No one thought that would be anytime soon. Frank and the rest of the household thought this would be a good time to try and find the trail Harvey had talked about. Dan thought they all could use that drink Barbra had mentioned. Two hours later Billy still had no idea he was talking to an empty house.

12:30 pm EDT, September 29, On the road to Alexandra

211

Carl spoke for the first time since they got in the car. "This would have been simpler at night, but none of us wants her out there attracting attention to herself, so we'll make it work. There's one state cop there right now. The checkpoint is actually two miles south of the border at a rest stop. It'll be on our right. It's in the middle of East Bum-Fuck. We're about a mile out.

Gianna thought, 'Evidently Carl knows where *everyone* is, not simply herself.' "Carl, that thing in your ear that looks like a Bluetooth, it's not really a Bluetooth is it? I figured out it's a flux-capacitor connecting you to an alien space station. *Everyone* knows they have way better technology than we do. That's how you know where everyone in the world is. Is there a chip in your head that provides you with video as well?"

"Gianna, I should know better than to try to put one past you."

Carl's tone was such that Reno stole a glance at him trying to read his face. Fuck if he could tell. Maybe it was an alien headset. If it was, he wanted one too.

Reno eased the vehicle into the rest area. The backup team pulled further in. Everyone exited the vehicles. The backup team resembled a bunch of country boys

212

out for fun. Their SUV had a camouflage
paint job. They were gathered around the
open hatch quenching their thirst from an
open cooler. Under a blanket next to the
cooler lay an assortment of serious
hardware. Gianna stretched imaginary
kinks out and whispered to Carl, "Me
first."

The cop leaning back on the trunk of
his car glanced up as she approached.
Glad for the break in his monotonous
afternoon, he offered an "Afternoon
ma'am."

"Afternoon, officer. Oh my stars
you're a Darling? Any relation to the
Reidsville Darlings?" Not waiting for his
answer, she bend down to straighten her
pant leg, her waist length hair tousled
by a breeze.

Carl quips to Reno, "A little T&A
works every time. The breeze was a nice
touch."

Standing ten feet away the air is
dead still. Reno smiled... he'd seen her
do that breeze trick before.

"Yes, ma'am the Crossroads Darlings
are kin."

"Oh my, what a small town North
Carolina is. Stephen Darling is one of my
dearest friends. He actually works for
me."

The cop stood up and grinned leaning forward as his voice became more animated. "Stephen told me about some of y'alls organic gardening skills. He told..."

Carl chuckled. "And there it is... the boy's engaged. This'll be fun watching her reel him in. Reno, we may walk away clean on this one." They watch her spin her magic. Reno noted to Carl he thought the the cleavage helped a lot.

Without missing a beat of the conversation, she beckoned them to her with a one inch nailed index finger. Introductions were made just as Alexandra's truck came into view. Some might say Alexandra was a half hour early, but for the extraction team she is *right* on time.

Alexandra was bustled to the SUV before she could reveal too much. Reno took over driving the truck. The rest of the team caught up with them five miles down the road taking their place in front of Reno with Carl, Gianna and Alexandra bring up the rear. They nearly home, yet Carl was still on point and would be until the gate closed behind them. His facial expression was focus. Those who didn't know him as Gianna did would find his countenance fucking frightening. Teasingly Gianna patted him on the shoulder, in a sweet sing-song-ee voice

214

in his ear she said,... "Don't be so sad
honey. Very bad times are at hand.
There'll be lots of people for you to
kill very soon.

chapter 10

BEWARE WHEN CHASING RABBITS

"What was it door mouse said..."

3:00 pm EDT, September 29,
Devil's Fork Gap
Smokey Mountains, Tennessee

Deputy Sanford found the door of the
trailer open. She thought stains on one
of the mattress and maybe the couch *might*
be blood, there were so many stains she
couldn't be sure. Before calling it in
she looked around for other indications
of a possible crime.

The stench hit her full in the face
as she rounded the corner. It was late in
the season for flies but here they were
crawling over and under a tarp that'd
seen too many winters. There was a puddle
of red gone nearly black seeping out from
under a corner of the tarp. It was held
in place by a cinder block. She used a
stick to lift the edge. At the sight of a
child's foot she nearly vomited. Backing
around the trailer she called it in. Two
minutes later the Sheriff came sprinting
up the drive heading for the gruesome
scene. She wanted to decline his request

216

to join him but didn't. The sheriff used the stick to flip the tarp up... He did vomit just missing her shoe.

That's when the circus began. Sheriff Willis called the Highway Patrol for help. They were better equipped to deal with a crime of this magnitude. Their crime scene unit arrive lifting dozens of prints from everywhere. Then FBI agents showed up. They were looking for a neo-nazi group suspected of fleeing into the mountains prior to the raid on their farm. The dispatcher told them the Sheriff was at a crime scene and how to get there. Theories multiplied by the minute. No one remembered how the fire department got involved.

The three dead adults were known crack heads with long arrest records. Additional prints belonging to a bad lot from Alabama made the suspect list. The medical examiner placed TOD sometime around midnight. Making the assault on the Goldbergs hours after the murders. Sheriff Willis was too happy to oblige when Highway Patrol wanted the case.

The FBI nosed around the scene then left to talk to the Goldgbergs and their neighbors. Their description the of the Alabama boy who'd escaped in the caddy matched the photo for the 4th set of prints found in the trailer. During the interview the agents got word the Alabama boys were wanted for having slipped past the Army at the Charlotte Processing Center. They'd been on a list of refugees to be sent to Lejuen. The four were also wanted for questioning in connection with the death of a young mother in Charlotte, the theft of her car, and the theft of a Cadillac in Hendersonville. Axelrod Jones, the most dangerous of the lot had escaped the US Army, and death in less than 24 hours. This crazy bastard was on a roll. Most likely feeling invincible about now... that could make him even more dangerous.

Agents Parker and Mendez had taken shit from upstairs for not having had the Tennessee Righteous farm under surveillance before the order for Martial Law came through. Now, this Jones asshole got dumped in their lap because of his connection to the Aryan Brotherhood in prison. Agent Parker wasn't happy with this turn of events. "I feel like we're chasing our tail with this one." His partner didn't agree.

3:30 pm EDT, September 29,
Dancing Goats Farm,
Moon Mountain, North Carolina

As the *Alexandra* convoy entered the Q's gates, there was a collective sigh of relief expressed by those waiting on the veranda. In the yard Amber was all but jumping up and down at the sight of her older sister. Violet and Sadie were equally happy to have their younger cousin safely home. Nick was so relieved to have Gianna safely home were he could watch her, he didn't mind being proven wrong for a change. The vanguard were glad to see their same number return as had left, no worse for wear. Theo, though not in the Q, which is irrelevant since he is virtually everywhere with his finger on the pules of the farm, was glad for the news of the safe return, since he has something worry-some to discuss with Gianna, in addition to the fact that Alexandra was home safe – one more thing he could check off his list. Keeping an accurate list is vital as everyone *should* know.

On his way to the barn Reno nodded to Nick sitting on the veranda with his boots propped up on the railing. Gianna caught Nick watching and flashed him a smile, the one that says '*I told you I'd be fine*'. The extraction team got busy hosing down the SUVs and topping off their tanks. None of them wants to hear Nick yelling... "Put your fucking toys away when you're finished with them!" He's been evil tempered since the Lady left. Carl grabbed a chair next to Nick. "Carl, ready for a beer?" Carl nodded, Nick yelled "Freddy, another pair of cold ones while you're in there." he turned to Carl "Things went smoothly I take it?"

"Like butter under a hot knife." The screen door slammed Freddy hands them their beers and walks away, leaving the

Boss and the Fixer to discuss the road trip in private. His feet take him down the steps towards the barn. He wants to hear how it went from Reno and the guys.

Nick was listening as Carl gave his rendition of the trip, but Nicks eyes are trained on the cluster of women as they make their way to the east portal. They remind him a of a kaleidoscope of butterflies. His eyes narrow as they trace the lines of a profile lit by the afternoon sunlight. Her laughter rises above the chatter of the reunion. His heart tightens as it so often does when he hears her voice. His heart tightens or his head explodes. She consistently elicited profoundly incompatible emotions in him. He reluctantly pushed the lady out of his mind. He wants to hear what he missed.

4:00 pm EDT, September 29, Elk Knob State Park, North Carolina

The FBI agents would've been pleased to know that at this moment Axel was making one of those connections, that changes the path of a persons life. He'd fled the botched Goldberg robbery going down the North Carolina side of the mountains. The Caddy's GPS gave him a run for his money. In the end he got it to show him the way to a state park.

In Tennessee Gene had been tipped off, the Feds were coming for him. He got out with nothing but the clothes on his back. He'd hitched from Tennessee to Elk Knob Park in North Carolina. When he got to the camp he wandered around the cabin looking for what, he didn't know. Then he found it, Hale had left a coded message for any members who made it out. Now, how did he get from here to Holly Springs? Overcome with frustration and exhaustion he sat on the step staring at the woods.

Just as water seeks it's own level so do low-lifes. In Elk Knob Axel stumbled upon Gene, who coincidentally was also on the run from the Law in Tennessee. Gene had a place to go but no car. Axel had a car but no place to hide. Gene said it was providence that brought them together on Meat Camp Road. If he only knew how true those words were. Axel said they'd leave for Holly Springs after dark. On their way out Axel stopped to switch out the Caddy's plate for a Tennessee plate he got off and old truck parked behind one of the cabins. Lady Karma had her far reaching fingers in this one...

4:00 pm EDT, September 29,
Planet Earth's Fucked,
Location Still Unknown

Today's Report of the Real World News

The Poles The Arctic Ice Sheets have begun to respond vividly to the one foot sea rise, which has has gone unnoticed by

99% of the earth's human population. Another foot of rise and the ice shelves will snap off one by one, like the chocolate coating on a Klondike bar.

Mean while back in **Antarctica**... the volcano that once lay sleeping under the Pine Island Glacier is now free and waking up thus making the air over the icy continent a *wee* bit toastier. A wee bit in the US means you turn your frigging air conditioner down. In the land of ice and snow with the midnight sun, a wee bit is a fucking deal breaker.

Currently there is a game of musical glaciers being played on Antarctica. The glacier that looses ends up in the ocean. Catastrophic Sea Rise rocks on!

My intellectual dilemma?... Who do we believe on the subject of sea rise: The assholes, who like the cereal company in the classic "Cujo", say "Nothing's wrong here."; or the scientists that have boots on the ground or rather the ice? I'm leaning toward the scientists BUT how the hell are we suppose to trust the science of silly minded people who name their research vessel Boaty McBoatface? What the fuck does that even mean? It sounds like something you'd hear from a five year old. 'Mommy this is my bath toy. His name is Boaty McBoatface!' Not feeling the trust here either."

Russia Moscow has admitted to an

accident with one of their nuclear power plants. More information will be forth coming... How very Russian of them.

Africa Ebola is marching it's way across the African continent... unchecked. Natural Disasters around the globe are hampering the delivery of medical supplies. Thousands refuse don't seek medical aid because of local superstitions. There are 5,000 confirmed cases, the death toll is over 9,000. The *hot beds of conflict* (a nice euphemism for wholesale slaughter brought to us by the WHO (not the band)) are expanding. The level of violence is escalating exponentially, exacerbated by (try saying that three times fast) the droughts.

Greece 200 are dead from mud sides on the acreage scorched in July's wildfires that ravaged the country.

Pakistan The extent of the cholera outbreak is the worst since modern record keeping began. It has effected 10 million people, blowing the former record holder, Yemen, out of the water. (oops too soon?)

Spain Wildfires have scorched a trail through the Andalusian region, decimating thousands of acres of the countries' olive groves. This is a crippling blow to Spain's olive oil production. Spain produces 45% of the worlds olive oil. Guess it's time to hide your Virgin.

China is wishing it had spent those billions on the infrastructure of Beijing, rather than building that illegal island.

Netherlands – Holland William might want to reach out to the LGBT community. He's going to need more dikes. (oops too far?)

England Londoners have been heard to say "We're are most assuredly going to need a larger set of gates". *And a bigger fucking boat!*

France Paris the City of Lights is now the City of Rats. Rodents out number the population eight to one. The rats are winning and not just in France.

United States As if the country hasn't had enough problems caused by water...

The Northeast is being pounded by powerful storms. One system is stalled over up state New York, Vermont, and Massachusetts. Cities and towns are being inundated with flood waters from rivers and streams overflowing their banks. There are mud sides in Vermont. Mud skiing could become a new Olympic sport.

Washington DC is falling apart at the seams. Power Grabs are the business of the day, not the welfare of the people. It reminds me of one of Lily Tomlin's skits about a box of animal crackers... "I heard a lot of noise, and I think they ate each other up." We can only hope.

Wyoming Yellowstone National Park has some new tourist features...six - mile long up to fifteen feet wide, fishers have opened up, emitting blasts of caustic steam into the air.

Montana, the *mine's bigger* state, reports two similar fishers just north of Pray, Montana. Theirs are two miles long and ten to *eighteen* feet wide. They also shoot geyser-like caustic steam, into the valley's air. Might be time to Pray in Pray. In Bozeman a massive sink hole swallowed half a city block. Only half?

Earthquakes abound...
Iran 6.9, **Australia** 5.8, **Turkey** 6.1, **Costa Rica** 5.9, **Portugal** 7.5, **Russia** 7.6, **India** 6.6, **Germany** 5.6, **Iceland** 6.4, **Colombia** 7.4, **Brazil** 7.8, and **Argentina** 7.4.
These are just the bigger ones. Yikes!

Volcanoes are erupting...
Everywhere! Mother Nature's spectacular firework displays can be viewed in; **Mexico, Washington State, Iceland, Ethiopia, Alaska, pretty much the whole soup bowl of island countries north of Aussy Land** and yes folks, **TuTu Pele** is still rather pissed.

225

Disclaimer:

Note to the readers of my blog:

Mother, does not type.

The levity contained in this blog, comes
from me not Mother. Just wanted it to be
clear that the irreverent cunt here, is
Me.

Sincerely,
The Typist

5:20 pm EDT, September 29,
Devil's Fork Gap
Smokey Mountains, Tennessee

Rory was taking a turn in the tower.
He needed to have some time alone to deal
with his thoughts and sort out his
emotions. Cindy understood what he was
going through. She was good that way. He
had retreated to their room for some
peace and quiet. The rest of the
household continued to argue loudly.
Billy even barged into his room demanding
he weigh in on some stupid point he was
trying to make to the group. Now, he was
in the tower, alone with his thoughts for
the first time in days. He admitted to
himself, he was scared by the changes and
the speed with which they were happening.
He'd been having chasing dreams the last
two nights. When he woke he couldn't
remember what he'd been chasing.

He was regretting having become involved with this place. Should have made a place for just him and Cindy back in Virginia. Based on information being passed on by the HAM guys, things didn't appear to be as chaotic back in his state. Up into Kentucky would perhaps have been a wiser choice. Cindy had spent a summer in the the Kentucky mountains. He remembered her telling him how much she had love the people she'd met. His anonymity might still be in tact had they gone there. He'd spoken with more members of law enforcement in the last week then he'd done in his whole life. He wasn't paranoid, he just didn't want to be on any government lists. This area was turning out to be not as safe as they all thought it would be. Five fucking murders, only one house away. There were nearly two more on the other side.

Harvey and Barbra were rather amazing people. Listening to their stories last nigh provided a breather for all of them. A normal evening with friends, wine good food, and laughter... he'd never again take these simple pleasures for granted. There was still a police presence on the road. No real point in hanging up here. That murderer was long gone. With cops out there he might sleep soundly tonight. On that thought he took himself to bed. The fact that is was only a little before six pm didn't even cross his mind.

6:00 pm EDT, September 29, Elk Knob State Park, North Carolina

Axel and Gene rolled out of the park slowly, not wanting to gain the attention of the ranger they passed. Gene watched the ranger's jeep through the side mirror. "He's not interested in us. Good thing we changed the plates. Not sure how we're gonna find Hale when we get there. We might need to find a place to park it for the night. Y'all don't mind if I catch some sleep while y'all drive do ya? Getting here was a bitch."

In the rear view mirror Axil watched as the ranger's jeep faded in the distance. Comfortable they had escaped unnoticed he said, "Y'all get some sleep I'll be fine."

The drive was uneventful. Few cars on the road out there at night. Fewer now, with the Army looking for runaways such as himself. Axel woke Gene when they eased into Holly Springs at half past eight. It had taken longer than the GPS said it would. They'd stopped for gas and too Axel was driving real nice like, under the speed limit. Axel pulled down the first side street he came to. He spotted a convenience store, one side of its parking lot was dark. Gene pointed, Axel nosed the Caddy in next to the fenced area where they kept the dumpster. He cut the engine, then lowered the cushy

228

leather seat, to catch some sleep.

8:30 pm EDT, September 29,
Holly Springs, North Carolina

Hale sent Bubba to the barn to
siphon gas out of the trucks for the Le
Sabre. They needed to make some money
soon. He told Tucker and Big John to take
turns standing watch while he was gone.
Most everyone else was already sleeping.
It'd been a rough few days, they were
beat to shit. He heard Bubba pulling the
car around the front. Hale took one last
look and left.

They worked their way to the
entrance of the Boy Scout camp. Bubba cut
the lights and drove slow and quiet. Damn
if his luck wasn't holden' strong. The
place was deserted. Around back they
found a window low enough to climb
through.

Hale went in and handed Bubba stuff
out through the broken window. In the
kitchen he grabbed a pot and filled it
with a set of knives and other useful
items. He went through the rest of the
rooms grabbing blankets, flash lights and
candles. In a closet next to the
bathrooms he found a stack of toilet
paper and such. 'Nice of them to stack
the garbage bags here too.' he thought.
It took two trips to get the bagged TP
and paper towels to the window.

229

When car was full Hale simply walked out the door. He hadn't used it on the way in because he was worried about an alarm. He hadn't seen any sign of one while robbing the place, so what the hell. The alarm box was hidden in the girls bathroom. The camp had been robbed before. The robber had cut the wires. Now, the alarm was in the last place they thought a burglar would look. Evidently they were correct. Hale and Bubba made their way back to the hideout feeling right pleased with themselves for having pulled it off without a hitch. No one would ever know they was there.

After after leaving the fruits of their labor in the care of Big John, Hale was feeling like he was on a lucky streak, they headed for town. He and Bubba were looking for whatever they could scrounge from parked cars. Hale figured they'd find cash he need for gas. They hit the Hampton Inn parking lot first. They came away with a case of beer and $18.00 in change. They moved on to The La Quinta next where they did better, scoring $52.00, a camera and a bottle of scotch. After such a successful night Hale thought it only fair to treat Bubba to a pack of chew and Camels for himself. They parked on the street next to a convenience store, while they were paying, two cop cars pulled in to the lot. Kinda casual Hale says to the clerk, "What all ya think is happen there?"

The teenage clerk answered without looking up. "I was taking out the trash an saw a creepy looking guy sleeping in that car. The owner has real strict rules about that kinda thing so I call him. I guess he called the cops. Here's your change." Hale and Bubba slipped out the door while the cops were trying to cuff the guy who wasn't making it easy.

Bubba snuck a peek over his shoulder at the way the cops were bangin' the guy about. "Poor bastard. Don't know ya but I feel for ya brother."

Hale had his hand on the car door when he heard someone call his name in a loud whisper. His hand instantly moved to his piece in the small of his back. Hale peered into the shadows.

The guy whispered, "Y'alls Hale right? I recognize the car and y'alls Tattoo. That guy they got is y'alls boy Gene."

Bubba had been keepin' an eye on the cops while the guy was talking. "He ain't lyin' they got Gene. Shit!"

Hale eyed the guy for five seconds then said, "Git in."

On the way back to the house Axel told them how he and Gene had ended up at the store.

"What I do not comprehend is why y'all is sittin' here and my boy is on his way to jail."

"I couldn't sleep. Took a walk to find some gas money. Me and Gene is 'bout tapped out."

"Shit! Me and Bubba just cleaned out som' cars at two motels for the same damn reason. Y'all can stay with us tonight seein' as y'alls car must be on it's way to impound."

Bubba was kicked back enjoying the night air staring out the window while Hale grilled Axel. Suddenly he bolted forward. "Shit, Hale y'all seein' what I'm seein'?"

Looking down the road toward the Boy Scout camp they could see the place was lit up like a carnival. "Shit! How the fuck?" Hale put the pedal down.

Once back at the house, proper introductions were made. Axel told them what he knew of Genes journey from Tennessee, and his own flight from Charlotte. He filled Hale in on all that'd happened in Charlotte and since. Over the bottle of stolen scotch, they commiserate on how bad it was for three good o'l Alabama boys to be cut down but by a pair of old jews was just adding insult the injury. He didn't skip how he and Gene had met. "Bout Gene saying it

232

was providence that brought them together. Gene'd told Axel all about the Tennessee Righteous he was looking to catch up with. That's how Axel recognized Hale by the Hitler tattoo on his neck.

Hale told Axel the history of the Tennessee Righteous and of their persecution by the FBI, including all the bloody highlights of their struggles before finding the old mans house. Hale even showed Axel the old man's treasures. They rattled on through the night, losing momentum with each passing minute. By dawns early light, Axel would be welcomed as a member of the Tennessee Righteous. Sally Anne would find them on the couch drunk asleep two hours later.

6:30 am EDT, September 30, Holly Springs, North Carolina

Agents Mendez and Parker got the call at around 2:00 am. One of the Tennessee Righteous was in custody in North Carolina. It got better, he was picked up in the stolen Caddy from Hendersonville with the guns still in the trunk, but wait there was more, the Caddy had tags on it from a truck belonging to another member of the Tennessee Righteous. That is what prompted the sheriff to call the FBI.

The Agents had spent the night in Charlotte. They'd gone threw Henderson to interview the owner of the Caddy. That's when they discovered there were four high powered rifles in a hidden compartment in the trunk. With this new information Axelrod Jones jumped to the top of the FBI's most wanted list. The home office was not happy to learn that this psycho was out there with this caliber of weapons. The agents went on to Charlotte to find any information the Processing Center might have gathered when they interviewed him. The Army personnel had nothing of value to offer. They were however pleased to be able to cross Silas, Craig and Wyatt of their missing refugee list.

Agent Parker couldn't believe he'd lost the bet and cough up the five bucks. Agent Mendez had bet him the groups were connected. It'd be a coupla days before Mendez figured out, that at the time of the bet they weren't connected. Parker never did get his five back.

The Agents arrived in Holly Springs around 5:00 am. That's when the jurisdictional pissing contest, to end all jurisdictional contests, began. Tennessee wanted to talk to the suspect about his connection to the five murders. Harvey couldn't be positive there wasn't a fourth man who'd stayed behind in the car, so ya that too. North Carolina wanted him for the theft of the Caddy and possible connection to the murder of a young mother and the theft of her car. Holly Springs wanted him for trespassing and to find out why he was in their town and were there other members of the Tennessee Righteous there? The FBI wanted him in connection with the Tennessee Righteous bust. And last but not least the Army wanted him for questioning in regard to the whereabouts of the escaped refugee Axelrod Jones.

This was going to take a while to clear up.

6:30 am EDT, September 30,
Dancing Goats Farm
Moon Mountain, North Carolina

Gianna had slept in. She was at this moment savoring her first cup of coffee and the silence. The girls had been like a flock of magpies from the moment Alexandra stepped out of the SUV. They had gone down to the Hundred Acre Wood to open Alexandra's cottage to air. Then for a reason she could not fathom they thought her house was the place to party all night. She'd sent them on their way at three am. She didn't even want to think about the mess they'd made of the library. "Well they could shag their sorry asses back here and clean it up today.

Shag there was a peculiar word. Here in North Carolina it's a dance. In New England it means something between a drag and a walk. In England it means fucking. My stars Cleo, when was the last time I

235

had time to simply sit and ponder the idiosyncrasities of a word? Is idiosyncrasities even a word? Well of course it is I just used it in a sentence, and if it isn't it should be. Don't you agree Cleopatra?"

The green eyed feline watched her human intently. "Yeow"

"Well then, it's settled. It's a word. Would you like some more cream my dear? And Cleo, your hair wants brushing."

Nick stood at the door watching Gianna. He wondered how long the conversation was going to continue. He'd come in at the shagging... Stepping into the kitchen he said, "Gianna, some days I walk in here and I'm sure I've walked into the Mad Hatter's Tea party."

Looking up into yet another set of green eyes Gianna shook her head. "Nicholas, nobody likes a smart ass this early in the morning. And for your information, we're having coffee and cream not tea. Would you like some? Coffee not cream, it's commonly known you drink yours black." Not waiting for his response she continued. "Furthermore; I would never invite you to a Mad Hatter's Tea Party, it just wouldn't be a good fit, you'd stand out like a ten foot Alice. However if you are a very good boy I will invite you to my next hookah party. I may even introduce you to the Caterpillar."

Nick wondered how may hidden messages were in that statement and smiled. "Cleo what's in her coffee this morning?" Cleopatra patently ignored his question. Closing her eyes she presented him with her best Cheshire cat smile "Gia, if the cat vanishes, I'm out of here. Did you ladies have a good time last night?"

Gianna furrowed her brow "They had far too good a time. I sent them packing at three. I don't know what gave them the idea that here was the place to party last night... till dawn!"

Nick shrugged, exhaled and replied, "That would be me."

Gianna gave him an incredulous look. "Have you lost your bloody mind? OR was tha my punishment for not taking you yesterday?"

Nick set his mug down a bit too firmly. "No, to both. Carmichael told me the cousins were planning a loud party. If you remember we're in blackout mode. Rather than taking my life in my hands and tell them no, or letting them set a bad example for the rest of the Tribe, I told Carmichael to tell them to have it here. This place is virtually sound proof. How was I to know you didn't want to spend the night with your kids?"

She narrowed her eyes at him. "Ahmmm I don't know... maybe by asking me?"

Matching her annoyed tone, "Well the whole 'not setting a bad example' went bust, when the night watch found them giggling their way to the Gypsy camp. Thank you."

Waving off his attempt at blaming her for the disruption she said, "Hey, they're all in their 30s and 40's, I am no longer responsible for their late night giggle infractions. You should see the bloody mess they left in my library. Was there a point to this visit or did you just come to spoil my wha?"

The defensiveness in her tone caused him to soften his response. "Yes, to the first and *never*, to the second." He recognized her combative tone for what it was... her shield. He knew she was hiding her upset. "Theo said you were very stoic when he told you about Sean. I know what Sean means to you. Gia, how are you really holding up?"

She ignored his question. The compassion in his voice nearly brought her to tears. She whispered, "I can't find him Nick. I think he's either, very ill or badly injured, but I'm not getting that he's dead... but that could be, my wishful thinking."

Nick set his cup aside and took her hand. "I haven't found anything either way. We're looking everywhere. There's an APB out on his car. Adrian has Ferret checking every hospital and clinic between Dodge City and here. There are hundreds of them for her to check. It will take some time."

Her voice cracked as she asked, "And the morgues too?"

Nick sighed. "Yes, she's checking them too. I spoke to Carl about situation yesterday when you got back. He's on it." Nick tilted her chin up to look in her eyes. "Gianna, I will find him. I got you."

chapter 11

IN THE AIR TONIGHT

*"There is danger in the air this night
They know and they wait"*

**7:00 am EDT, September 30,
Planet Earth's Fucked,
Location Unknown**

Today's report the real world news

Yes, people of the earth, today's news is more grim than yesterday's. As it has been, every day since the Autumn Equinox when Mother sent out 4.5 billion emails. Are we seeing the pattern here yet? Many of you are still... not getting the math involved with sea rise. You still think an 11' rise means the you'll have to pull you beach towel 11' closer to the parking lot.

In other beach related news, the Totten Glacier in **East Antarctica** is wading in the surf of this week's 1/2' sea rise; last night she added a Maryland size iceberg of her own to the mix. Remember folks, when all of East Antarctica melts it will push those silly sea rise numbers up to 15'.

At the top of the world Greenland is serving up ocean cocktails with lots and lots of ancient iceberg cubes. This morning we're halfway to the foot of rise mentioned just yesterday. Research teams have begun to move off the ice shelves. Loud rumblings emanating from beneath the ice have precipitated this wise move. The thinner edges of several shelves have already launched themselves into the Atlantic.

Netherlands is still battling wildfires that have now burned 20,000 acres. The air quality has plummeted from the smoke. People are being warned to stay inside. Do they have airtight homes? What happens when the air in the home runs out?

Russia Still waiting for that update on the 'issues' with the nuclear power plant. In case any of you missed yesterday's blog, There is one of those nasty rumors trending that the top Russian government officials have left Moscow for the East Siberian Sea. Most likely they're going for the sun & surf since the whole arctic region is experiencing a heat wave.

Brazil & The Philippines are on the top of today's shit list because the number of murders of environmentalists and indigenous tribal members continues to rise. You may recall the reports out on Brazil and the Philippines back in July, of the capture and mutilations perpetrated on the Gamela people. Many had their hands cut off in retaliation for them protesting the destruction of their lands for the production of fucking palm oil and cattle. Cutting swaths through the vegetation on an island jewel, then murdering those that would save it, makes Mother very very angry.

The European Union gets a big fat black eye folks for being in cahoots with these two amoral countries. Money, Money, Money... agreeing to push back the referendum 10 mother fucking years! Really?

You know what... *Fuck You People!* It's like talking to a box of hair!

New tactic, going off script:

Rather than talk about what has happened I will tell you what's *going* to happen. I know you're easily bored so I'll make it fun for you. Hmmm a song... Here's one I can work with. Not about my preferred gender, but this is not about me. Hold on, need to do a wee bit of a rewrite. Okay, got it.

You only get one clue: There is one double-entendre.

The Goddess, Mother Nature,

Called to Apollo high above the sky
She told him make it greater
Tonight three billion die

Calamity's are rising
Her patients are getting low
So mote it be at half gone ten
Her sky'll start raining men

Solving this riddle could save your life.

8:00 am EDT, September 30,
Devil's Fork Gap
Smokey Mountains, Tennessee

Rory had woken when Cindy got in bed at 10 pm. She said they needed to talk. They talked for hours. She too was frightened. They questioned their choice to become part of the mountain compound. Yes, they felt and maybe it was, the right choice when they made it, but not now. They weighed the $40,000 they'd put into the place against what life was turning into there. Reports of conditions in Virginia were better than here but they couldn't be sure of what they'd find if they went home. They talked about their need of still wanting to be safe away from the crazies. They explored the idea of heading to Kentucky. The decision to leave happened around 6 am. They hoped the others would understand and give them some of their share of the supplies. If they did, Rory thought he'd ask Harvey if he would sell them one of their trailers with the sides to transport the supplies in. They broke the news to the others over breakfast. The others were sad but of course they would give them as much as they could carry. Harvey did sell them a trailer, he even helped Rory fashion a plywood cover for it.

Pauline filled a cooler with foods easy to eat on the road. When she'd finished with that she made up a basket with fresh biscuits, bread and chocolate cake she'd made the night before. While Pauline tended the food, Betty Lou and Tracy filled boxes and bins with supplies from the basement pantry. The guys packed the bins in the trailer along with camping gear and three 5 gallon gas cans. Bedding and an air mattress went in on top. The bed of the truck held their suitcases, six 5 gallon water jugs, and the food Pauline had packed.

8:00 am EDT, September 30,
Dancing Goats Farm,
Moon Mountain, North Carolina

Gianna was in the Shack to see if there had been any word on Sean's whereabouts but Ferret wasn't at her desk. While she waited, Gianna picked up a copy of today's **The Planet's Fucked blog** off the desk. She was reading it when Ferret returned.

Ferret froze when she saw Gianna standing by her desk. She looked at the

paper then at Gianna. From under her
eyelashes Gianna studied the girl. She
trusted her, but her reaction to Gianna's
presence is what had her attention in
this moment. Gianna's eyes shifted down
to the paper in her hand and then it hit
her. Looking at Ferret she said. "Ferret
I haven't had time to talk to you in this
insanity. Let's go to the office shall
we?"

Ferret opened her mouth to protest.
The look on Gianna's face made it clear
this wasn't a question. Ferret closed her
mouth.

Inside her office Gianna walked to
her chair, turn, put both palms on the
desk, leaned forward and said, "You
little shit." A smile hovered on her
lips. The double-entendre is men isn't
it. You know my dear, it's very bad form
to not properly introduce yourself. How
long have you worked for Her?" Gianna
could see the girl was retreating into
herself. "Let's try this another way. I
work for the Goddess." Tapping the blog
printout, she continued. "Evidently so do
you. Here, we share our knowledge.
Ferret, you're among sisters. You're safe
here. How does your information come to
you?"

Ferret relaxed a *wee bit*, a phrase
she was fond of using lately. "On and off
since I was a kid, I've had dreams. Since
the first night here they've been getting

245

longer and more vivid. I lost my shit
this morning. I've well it's like I wake
up understanding what I should write that
day. This morning I was typing, hoping
anyone would get the words and see what's
in my dreams. The realization that they
don't, hit me like a slap in the face and
I so I lost my shit. What I wrote is so
not how I write and to give away personal
information was just so crazy."

Gianna sat on the edge of the desk.
"Take a breath - it's a lot to know. I've
known this was coming most of my life.
You dreamed men fell out of the sky
everywhere, yes?"

"Yeh, the riddle is what I dreamed.
It's some fucked up shit."

Gianna smiled. "I think this
morning's blog is perfect. You wrote what
Mother wanted said. I believe here on the
farm, we're safe from what's coming but
it's never wise to be over confident with
your interpretation of the messages.
Everyone will retreat to the shelters
tonight to be safe. Does anyone know it's
you that writes the blog?"

The girl's eyes widened with fear as
she shook here head no."No."

"Did you write the email too?"

Ferret took a deep breath and
exhaled. "I don't know. It was the

Equinox so we had a party. I passed out on the floor. Last thing I remember was fighting with this guy Drew over a pillow. Best I can figure it must of been around 9:00 pm when I fell asleep. I woke up at 4:00 am asleep on the keyboard. No memory of how I got there or when. Everyone else was still crashed out. I opened the email and freaked the fuck out. I've worked for days trying to trace it. Nothing. I'm good, but not this good."

Gianna stood and placed reassuring hand on the frightened girl's shoulder. "You baby girl, may be the first case of *automatic* hacking! I think you should go find Adrian and tell him everything. Let him check your work. I'm not doubting your skills but here we double check everything. We watch each other's back. I need to talk to Nick. There's a great deal to be done today. You will call me if you find anything on Sean?"

"Yes. Can I ask a question?" Gianna nodded. "Who is Sean that so much effort is going in to find him."

"Sean and I have so many lifetimes together I've lost count. Most of them we have been siblings. That's why I call him my brother from another mother. Let's get back to work. We all have a lot to do before half past ten. If you want or need to talk, go down to Gypsy camp and find my daughters and niece Alexandra. They work for Mother too. If nothing else you can show each other your tatts."

Ferret walked back to the Shack, dreading having to telling Adrian what she'd been up to. He was going to kill her for putting the farm at risk. She hadn't. She was good and careful, but he'd yell anyway."

Gianna called Nick "Where are you? I have a potential 911 situation."

"I'm outside the Q gate meet me in the kitchen."

Nick was waiting when she arrived. She tossed the paper on the table in front of him. "Houston, we have a fucking problem."

Nick glanced at the paper. "Yea I saw it this morning. What about it?" He was relieved her 911 wasn't bad news about Sean.

Gianna pulled out a chair and sat. "You might want to sit too. Ferret is the blogger. She may have also sent the Mother email. She doesn't remember doing it. And before you ask, yes I believe her. If she was using a pencil and paper we'd call it automatic writing. Her information comes from her dreams."

For a second Nick wasn't sure this news wasn't worse than bad new about

Sean. They discussed the possible meanings of the riddle, Ferret, the odds of them being hit, and what could cause men to rain from the sky. They agreed on sheltering underground tonight. An EMP was the most likely scenario, so they prepared for one. Gianna went to get the Tribe ready. Nick went to inform his men. Then he'd see Theo about the security of the shields in the big house.

9:00 am EST, September 30,
The World does Appear to be Fucked
I'm Still Not Telling You Where I Live

Moscow, Russia There is mass panic, confusion and death. The nuclear power plant that had 'issues' has become the worlds worst nuclear accident. The surrounding countries are overwhelmed by their efforts to evacuate their people, as the winds carry radiation saturated clouds their way.

China is not getting the relief assistance they have requested and desperately need. The UN and WHO have told them there is no one to send. World wide, countries are struggling with their own cataclysmic events.

Brasilia, Brazil has discovered illegal refugees from Africa have brought them a gift... Ebola. There are cases reported from Sao Paulo, where they entered the country, to the capital, Brasilia. They don't yet know how many of the infected have escaped capture and traveled to outlying areas.

Pakistan Has yet to discover the source of the cholera that continues to spread throughout the country. 60% of their military have come down with it.

The Middle East The entire region is being pummeled with round-the-clock earthquakes, some as large 7.9. There is widespread destruction in cities and towns. People are camping outside because most buildings are no longer safe.

Coastal Countries Are being flooded. The earth's waters are rising by the hour. Having reached a 1 1/4' foot rise in less than 48 hours it shows no sign of stopping. In some areas it is accelerating faster. Evacuations on this scale are next to impossible.

South Eastern United States The small abatement of the water in all the coastal states affected by hurricanes Rafael and Sara, has been reversed and continues to rise.

Southern Florida where many hurricane evacuees fled to, is taking on water faster than almost anywhere else in the world. Miami Beach roads are all flooded. The water is two feet deep. Evacuations there are being hampered by a tropical storm hanging off the coast of Cuba.

The Mid Atlantic The national
Weather Service expects slow moving
category 1 Hurricane Tony to brush the
coast of Virginia and Delaware by this
evening.

Wyoming & Montana The fissures are
expanding and several more have opened.
Pray, Montana has been evacuated due to
the toxic steam trapped in the valley
there. The death toll is 45.

Arizona & New Mexico There is
prevalent flooding from a storm that came
in off Baja California. Flash floods have
already killed 92 between both states.

The middle of the country is
experiencing a heat wave with
temperatures reaching 110' in some areas.
A 100 heat related deaths have been
reported over the last 24 hours.

West Coast of the United States It's
flooding. Areas hit by the tsunamis are
flooding faster. Many cities and towns
are gone.

**9:15 am EDT, September 30,
Holly Springs, NC**

All the agencies who wanted a piece
of Gene have worked out a list of the
questions they needed answered. They'll
take turns interviewing him. Once they
have all the answers they are able get

251

out of him, the Army will take him to the brig at Camp Lejeune. The FBI has given the Holly Springs police a list of the cars and plates registered to the Tennessee Righteous members they are hunting. They all agreed the FBI will have first crack at the suspect. It's going to be a very long day for Gene.

9:15 am EDT, September 30,
Mountain Compound, TN

They spent the morning going over maps and adding last minute items to Rory and Cindy's truck. Rory hoped the load wasn't too heavy for the old straight 6 in his restored 61 Ford. They plan to have lunch before they get on the road. Rory and Cindy will drive straight up to Virginia and then decide where they will go from there. It's about an hour to the state line from the compound.

9:15 am EDT, September 30,
Cumberland Gap, KY

Fern also had a dream last night. She was in a deep root cellar talking on a phone. A radio was playing. The wires for them were draped along the walls. When she walked up the many stairs and opened the door, the night was still and dark as far as she could see. She sent Duncan to pass the word to put the things with wires underground. Then get their lamps and candles ready - God was going to put the lights out tonight.

9:15 am EDT, September 30,
Washington, DC

The government thinks things are
getting under control. Martial Law is
working. The water in the southern states
seems to be receding a few feet. The
riffraff was almost evicted from the
country. The borders were locked. They
are feeling pretty good about themselves
today.

9:15 am EDT, September 30,
Bozeman, Montana

The members will be arriving
tonight. The staff is busy with
preparations. The security team is
checking the runway for debris. Across
the globe the twelve men spent the day in
anticipation of the nights' gathering.
They are scheduled to arrive at the ranch
between 6:30 pm and 1:00 am MDT.

9:15 am EDT, September 30,
Culpeper, Virginia

The congressman has a meeting
planned for the afternoon with David and
Charles. Ammar will be joining them a
little later. They want to finalize a few
things before the big meeting tonight.
They'll be flying out on Ammar's jet at
10:00 pm EST.

Hale nursed his hangover with a handful of aspirin and a cup of instant coffee. Sitting on the ruins of the back porch he studied Axel standing over by the well washing off a week's worth of grime with the aid of an old bucket from the barn. Hale felt Axel would prove to be a worthy member of their group. He recognized the ruthlessness in him. Hale could use that.

Turning his mind to the more pressing issues at hand he thought they best stay clear of town for a few days. He hadn't expected the cops to find out about the Boy Scout camp break-in as soon as they did. He felt real bad that Gene had made it all the way here only to be caught when he was about to rejoin the group. Guess it was a case of crap luck. He hoped the cops had impounded the car thinking it was Gene's. Could be they were only holding him for trespassing. They might not have run his prints on such a small bust. He'd send Big John into town to sniff around in case they turned Gene loose.

If they had run his prints then the Feds would be showing up for Gene pretty quick. Hale knew Gene would give them nothing but it was best the members stayed out of sight. They still needed money and food. Tomorrow he'd take Axel and make a run north to Mount Airy. He needed to remember to take the phone with them so it could charge off the car. He didn't like getting so close to the border. They might be checking for refugees in the towns along the North Carolina/Virginia border.

Here at the farm there were other problems to tend to. Sally Anne asked if they could steal a chicken or two. Tuckers' snares brought in a pair of rabbits and a possum but fresh eggs would really help. He'd send Tucker to scout beyond the back woods for a place with a chicken coop. The boy was like a weasel the way he could slip in and out of places. Better send Ethan with him. He might need someone to hold his catch if he found more than one place to raid. Not much else Ethan was good for at the moment. He was healing good but he was useless and restless. Better have Tucker set more traps before he went. Hale had twenty-two mouths to feed. Sally Anne's kid's food would be gone soon. He didn't want James Blaylock seeking revenge on him for having let Sally Anne and his kids starve. They were going to need more than two chickens.

**1:55 pm EDT, September 30,
Dancing Goats Farm
Moon Mountain, North Carolina**

After his meeting with Gianna, Nick had the security cameras pulled. All the electronics in the Q were put in the bed of the Dark Lady pickup. The men assembled a cage of copper screened panels and drove her inside. The seams were sealed with metallic tape for good measure. Then they built Faraday cages for the SUVs and other vehicles that could be affected by an EMP. Most the vehicles were computer, free but Reno had them pull the batteries and put them in the cages. They had no idea what was coming, why chance it?

There were components for ten more of these Faraday cages around the farm for items like the forklift. The vanguard and regulars made the rounds assembling as they went. Some of the buildings like the Shack had shielding built into them. The seams were checked for breaks. Almost every building had a box or cage for important items that needed to be protected from an EMP. The Tribe spent the day moving electronics inside them.

The winter windows of Plexiglas were put in their frames on the greenhouses. The quilted freeze blankets were pulled over the frames. Amber was sure no one wanted a serving of organically grown veggies seasoned with a dash of radiation.

In the kitchen Simon and his crew moved food that was not in the walk-in cooler or the steel paneled pantries. The pantries had been constructed to keep their contents safe from tiny invaders.

Neither Simon nor Gianna liked sharing their supplies with the occasional field mouse no matter how cute they were.

Once in a while one would seek refuge inside to escape the pride of felines that roamed the farm. Simon wasn't particularly fond of them either but he did admit they generally did their job well.

The Water Wizard covered the lids of the underground cisterns with lead aprons. He lamented there was nothing he could do for the the streams and ponds. Tomorrow he'd bring Alexandra a water trough to put out in the Hundred Acre Wood for the herd of deer that lived there. Gianna's small koi pond got an apron too.

Alexandra and Lizzy covered the hay in the barns with more of Amber's freeze blankets. They added feed and water to the pens in the animal bunker to have it ready when they herded the beasties in for evening feeding. Then they locked the feed room. It was built like the pantry for the same reason.

Miles of gaffers tape sealed every window, door and crack on the farm. By the time the evening meal was done the farm was, as Axel would have said, sealed up tighter than a gnat's ass.

10:00 pm EDT, September 30,

Devil's Fork Gap
Smokey Mountains, Tennessee

The remaining members of the mountain compound had missed the blog post when it was first posted. Everyone had been busy getting Rory and Cindy on their way. Dan found it around on 1:00 pm.

To everyone's amazement it was Betty Lou who found the double-entendre. "It's men y'all. Men can be men and men and women together are called mankind."

Frank felt it would be an attack and our planes would be shot down. Dan said no, an EMP would have a wider effect. The blog was talking to the whole world. All three women agreed Frank was thinking too small. They sided with Dan.

The men and Tracy had spent the rest of the day moving all the things that would be affected by an EMP into the food store room. There was some space left by the supplies given to Rory and Cindy, they shuffled stuff around to make more. Betty Lou gave Pauline a hand in the kitchen canning as much as they could from the huge chest freezer in the garage. It was easier with power than it would be without, if there was an EMP. Besides, if they waited till after they might not get it all put up before it went bad. At 8 pm they stood back admiring their efforts. It'd be tight but

they'd be able to squeeze the six of them
in with the the food and equipment. In
the garage the freezer now stood half
empty. They showered and ate. Afterwards
Dan checked the garage one more time. He
didn't know how bad it would be. They
might lose the vehicles with their fancy
computers. He disconnected the batteries
and put them on one of the wood stacks.
He checked the duct tape around the doors
and windows again. He'd checked the
filter on the intake fan in the store
room next. It was his last job before
they closed the door at 10:00 pm. They
spent the night either dozing or reading.
No one wanted to talk about what they
might find when they opened the door in
the morning.

**The pathetic state of the worlds
population...**

Mother's mysterious email has been
forgotten by 99.9% of the world's
apathetic population. All 99% of them
will pay for their indifference with
their lives within the next 30 days.

Only 3.5 million, the Earth
Stewards, understand the message. 68
million preppers understand it's a
warning but not the full implications of
the context. They have gone to ground but
have no idea what is coming or from whom.
These two groups are the only ones giving
any credence to the Typist's latest blog.

The brains of the 99% have become more Psy-borg Hive than human. Indoctrinated by technology, their primal instincts have gone mute, silenced by their willing absorption into the digital dimension. Waking and sleeping they are more preoccupied with the day to day events unfolding in their virtual worlds, rendering them instinctual cripples in this physical world. Their flight or fight instincts reside solely in their cyber-selves. Now, when confronted with tribulations in the physical dimension, such as those created by the current rash of catastrophic Natural Disasters, they are no longer capable of saving themselves. They are billions of Sheeple waiting to be herded to safety.

... which may or may not happen. For all but a handful, it won't.

This day was filled with a frenzy of activity for those known as the Preppers and True Earth Stewards; securing their caches within Mother's breast, herding their beasts into caves and cellars, and as the ancient Israelites in Egypt, praying death passes by their doors this night.

Chapter 12

THIS IS IT

*"One of Mother's miracles,
Also the chapter in which
we meet Audrey"*

**10:25 pm EDT, September 30,
Washington, DC**

The White House is notified that a coronal mass ejection will hit the earth's atmosphere in six minutes. Scientists everywhere cannot explain how they've missed it nor do they have the time to figure it out. This comes right on the heels of a bulletin from the National Weather Service that Hurricane Tony, has turned and is headed for DC. The decision is made to shelter the president and vice president along with several of the cabinet members in the bunker beneath the White House. The staff, right down to the last maintenance worker, is told to go home. They don't know it yet but what the president has given them is... a chance to survive.

Sirens blare across cities and towns around the world. Most fall on deaf ears

261

whose owners think it's a test. In fact
it could be viewed as a test, a test to
verify the depth of their stupidity.
Others leave the shelters to look at the
pretty lights in the sky, clapping at the
brilliant flashes of bright white and
blue they see. Oblivious to the reality
that the flashes happen when stray
particles of radiation pass through their
eyes.

10:31 pm EDT,

In the US alone, 7,308 aircraft fall
from the sky. The over 500,000 people in
those aircraft die on impact. It is
indeed raining men.

A military jet lands on the oval
office, another on the pentagon. Wall
Street is not hit by a plane. It burns in
an inferno caused by one.

A private jet skids into the mouth
of the Luxor's underground garage. People
who see the explosion say it looks like
an ancient funeral pyre.

Ammar's jet had taken off before
10:00 pm. The pilot wanted to get ahead
of the storm. In their final moments,
four of the men who believed they would
rule the earth, understood how profoundly
they had underestimated Mother Nature.
Their jet's left wing embeds itself in
the 99th floor of the Willis Tower and
the cabin spins downward setting the

shore of Lake Michigan ablaze. Perhaps
the last image burned into the retinas of
the four conspirators is that of Lake
Michigan, whose water they have so
wantonly polluted. The congressman
remembers the woman from the gas station
as he is roasted alive in a slick of jet
fuel.

Millions more die on the ground than
passengers in the planes. Planes crash in
cities, their fuel igniting whole city
blocks. Burst gas mains feed the
conflagrations. Medical flights crash on
the rooftops of hospitals scorching the
buildings from the inside out. Suburbs
become tinder boxes.

Two billion are electrocuted
instantly while playing in cyber space.

The undulating of the planet's
magnetic field causes the Pacific Plate
to grind against the North American
Plate. The Cascadia Fold, *folds*, starting
a chain reaction the end of which will
not be seen for years.

The power grids world wide are gone.
Not mendable by any stretch of the
imagination.

Nuclear power plants who got the
message in time are able to SCRAM. A few
are not so lucky.

The Hoover Dam like thousands of

others, cracks and then crumbles. The mighty Colorado River flows free and unfettered once again. The onslaught of tons of water bursting down takes out another few thousand instantly. More will die from flash floods over the next hours. On Second Mesa The Hopi dance in prayer.

The EMP could have been the strongest ever recorded, If there had been anything left to record it on.

In the Atlantic off the coast of DC, Hurricane Tony is racing toward the mouth of the Potomac River, thrusting before him a monstrous tidal surge. Maryland's 'tail' isn't even a blip on his radar. Though there is no way to monitor his progress, he's now a category 4 hurricane and traveling at 27 mph. Sea rise passed the two foot mark an hour ago and continues its rapid ascent, adding volume to the surge.

In addition to the two that hit the White House and the Pentagon, five more planes crash inside DC. The driving rain from Tony is helping to extinguish the non-fuel-based fires. The 45 firestorms being fed by natural gas lines and gas station tanks are still raging.

Old Abe has waves splashing at his feet and there is a shark doing laps in his reflecting pool. The tidal basin has engulfed the MLK memorial and is flooding the Bureau of Engraving and Printing. The Constitution Gardens are now the Constitution *Water* Gardens.

The New York Subways are flooding as Wall Street burns.

Wilmington, North Carolina is taking on sea water. The refugees in Camp Lejeune are standing in two feet of water.

**10:35 pm EDT, September 30,
Holly Springs, North Carolina**

Agents Parker and Mendez had left the station only fifteen minutes earlier. They are standing in the lobby of the Motel when the lights go out. While the staff are trying to find out why the emergency generator isn't coming on, a commercial flight drops down on top of the new police station, a fireball lights up the night sky. The explosion shakes the motel, shattering several lobby windows. The agents race through the broken door. Mendez is trying to unlock the car door as he runs, the fob wouldn't work. He uses the key, lets himself in and hits the power lock for Parker. It doesn't work either. A very bad feeling washes over him. He puts the key in and turns it, as he fears, not even a click. Parker is banging on the window asking him to hit the locks. Mendez gets out. Over the roof to Parker he says, "It was an EMP."

Shaking his head Parker points toward the smoke billowing skyward. "No it's not! The explosion knocked the town's power out."

Mendez slides his partner the fob. "This doesn't work. The locks don't work, turn the key not even a click. That's why the back-up generator didn't kick in. It's wired into the electrical system."

"Shit no, don't tell me that. Lets go." Parker takes off running toward the fire.

Mendez catches up with him three blocks down. "Why are you stopping? Out of shape old man?" The look on Parker's face makes him turn toward the fire. Then he understands the look of horror on his partners face, the place they were standing minutes ago is gone. Almost eight square blocks are on fire. No one is doing anything to put it out because the plane has also set the firehouse across the street ablaze.

10:35 pm EDT, September 30, Tennessee Righteous Hideout, Holly Springs, North Carolina

The EMP had no immediate effect on the people sitting on the front porch. The explosion and the fireball, however, got them all on their feet or running out the door. They all speculated on the

cause for fifteen minutes before Hale
decided he, Bubba, and Axel should go see
what the hell has happened. Hale sends
Bubba to the barn for the Le Sabre, which
was his only choice though he didn't know
it. The computers in the newer vehicles
are fried.

Hale park on a side street at the
edge of town. They work their way towards
the crowd gathered near the fire. Hale
and Bubba took it hard when they see how
Gene had died. The townspeople are in
shock. Many can be heard wailing over the
loss of loved ones. Some are crying for
the sheer impact it will have on their
town. Hale says they should head back to
the hideout but not before they siphon a
few gallons of gas while the people are
consumed by their grief.

10:55 pm EDT, September 30,
Dancing Goat Farm
Moon Mountain, North Carolina

Six men had volunteered to stand
guard outside while everyone else went
underground. Carmichael was the only one
of the vanguard Gianna would allow to be
among the six. He had begged and pleaded
like a little kid until she'd relented.
Nick was beyond pissed when he heard he
couldn't believe she had given in. They
argued over her decision. Gianna stood
her ground. "Nicholas, we're in here
blind to whatever is going to be
happening outside. There are only six men

to protect us and the entire farm." From the look on his face she knew this was an argument she might loose. "I know the first thing you're pissed about is you think you should be one of the men out there. I can't let you go. Nick, how would I keep this place safe without you?" The muscle in his jaw twitched. She knew he knew she was right. "If there is a breach, you know dam well Carmichael take will out at least half of them, no matter how many there are. Yes, I know I'm risking our best sniper." She put both hand on his chest and stepped in for the close. "Nick, he doesn't want to be treated as broken. This is what he does best let him shine;... for his sake as well as ours."

Nick threw his hands up in surrender. "I can't frigging argue with *that* speech. Let him go." He walked away wondering, not for the first time, how the fuck she won 9 out of 10 of their '*differences of opinion*'.

Now someone was banging out a message in Morse Code on the other side of the bunkers' steel door. Barry AKA The Mad Scientist pushed people aside to get to the door to translate. As if he was the only one there who knew Mores Code "It's Carmichael. It was an EMP. Interesting, wonder what the source was? He says it's all clear now. And he knows this how? He's probably right depending on how long ago it happened. Let me check something." Barry taps a message to Carmichael. One comes right back. Barry listens and announces, "All clear. He's got a safe reading on the Geiger counter. Everyone should get to their houses and stay inside just to be safe. It hit just after ten thirty like the blog said it would... that's fucking spooky..."

Not unlike Persephone's yearly ascent, the people of Dancing Goats Farm climb the stairs into the welcomed chill of the crisp night air to a world profoundly changed.

Outside, Amber looks around her. "Hey Tyler, doesn't it seem quieter somehow?" Not waiting for a answer which may be too long in coming, she takes her daughter's hand. "Come on, Angelena, let's get you in bed." They, like the others, make their way back to their homes.

Gianna asks "Lizzy, do you and Alexandra need help bringing the animals up?"

"Yes ma'am. Three or four will do. I'm not letting them out just up into the barns. They're kinda cramped for space right now."

Nick signals to four of his regulars to follow Lizzy. "The animals need to be brought up from the cellars underneath the floors of the barns. Follow Lizzy."

He sends the vanguard to the Q to secure the front walls. Twenty-five men are sent to their posts around the perimeter. The five who stood guard with Carmichael follow Nick to the Q kitchen to be debriefed. By noon tomorrow Dancing Goats will be back up and running as if nothing had changed. Unfortunately for the people of the world, outside the cocooning walls of Dancing Goats Farm, *everything* had changed.

11:30 pm EDT, September 30, Damascus, Virginia

Rory and Cindy made it as far as Damascus before the lack of sleep began to affect his driving. They'd been running on adrenaline all day. At 2:00 pm Cindy said, "If the world is going to hell let's treat ourselves and stay some place lovely." They found the Laurel Mountain Inn a charming B&B. The owners said the Inn was empty so they had their pick of the rooms. Once inside they dropped their bags, showered, climbed into a darling half poster bed and sunk into a deep sleep. They missed the messages from Dan about the 'maybe' EMP. They slept like babies as the world went to hell.

12:00 am EDT, October 1,

If the internet still existed the morning blog would have read like this:

The Report on;
Just How Fucked Planet Earth is *now*

Late last night the Sun God Apollo slammed the earth with the mother of all coronal mass ejections. My guess is that 3 billion people died between 9:00 pm EDT and midnight. Figuring that around 1 billion have died since Mom got pissed on the 22nd, that should leave maybe 4.4 billion left. I might be a few hundred thousand off but 5 million died in Beijing alone. It's not like I can check with Google this morning.

For some of you this next will be good news for others maybe not. Guess it would depend on your political affiliations. **The president, vice prez, and 4 of the cabinet members** who hunkered down in the bunker under the White House are most likely dead. A plane fell on the Oval Office and set the rubble afire. At present, Hurricane Tony and the Atlantic Ocean have the **White House** rubble sitting under three feet of water. Don't know how water tight that bunker is but it can't be good if the air intake is under water too.

The west coast is not worth talking about at present, because the coastline is changing shape every few hours. I'll have to get back to you on that when things settle down... pun intended.

Word from way down south is South America is no longer connected to the US. The Panama Canal has become irrelevant. Not sure there still is a Panama. Think we may have lost a country or three there.

Speaking of down, **Montana** has another big ass sinkhole. One opened up south of Bozeman and swallowed some rich guys' hacienda and half of their runway. The surviving members of the security company reported a jet was landing as it happened. The pilot tried to stop but slid off the edge. Guess it's rather deep because it exploded when it hit the bottom. I don't actually know how far a jet has to bounce to explode. Really starting to miss Google.

England has shrunk and will continue to do so. Watch out Ireland, now they'll want the rest of your country.

Russia will henceforth be known as the Glow-In-The-Dark Lands. Because the Top was at the bottom in an island bunker, not all of the Nuc plants got the SCRAM shut down message... I hear the East Siberian Sea is one of the places the water is rising fastest. Kinda like our **Florida** which is swiftly becoming a State comprised of swamp islands.

India is losing land and people at the rate of a foot an hour. I don't know how many actual feet they're losing in an hour, but they have quite a few of them. They are the only country of two to have over a billion people, second only to China. Really? Haven't you people heard about birth control? Well those were the numbers last week. Now... again at a loss without my Google.

I can't contact the defunct **FCC** for the actual number, but generally speaking the cities with airports have the greatest damage from planes falling out of the sky.

In North Carolina one fell on the state house. Let's hope the assholes who created the 'bathroom bill' were in there having another one of their secret emergency late night sessions. The Queen City, Charlotte, has lost her crown. Three fell there. One landed on the largest refugee processing location. The other two centers were lost in the fires caused by the other two planes.

If the satellites still worked NASA (if it was still there) could tell you the ice is on the move. The effect the CME had on the earth's magnetic fields was like... earth had been dropped in a Yahtzee cup and tossed about with the dice. Sixteen new chunks of ice the size of states or small countries are now adrift. An folks, they be driftin' to warmer waters. My source tells me we're at 3 ½' sea rise. Which is kinda of a big jump since yesterday... don't you think?

Oh, sorry, I forgot you don't think. That would be how we got here.

When the sun rises on the east coast the real madness will begin. The stores that aren't already, will empty of food and water. Inland towns will be overrun by those who stayed too long at the beach. Some state governments may still be functioning. It will be weeks before we know if there is a functioning sort of federal government. Civil unrest will rule in most places.

Gather your family and neighbors. Work together to help each other survive. Know this... *Mother is not finished.*

5:00 am EDT, October 1, Tennessee Righteous Hideout Holly Springs, North Carolina

Hale had been up since four. He figured now would be a good time, before the town reorganized, to take what they needed. He didn't know how many cops were in the police station when it burned. Talk in the crowd was a lot of them because they had captured a famous criminal. The FBI had sent agents to fetch him. He guessed they was talkin' about Gene. Maybe the Feds had already left with Gene. He might yet be alive. Hale needed more information. He woke Big John and told him he was gonna take a run to town. He woke Axel and Tucker to take with him. Out in the barn he climbed in his truck but it wouldn't crank. No lights or radio either. He tried the other vehicles with the same results. "Shit we was attacked by an EMP bomb. That's what caused the plane to drop outta' the sky like that. Let's go. We gotta find out how bad it is." On the way Hale told them about his idea of striking while what cops that were left kept busy with the plane crash and shit. When they arrived in town the three of them wandered though the crowds pickin' up what information they could. They'd start listenin' for places that'd be empty cause the owner died in the crash.

They learned there were only three cops left and the two FBI agents, who were now stuck here. Even the Mayor had been in the station it when burned. The FBI guys were running things for now. Mr. Taylor had brought his HAM radio set in and had set it up in the Town Hall. They found out it wasn't a bomb but a giant solar flare. The whole world was hit.

The FBI wouldn't let the owners open the food stores. The Feds were making sure everybody got a chance to buy a share of the food. A table was set up where people could sign up. Even the two motels had to give an inventory of what they had to sell. They had people with wells bringing in water for the town folks who didn't have one.

There were a pair of old farm trucks

with water tanks in their beds. They watched as people used a small gas generators to pump the water on the edges of the fire to keep it from spreading.

One of the cops was in charge of a gas and propane collecting team. They were siphoning it out of city vehicles to be used at the discretion of the agents. The agents had gone into the hardware store and the food store to buy all the lamp oil and candle making supplies. A group of ladies were melting wax on a propane burner and making candles. The city paid for the supplies and would be passing them out equally as with the food.

They left town with a lot of information but no gas or food. They wouldn't be gettin' on any list neather so they better get what they could while folks were busy in town. They hit the farm where Tucker had got the chickens first. They found five gallons of gas in a shed before an old coot came after them with a shotgun. They laughed as they sped away. It wasn't like he could call the cops. Down the road they raided a farmhouse belonging to one of the dead cops. Got away with two shopping bags of food and a jar of homemade hooch. They tried one more and grabbed some deer from the freezer in the garage before the woman came out with a rifle. Unlike the old man, she started shooting. The deer haunch Axel was carrying saved him from

taking one in the ass. They thought it
best to head back after that.

By 10:00 am, they were all sittin'
around talkin' about what all was goin'
on. They had more food but it wouldn't
last long. Then Ethan brought up the
place he and Cal had found. He was sure
something big was going on in there. And
one of the guys that shot at him and Cal
was an african. That settled it for Axel
and Hale, who had been enjoying the last
of the scotch. They worked out a perfect
plan to get inside and take them.

12:00 pm EDT, October 1,
Dancing Goats Farm
Moon Mountain, North Carolina

The farm had survived just fine.
Everyone was as busy as the day before
putting things to rights. The Mad
Scientist insisted they needed to wash
things down with bleach, then went back
to his lab. Violet rolled her eyes at his
back and shook her head. "*Really*! I'm not
washing down the buildings in the Q or
anywhere else!" She, Sadie and Lizzy were
on duty in the Q today. As Lizzy started
the go-cart Samira ran up and begged to
come with them today. Violet and Lizzy
thought no but Sadie overrode them and
pulled the girl in the cart. Samira was
one of what Gianna had called the 'Airy-
Fairies'. Healers, psychics, creators of
peace and love. They worked with the Fae
and the earth spirits on the farm. Gianna

277

also called some of them born-again hippies. Being an old hippie herself, she would know.

Nick was just pulling out of the Q gate when the women stepped out on the farmhouse veranda. Lizzy asked "Where the hell are they going? Does mom know about this?" She called Theo to check. She hung up and said, "The *Brain* says she does know and is ripping mad about it. Give her a wide berth if we want to keep our hair. Theo said she about screamed his off when he told her."

Before leaving, Nick had assigned most of the vanguard to reinstalling the cameras around the 1000 acre property. They took more time to put back up than they did coming down. Every camera had to be tested. Some wires had fried and had to be replaced. Tiny was in the command room in the cellar of the farmhouse making sure every one of the 200 cameras worked properly. Carmichael was in the hay loft. Down below in the barn, Reno, Mikey and Antonio were breaking down the cages, testing the equipment and vehicles. One of the dirt bikes was running a little rough. "Reno one out of four's not bad." Mikey joked. He knew Reno was obsessed with having every machine in perfect running order.

Nick and Charlie were going to Holly Springs. Before dawn Nick had talked to FBI agent Mendez on the HAM radio. They agreed their conversation should not be continued on the open air. Nick knew Mendez. He had done a tour with Nick maybe fifteen years ago. Under a blanket in the back of the jeep were a few of Nicks toys. The town's guns and ammo had been stored in the police station. Nick couldn't leave a brother Marine out there naked.

12:00 pm EDT,

In the farmhouse Lizzy and Violet were making lunch for themselves and the five guards in the Q. Sadie was sitting on the counter regaling them with a Boston story. Samira was wandering around the garden. Presently she was talking to a rose bush.

In the scrub at the edge of the woods across the road from the Q's gate, Hale, Bubba, Axel, Big John, Willy, Tucker and Ethan lay-in-wait.

Hale had sent Tucker to drop five of the guys at the woods, near the gate Cal had broken through. They were to work their way down the trail, cause a disturbance, so the guys inside the gate would run to see what the commotion was. Then Ethan and Tucker would get the women to open the gate by saying he'd been shot and needed help. They'd send a sixth man to tell the first five when Hale and the rest of them had arrived. The Le Sabre was big but it wasn't big enough for what

Hale called *'the assault team'*. He was positive with fourteen men they would outnumber the guys behind the gate. While they waited for Tucker to return, Hale and Axel had dipped into the stolen hooch after they'd finished the last of the scotch. Somehow, they'd ended up trying on the SS uniforms. It was drunkenly decided the sight of six SS officers would really scare the shit out of whoever was behind the gate. That settled, off they went to execute their fateful, poorly planned assault on the Q farm.

When the first part of the assault team got to what should have been a cattle gate they found instead a 6' high gate of sheet metal. There was no way to climb the slick surface so they went around the outside of the chain link fencing. They hid until the sixth guy showed up then they tried to climb over the fence with the razor wire on top. Pete and Freddy were on the inside of the wall opposite the breech in progress. Freddy was on the ladder tucked up in a tree hanging the camera. He called Reno on the radio, "There are six assholes trying to get over the fence into the zone. We're across from the Hall."

Carmichael having heard the call, came flying down the stairs as the other three jump on the bikes - he's right on their 6. Reno swung the gate open just enough to get the bikes through yelling to Samira to close it after them.

In the kitchen Lizzy asks "What's going on out there?

Sadie answered "Reno and the boys are working on the bikes. They're probably taking them out for a test drive."

Violet looked over at her sister. "Really? Lunch is almost ready. By the way where is your Samira girl?"

Sadie snorted at her sister. "How is she *my* Samira girl? I just saw her a few minutes ago. She was petting a rose bush." Sadie walked over to the window to check. "Oh Shit! Fuck! What is she doing? VY!" Sadie flew out the door with Violet and Lizzy on her heels.

Samira had fallen for Hale's ruse. Her chocolate brown toes are quaking in their sandals... Tucker has a gun pointed at her chest. Ethan sees the three women running towards them and raises his gun in their direction. The sisters halt ten feet away; Lizzy is behind them... Sadie slides one step to her left. Hateful ugly things are spewing from Tucker's sick twisted face, aimed at Samira and her race. Ethan says "See I told you they fraternize with africans."

Violet slants her eyes at her sister. Quietly she says "You take left I'll take right." Samira is sobbing in humiliation and fear. Violet looks Ethan in the eye. "Hey twat-waffle, you a pussy like your buddy? You like frightening little girls too? Grown women too scary for you?"

Tucker turned at the insult. The second the gun was off the girl Sadie said, *Yes please...*

So intent were the men in their abuse of Samira, the fools never saw Lizzy slip a Glock 19 into each sisters waiting hand. Sadie liked center mass. Violet preferred the zombie shot right between the eyes. As the men hit the ground Sadie said, "It's amazing how quiet these are don't you think sis?"

Lizzy took the radio off her hip. "Mom."

"Yes Liz."

"Mom, Violet and Sadie just killed two snot-zis. They were inside the Q."

"Did they get any on them?"

Looking at Samira who is now on her knees shaking. "Ah, no but someone in here is a little freaked."

"I'll be right there." Gianna had been on her way to check on the Q because asshole Nick had run off on a *social visit*. Thirty seconds later Gianna stepped onto the veranda and took in the scene. There are indeed two dead snot-zis lying in the yard. Tiny couldn't hear the shots in the control room, but he'd glanced up at the split screen monitor for the front yard and outside the gate and ran.

Gianna looked over her shoulder at Tiny as he whispered "There are 6 outside the gate in SS uniforms. They're armed. Six more are trying to breach the zone. Reno and the other three went out after them. I'm all you have ma'am."

Quietly she said "Get Audrey."

As Tiny heads to the barn. Gianna looked at her daughters. "Lizzy get the girl. You two take bodies up and throw them over the gate." Freddy and Pete came tearing around the house. Gianna pointed to a body.

Lizzy yanked the girl to her feet. "Shut it. Now. Not another sound out of you." She moved her back near the veranda.

The sisters grabbed one body, the guys the other, and they head toward the stairs to the tower. Freddy and Pete got to the top as Sadie threw the first one over. The guys sent the second one right after it. As the bodies hit the dirt outside the gate, a calm disembodied voice flows from the speaker hung on the outer wall. "Go away. You are not welcome here." Ten seconds ticked by "Please don't make me send Audrey out there. I promise, you won't like Audrey."

Hale is stunned silent at the sight of his friends' bodies and the realization that his perfect plan had gone so wrong. Then he found his voice. "Fuck you. Lesbian cunt. Y'all fucking lesbian hippie nigger lovin' cunts gonna pay for this. All y'all are gonna die. Y'all killed three of my men now."

The voice from the speaker now with a razors edge to it replies. "Remember... I did ask nicely."

The gates of the Q slowly swing outward, revealing six heavily armed (or so they thought) miscreants, ridiculously clothed in filthy, stained, moth eaten Third Reich uniforms. They looked up. To a man, they pissed themselves. And then Audrey spoke...

Gianna leaned around Audrey. "I need you lesbian and or hippie cunts to dump the bodies and parts in the hole. Pete get a flame thrower and burn them. Freddy get the bobcat out there. I want the hole filled in and graded it. We don't need a snot-zis speed bump in the driveway. Tiny put Audrey back in the barn. Oh Tiny, turns out you were all I needed." Reno came into view running from the zone. As Gianna's walking away she says "Reno take a team out. Make sure there aren't any more of those dickless wonders hiding in the bush."

"Yes ma'am. Ma'am what should we do if we find any?"

Gianna stops, turns to face Reno, raises an eyebrow and says sarcastically... "Well, you could bring them back here. We could bring Audrey out again; Make another big hole and send another crew out to clean it up... OR *YOU COULD JUST SHOOT THE FUCKERS*."

Reno grinned ear to ear and nodded. "My pleasure ma'am. Just making sure that's what you had in mind."

As she starts to walk away again she says "And Reno get six guard out here to clean this shit up." Carmichael who'd come around the corner after Reno is waiting for his orders. Gianna points at him then at the ground at her feet. Ten of the guard come rushing in from the farm. Gianna points. "You six get out there and clean this up. Carmichael follow. Violet, Sadie you two with me. In the house. Now! Carmichael get that moronic grin off your face. People died here."

Violet pushing her luck says, "Mother are we sure snot-zis qualify as people?"

"Violet! Do not encourage him!"

Lizzy grabbed the girl by the arm and yanked her up the steps. Samira starts to whimper. "Don't start. Not a sound out of you. You broke the cardinal rule. You let killers into our home. You'll be lucky if she doesn't feed you to the hogs." as she pushed Crystal in the house.

Reno helped Tiny back the tank into the stall. He grabs his radio off his belt. "Mikey, you and Antonio take the garbage ten klicks out and dump it."

"Got it."

Once Audrey safely tucked in her stall Tiny eyes Reno and asks, "Are you sure about that order?"

Reno shrugged "You heard the Lady. She said to kill the fuckers."

"Yeah but she didn't know you had them already."

Reno stopped and with a 'what the fuck' look on his face said, "So you're saying I should drag them in front of her, give her a chance to go soft? Then what? We have to give them a room at H&G's? How long do we have to feed them for? Until they turn good? That's never going to happen. They would have shot that girl and you know it. I would have loved seeing the sisters taking them out."

Tiny nodded. "You can, I recorded it. I couldn't watch the front and deal with all the cameras too, so I just hit record. Figured I'd scan it before the Boss got back."

Reno stared at Tiny for a full thirty seconds. "Tiny you know we can't let them go. They're sick fuckers. The Lady's right. Those fuckers we shoot."

chapter 13
DUST IN THE WIND

*"Things have...
deeply and seriously changed"*

**12:00 pm EDT, October 1,
Holly Springs, North Carolina**

If he didn't know better Nick could
have mistaken it for just another
beautiful Autumn day. The homes and farms
along the road to Holly Springs looked as
they ever did. Children running through a
hay field. Cows grazing in the pasture.
Chickens squabbling in the yards. His was
the only vehicle on the road but that was
not uncommon here in the country.

The stark contrast that greeted them
as they rolled into Holly Spring said the
world had gone horribly wrong and may
never be right again. The acrid stench of
the still smoldering wreckage hung in the
air, windows and shops fronts opaque with
an oily layer of soot, there were no
moving cars. The people walked, some
walked as if in a trance, the tragedy
that had consumed so many of their
friends and family etched on their faces.

The charred berm of rubble that was just yesterday their main street, kept the pain new, burning in their minds.

The old wooden wagon used for hay rides at the Harvest Festival was parked across the front of the post office. The familiar tractor had been replaced with a team of draft horses who added to the scene of destruction by snapping off the tops of the flowers in the planters leaving jagged stalks behind. Charlie broke the uncomfortable silence. "There's a sight we don't see in town any more. Those are nice looking horses."

Lips pressed tightly against his teeth Nick nodded. The faces reminded him of the those he'd seen in war torn countries he'd served in. But these faces were here, in his country. He would do what ever it took to keep this misery from the faces of his people on the farm. He pulled the jeep up in front of the Town Hall and glanced around. He saw neighbors sharing water, food and comfort. People working together to survive.

Charlie said "I'll stay here with the toys. I don't care much for the FBI anyway."

That brought a half smile to Nick's face. Charlie not *liking* the FBI was an understatement. All the men knew never to let Charlie get started on the subject of the FBI. He'd rant for hours once he started.

Nick walked through the doors and removed his sunglasses. A woman in yoga pants and a flowing flowered top smiled up at him from a make-shift reception desk. Nick pegged her as *a west coast transplant*.

"May I help you?" she purred, batting her eye lashes.

Nick inwardly cringed *'Christ! Not another one'*, "Afternoon ma'am, I'm here to see Agent Mendez or Agent Parker if he's not around."

This set her all a-twitter. "Ohhh you must be Captain Lorenzini! Agent Mendez asked me to keep an eye out for you. He said I couldn't miss you, you'd have that Special Forces look about you. Oh, he was so right."

Nick stifled a grown. "Not Special Forces ma'am. That's the Army. Special Ops Command... Marines. Can you tell me where I can find him?" and because she looked confused he added, "Agent Mendez ma'am."

She got up so quickly she almost flipped her folding chair. "Hazel would you watch the desk I have to escort Captain Lorenzini to the Agent's office." Without waiting for an answer she started

290

across the floor. People were staring at Nick after her too loud request to Hazel.

He followed several paces behind her avoiding the chance for her to wrap her arm around his. He knew the type and wanted no part of it. Watching her navigate the marble floor in six inch heels. Nick thought *'If she gets any more sway going, those high heels are going to slip out from under her and she'll be on her ass.'* There was a time he tolerated these fluffy broads, now they just annoyed him. He'd been too long on the farm living with the Amazons. They looked sexy mucking out the barn.

At the end of the hall his escort stopped in front of a door marked Mayor. Nick suffered through her gushing introduction peppered with more of her sappy smiles. Agent Parker had to thank her and tell that would be all to get her to leave. Yes! she flashed Nick one more of her, all you have to do is ask, smile at Nick on her way out. After the door closed Nick said "Tell me there's a back door out of here. Otherwise I'm going out the window."

Rick Mendez grinned at his friend as he walked around the desk. "This is Agent Al Parker, my partner. Al this is Captain Lorenzini. So Nick, welcome to hell. Sit."

Nick shook his head. "Glad to see

291

you're still with us. You've got a hell of a mess here, but I caught a glimpse of your training on the way in. You've got things are under control. It's not as bad as it could be. You're both doing a good job with what you've got. I brought you what I could spare. You can't be the sheriff without a big gun." Nick's Catsear crackled. "Excuse me." He adjusted his earpiece. The reception wasn't great but Reno's message was clear enough. Nick looked at the agents. "Sorry guys, I have an emergency." He stepped to the window and waved Charlie in.

Mendez read the level concern in Nick's eyes. "Can we help?"

"Something's happened at the farm. I need to get back."

Agent Parker asked, "Were they attacked?"

He hesitated a moment. "Ah Yes." Nick eyed Mendez. "Marine to Marine, I'm not going to bullshit you, but don't ask questions an FBI agent doesn't want to know the answers to."

Mendez thought about it for three seconds. The Corps comes first. "Nick whatever it is, You know I've got your back. Did your men kill someone?"

Nick shook his head. "No, my men are disciplined. I wouldn't be concerned if it was my men... the women did."

Parker's mouth fell open. Mendez started laughing. In between chortles he asks, "How many?"

"Eight armed men."

Nick can hear the clip clip of Fluffy's heels running down the hall. "Sir! you can't just walk in here! What are you carrying? Sir!"

Nick yanked the door open. Charlie handed him the two bags, turned and left. "It's okay ma'am, he's with me." Then he closed the door in her face before she started smiling again. "These will keep you both armed." He placed the rifle bag on the desk. With his hand still on the bag he said "Let's *assume* these have been *grandfathered-in.*"

Mendez unzipped the bag and Parker's mouth dropped again. Inside were four AK-47s. Mendez whistled and looked at Nick. "You do know how to take care of a brother Marine."

Nick put the smaller bag on the desk. "And of course *whatever* is in here is also *grandfather-in.* We'll, keep in touch. I need to address that issue at home."

Mendez came around the desk and shook Nick's hand. "Seriously, thanks for these. Parker, I'm going to walk him out. Put those in that closet and lock it before Betty Boop out there comes nosing around."

Nick laughed. "Betty Boop, that's about right.

At the sight of the jeep, Mendez looked at Nick and narrows his eyes. "I think there's more to this farm then just being a home for retired Vets. Kick ass fire power, crazy women shooting people... what else is there that you haven't told me about? When things calm down a bit I need to come by for a beer, so save me one... or do you brew your own on the farm?" laughing again.

"Yes we do... and they're not crazy women. They're well trained, by me, Amazon warriors and without their mother, 90 Vets wouldn't have a home."

Mendez went quiet and serious. "You have a Company of trained men? Well, Nick, I feel a fuck of a lot better hearing that. I thought Parker and I were stranded here, with our asses out, all on our own. How far away is this place from here? How do I get there?"

Nick grinned "Close enough. If I told you I'd have to kill you."

This started Mendez laughing again. "Hey we'll check in every day at 08:00

hours. If you don't hear from us come running. Oh and if it goes to hell here I'm coming to live on your farm."

As they're leaving town Nick can see from the look on Charlie's face he's working up to giving Nick a ration of shit. "Look Charlie, I know all you see is an FBI agent but underneath he's a Marine first."

"Well you didn't tell me he was one of us!"

"There's a lot I don't tell you."

"Right! Like what's this shit about crazy women shooting people?"

Nick braced himself. "It seems it's been a busy day at the Q. The sisters shot two men that got inside and Gianna took six more out with Audrey. And I think Reno cleaned up a six pack in the woods. That's all I know until we get there."

"WHAT THE FUCK! FUCKIN A! We leave for an hour and the whole place goes to hell."

"Actually I don't think it went to hell, none of ours got hurt. More like all hell broke loose. The connection was bad but I think Reno said nazis."

Charlie's fist pounded the dash. "I

missed killing nazis? Fuck Me!"

While Charlie lamented his loss all
the way home, Nick worried about what he
almost lost. He should have been there.
She opened the gate to six armed men. He
should have sent Reno to deliver the guns
to Mendez. He yelled at her for going out
without him, then he wasn't there when
the place is attacked. She could have
died today because he wasn't there to
protect her.

1:30 pm EDT, October 1,
Devil's Fork Gap
Smokey Mountains, Tennessee

At 6:00 am the three couples
stumbled out of the storeroom. They
really hadn't gotten much sleep.
Cautiously they made their way through
the house. The only thing that stood out
was the lack of power. None of them were
hungry. With nothing else to do all night
they'd snacked on and off from the cooler
of food Pauline had packed. The women
said they were going to bed.

Billy hauled the generator out
while Frank and Dan carried the parts to
the HAM radio. They set it up on a table
in the garage so they could run a cord
from the generator outside the door. It
was cold in the garage but they were in a
hurry to hear what had happened. They'd
have to figure out a better arrangement
for upstairs later. Billy went up and

started a fire in the wood stove in his
and Betty Lou's rooms and another in the
fireplace in the living room. He didn't
want to go in the other bed rooms while
the women were sleeping. Dan and Frank
could do that. He put a kettle on the
woodstove and went back down to see what
the guys had found out.

Frank had just contacted someone.
Dan told Billy there was almost no one
on. The guy on the other end was in
Greensboro, North Carolina. He said there
was a government in his state but only
HAM radios for communication. They're
saying it was a massive CME and the grid
is down everywhere. A hurricane tore up
DC and there are rumors the president and
the vice are dead. The ocean is rising.
Fayetteville is under water. Out west the
Hoover Dam broke. He said it's crazy
outside. He's so glad he prepped. There
have been gunfights over food. The guy
said he saw fools running down the street
with TVs and high end electronics. He
couldn't think why the hell they'd steal
stuff they couldn't use. He didn't know
about other states but Duke there in
North Carolina was trashed. A plane
crashed into one of the power stations,
cooked the whole system. He guessed that
was one way to stop them from burning
coal and polluting the rivers. Even
started house fires. Looting is really
bad everywhere.

He said he'd only been in touch with

six other HAM operators. They agreed to make a list of info they each got so they could pass it on to others. Frank agreed and signed off. The guys pulled the generator in and carried everything upstairs. Billy went back down to double check they were locked up tight. Dan and Frank built their fires then the three of them sat in front of the fireplace drinking instant coffee. They talked over what the guy had told them. They wondered how Rory and Cindy were. The three of them fell asleep in the living room.

Tracy was the first one up. She found the men crashed out and thought they looked so peaceful she'd let them sleep. She put a few pieces of wood on the coals and went to the kitchen for some coffee. She was really proud she'd remembered to bring her French press. She was just taking her first sip when Betty Lou wandered in. "Hey Betty Lou how did you sleep well? Coffee is still hot."

"I slept real good. We made a good choice with that woodstove. It was still plenty warm when I got up." Betty Lou got her coffee and cream. "The fridge is still cool. Maybe we can plug it in for a bit and make a lot of ice. Like bowls so we have blocks of ice for the fridge. What do y'all think?"

"That's a great idea. Like the old ice boxes."

"We need to get to the meat in the big freezer too. That must be pretty cold still. Let's bring some up to defrost inside the fridge. And I think we should wrap the whole thing in a blanket to protect it from the heat while we cook."

Tracy looked at her friend with a new respect. "Damn Betty Lou you're just picking up on all the little things everybody else missed. They're small but will make a big difference. Thanks to your quick thinking on the riddle yesterday we still have our electronics. You are queen of the preppers today."

Billy had gotten up just after his wife. He stopped in the hall outside the kitchen to fix his sock. He could hear the girls conversation. 'Damn, Tracy's right.' For the first time in years he was proud of his wife. The others trickled in one by one. More coffee was made. Pauline heated some ham and cheese biscuits she made the day before. The girls got to talking about what they would cook and can today.

The men talked about how to set the radio up. There was a small balcony off the kitchen. They would put the generator there. They would run a cord to the window in the office. They congratulated themselves on finding a way to keep the generator safe from thieves and still not kill themselves with the fumes. To everyone's amazement Billy said they need

to give Betty Lou a hand for figuring the
riddle out. They all did. Betty Lou
smiled at her husband and Billy
remembered why he married her. Yep Billy
felt this was not going to be so bad.
They'd be fine till things got right in
the world outside the compound. Then he
leaned over and kissed his wife.

2:00 pm EDT, October 1, Damascus, Virginia

Rory and Cindy Got up about 10:00
am. They wandered down and were blown
away when the owners told them what had
happened while they slept. Beth heated
them some left over meatloaf and mashed
potatoes on the cast iron cook stove in
the kitchen. Ann had bought it for her
for their anniversary. Beth had used it
as a hutch until this morning. The women
had gone out to the store early and had
to fight for everything they got, which
wasn't much if this was how life was
going to be. They had some bulk items
like flour, rice and sugar because of the
meals they had to make for the guests.

Cindy and Rory shared their story
with the women. They were not sure what
the hell to do now. They could go back to
the compound maybe. Rory didn't think
they would get far with their supplies
before they were robbed, maybe even
killed. Beth and Ann invited them to stay
on at the Inn at no charge. It was a big
place for two people to try and protect.

They asked Rory and Cindy barter shelter for to teaching them about how to survive.

Rory and Ann went outside to assess what the building needed to make it more secure. Ann had a dozen sheets of plywood in the shed for a project she didn't get around to. There was also a small gas generator but she had no gas. Rory smiled and went over to the trailer and pulled out one of the gas cans. While doing that he realized they needed to empty the trailer and the truck right away.

The basement level of the house was above ground on one side. Rory backed the trailer up to the door while Ann got the other women. They found the two teams worked well together. Beth and Cindy made room in the basement and emptied the trailer and truck. Ann and Rory made shutters for the downstairs windows. Rory was impressed with Ann's tool collection. She said "You mean for a *woman*?"

"Hell no, this stuff would be impressive for a guy or a woman! But when we're done, let's move it all into the basement."

After Cindy and Beth had emptied the truck they moved to the garage in search of anything of value. They rolled Ann's Civic out into the guest parking area to make room to sort. They went through boxes and plastic bins like it was an

Easter egg hunt. Cindy opened a box and said "Holy crap."

Beth looked inside the box and said, "That was my dad's I just, couldn't part with it."

"Well it's a damn good thing you didn't. Help me get this in the house. And don't drop the little box they're all glass."

They'd found all sorts of stuff Cindy thought might be useful to have or to barter. As they worked she explained why she put each item in the 'to the house' pile. Beth got a crash course in prepping and living off the grid. When they were done Cindy backed the truck in the garage. The two women were pushing the trailer around the back of the garage when Cindy saw a shape sticking out from under a tarp she thought she recognized. She lifted the tarp and "Holy Fuck!" slipped out before she knew it. She look at Beth expecting her to be shocked.

Beth was laughing so hard she almost peed her pants. "I don't know what's better. The look on your face when you thought you'd offended me or the fact that you swear! Ann and I mind our language around the guests. Alone we swear like longshoremen."

"That's a relief! What is this doing under this tarp?"

"It's another of my wife's projects. It doesn't run and no one around here seem to know how to fix it."

"Well if we can find the parts, my husband can make it go. Rory is a brilliant mechanic."

They both looked over at their mates. "I can't believe she's letting him use her tools. No one touches them. She fired a workman last summer because he borrowed her saw. It took me two frigging weeks to find someone to finish the job. So them laughing it up passing tools back and forth is not anything I've seen my wife do. And I've known her since high school." They finished putting the trailer away and locked the garage.

6:00 pm EDT, October 1,
Tennessee Righteous Hideout
Holly Springs, North Carolina

Sally Ann was starting to get worried. They'd been gone five hours. 'Ya think they woulda sent word if they had taken the place.' She looked at the six men scattered around the living room eating the rice and beans she'd made. 'What if it had all gone wrong and they were all in jail or dead?'

Shit, Jim had taught her to hope for the best and plan for the worst. She didn't think the worst he was talking

303

about was anywhere near as bad as this. She went upstairs to the front room where those assholes had changed into the SS uniforms. Hale the drunken bastard had left his pants on the floor... and the money in the pocket. Hale was dumber than a bag of shit when he was drunk. This is all the money the group had. 'If that no-count Jeff had found it he be walkin' to the liquor store right now, Apocalypse or not.' She hid the money in her bra and left the pants where she found them.

Back down in the kitchen she sat at the table and assessed each of the men: Jeff was a drunk and couldn't be trusted, Jimmy Ray was nice enough but slow in the head, Mick could be counted on and might be of some use, Ash about the same as Mick, Colter was the one who tried to take her kids food back at the cabin, he was an asshole, he'd bolt as soon as the food ran out, and Tommy was just a kid maybe 16, all he talked about was finding a piece of ass.

If they wasn't coming back she needed to loose the dead weight to make the food last longer. She got up and went in the living room. "Y'all listen up. Some thinin' not right. They should have been back by now or sent word at the least. We need to find where the car is at. We're runnin' out of food too. Ash and Mick y'all go check Tucker's traps."

Colter snarled, "Why them."

"Cause they are the best shots in the room and y'all know it. You other four head out for that farm. They had to stash the car near by there. Colter, Hale told me he was leavin' the money in the glove box in case some thin' went wrong. I know we can trust you to get the car and the money for us all."

Colter jumped at the chance to take the money and run. "Y'alls right Sally Anne. I'll take the rifle, y'all get your shot guns."

Sally Ann gave him her fuck you face. "No Colter. Y'all take y'alls shotgun. That rifle belongs to my husband. It stays right here to protect my children. Y'all don't steal a man's gun. Even if his wife is the one holdin' it."

"Sally Anne is right about that Colter." Ash felt he had to stand up for her after she named him the best shot in the room.

Grudgingly Colter gave in. "All right y'all lets go find our money and our car." He grabbed the map Ethan had made off the table on his way out.

Ash and Mick went off to see if they could find the traps. After they'd all left, Sally Anne wrapped a blanket around her and sat on the front porch. She felt

that it had gone better than expected.
She knew Colter would take the bait. He
was walking right now thinkin' he was
gonna find the car and the money and keep
on down the road. She knew there was no
money there. It was a 50/50 shot that
he'd bring the car back. She be no worse
off than she was now and she wouldn't
have to share the last of the food with
them. If he did bring the car back she'd
take it tomorrow night while they were
sleeping. She'd hid the half quart of
hooch Hale and Axel didn't drink. She had
a few oxy in her bag she'd add to it.
They'd never hear her leavin' with her
kids and the food. A girl's gotta do what
a girl's gotta do. She looked t the night
sky and wondered where her husband was
tonight.

7:00 pm EDT, October 1,
Dancing Goats Farm
Moon Mountain, North Carolina

Reno was in the command room. He'd
been hiding there for the last hour. It
had been a shit storm from the minute
Nick and Charlie came through the gate.
Nick had the entire company out in front
of the barracks for an hour.

He started out with, "What happened
here today is the perfect example of what
should never have happened. Every fail-
safe I put in place to secure the safety
of the people that live here FAILED! You
All Failed today."

At one point he threatened to kick everyone of them out on their ass. It wasn't pretty. He accused them of being candy asses, something most of them hadn't been accused of being since in boot camp.

After an hour of this Nick had gotten louder and madder, then the Lady showed up and shit got *real* crazy... she interrupted him in mid rant.

Nicely, "Nicholas I think you should take this inside the Hall or barracks please."

Loud, "Do not tell me how to discipline my men, madam."

With a sharp edge to it, "You may discipline them as you see fit. I'm simply asking if you would do it inside a building." Then because he just stood the glaring at he she got loud "Because you're scaring the shit out of the people who aren't your men!"

Drill sergeant loud, "If you had better control of your people we wouldn't be having this fucking conversation! They need to be scared. They need to be very fucking scared because if what's out there gets in here they'll be dead not scared!"

That snapped her last Gypsy nerve.

Her voice dropped to a rasp. "If you want to stand in front of your men and show your ass that's your choice but YOU'RE NOT SHOWING THEM MINE!" Then she grabbed a handful of his shirt and led him to the east portal. At the door she turned and said, "Reno, your Captain has urgent business with me in the Q. Put the company back to work." The last thing Reno heard was... *"Nicholas-have-you-lost-your-mother-fucking-mind?"*

Reno thought when Nick got back he was going to court martial Tiny and Carmichael. He thought he might be gone too, for having given the order to take out the trash.

As the men were going back to their jobs, Violet, Sadie, and Alexandra showed up, and wanted to know why it had suddenly gone quiet. Had Nick's head exploded? Reno told them what just happened. They looked at each other and they all shook their heads knowingly.

Alexandra said, "Nick's in deep shit."

Violet said, "Nicholas is in time out with Mother...this is not good."

Sadie said, "Reno, If you can hear my mother yelling, you're okay. When her voice drops down to a whisper and you have to lean forward to hear her... just keep bending over, put your head between

308

you knees and kiss your ass good by."

What ever happened in the Q, Nick returned an hour later and calmly asked him, Tiny and Carmichael their side of the story and that was it. Reno watched the footage of the snot-zi take-down. After the fifth time he'd watched it, he wished there still was an internet cause this really should have gone viral. Reno played the screaming match over in his head. She could always wind him up but she could always reach him when no one else could bring him back from the edge. In retrospect he had to admit the dynamics between the two of them had been really hot. Too bad they weren't a couple... they could've had some incredible make-up sex.

8:00 pm EDT October 1, Holly Springs, North Carolina

Agent Rick Mendez sat in the dead Mayors chair with his feet on the desk. Closing his eyes he drifted into a shallow sleep.

Betty Boop and her clip clip clip no longer echoed through the halls. The main street was relatively void of people. At dusk the hay wagon had ferried people back to their homes, their food rations in paper sacks clutched on their laps. For the most they were emotionally numb from having come to the realization there would be no one who would come to save them. They went home empty, to their dark cold houses to hide beneath their covers in sleep. Some would not wake. Crushed in the night by the burden of being solely responsible for their own existence. Others awoke screaming having relived the horror they'd seen. Others still would dream of life as it had been before... Before when they greedily helped themselves to all of the earths bounty. In return they gave her filth, poison and scars. When the food ran out and winter came with her icy breath, many would die dreaming, never having owned their crimes.

Rick Mendez woke with a start. "What the hell?"... Some asshole was shooting a rifle in the street right outside the window, followed by the sound of muffled angry voices, footsteps running down the pavement. Not fully awake he tried to get out of the chair not realizing his feet were still on the desk. He sort of flipped-rolled out the chair and hit the floor hard. "I'm awake now!" he said to no one. The fumble actually saved his life. The next shot pierced the window passing through the chair and stuck in the plaster on the far wall. "I'm under attack and I'm talking out loud to myself." He could hear them ramming the brass doors in the lobby. He crawled to the closet, fumbled with the key and pulled the AK-47 out of the bag ramming the magazine into the well. Though he didn't have a chance to check them out after Nick had left, it wouldn't have occurred to him that it would be in anything but impeccable working order coming from Nick. He heard the lobby door give way, thirty seconds later, they crashed through the office door. The absence of ambient light in the office gave Mendez the advantage. Rick took all eight of them down before they realized he wasn't in the chair. He gathered their rifles locked them in the closet and ran for the motel.

More gunfire was coming from the direction of the motel. People were screaming. A block from the motel a man launched himself from a doorway catching Mendez broadside. They crashed sideways into a parked car. They wrestled for control of the rifle. Mendez let go with one hand, the guy swayed backward giving Mendez the room he needed. He pulled his Glock from his shoulder holster and shot the bastard in the face. Mendez ran toward the motel. There were at least twenty-five bodies scattered around the parking lot, some had been shot in the back as they ran. Mendez found his partner dead on the kitchen floor. He'd been defending the staff who were also dead. Mendez raced back to Town Hall. The HAM radio was still in the room down the hall from the Mayors office. Mendez Collected the guns and bags Nick had brought him and returned to the room with the radio. He waited until the street had gone silent for 15 minutes then he

311

started the generator, they'd moved inside for safe keeping. As he worked he said, "Nick, I hope you have someone with ears on over there." He sighed "Now I'm talking out loud to people who can't possibly hear me!"

8:35 pm EDT, October 1,
Dancing Goats Farm
Moon Mountain, North Carolina

Reno was watching the recording of the snot-zi take-down from the outside camera when the Mayday came through from Mendez. The second he heard him say he was under attack Reno hit the alarm that went off in Nick's room on the second floor of the farmhouse. Reno switched on the intercom so Nick could hear what Mendez was saying. Nick told Reno to sound general alarm in the barracks. Nick gave Reno instructions for Mendez and ran down and out to the barn. Reno told Mendez to turn the generator off and find a safe place where he could see the street. Sit tight they were coming for him. They were 15 to 25 minutes out.

Tiny came into the room as Mendez signed off. "Top side Reno, the Boss wants you."

When the alarm went off in Nicks room a red light flashed on a box on Gianna's night table. She called it 'The Bat Phone'. When the general alarm went off in the barracks the box began to ring

312

like a fire drill. Gianna was up
instantly and down the stairs dressing as
she went, while Reno was still giving
Mendez Nick's message. Twenty seconds
later she charged through the backdoor of
the farmhouse as Reno stepped into the
hall. She nearly knocked him over.

"What the *Hell* is going on Reno?" He
filled her in as they ran through to the
veranda.

At the steps Reno put his hand out
to stop her following him. "Ma'am I think
it's best if you wait here." Then he
hustled across the yard to the barn door
where Nick was giving the Sergeant orders
for the protection of the farm.

The man left as Reno came alongside
Nick. "Reno, good catch. I'm taking
twenty. Half regulars and half vanguard.
The rest of the guard stays with you."
The Dark Lady was at the gate. Behind her
were two jeeps, two SUVs and Pepé the
souped-up monster wheeled, tricked out
truck. Reno followed Nick to the truck.
He told Nick Mendez had called from the
Town Hall. Nick pulled the drivers door
open and turned back to Reno. "You did a
good job today." as he was speaking to
Reno, Nick saw Gianna standing on the
veranda - back lit by the yellow glow of
the fog lights - her hair lifted by the
night breeze - her hands defiantly on her
hips. Nick's heart tightened and he
smiled. Reno turned to see what could

make the Boss smile at a moment like this. Nick said, "The Amazon Queen sending her men into battle... *there's* an oxymoron if there ever was one." As he got in the truck he said something Reno could barely make out over the revving of the engines. Reno thought Nick had said 'Keep them safe for me.' By the time Reno had retraced his steps to the veranda he wasn't sure, Nick might have said 'Keep *her* safe for me.'

8:55 pm EDT October 1, Holly Springs, North Carolina

Mendez had worked his way to the roof after talking to Reno. It had a steel door with a cross bar. He had heard snips of what Nick had said over the intercom. He'd called a general alarm. Rick knew from personal experience, the minutes spent waiting for an extraction were the longest minutes in a person's life. Rick distracted himself by speculating whether the alarm was because of his extraction request or if this fucking insanity was happening there at Nick's farm too. Where ever *there* was. Where ever it was he hoped *there* was close to here. No sooner had that thought crossed his mind when he heard more gunfire and yelling coming his way. It looked like a mob of about twenty-five coming down the street. In six minutes they were on the steps below him. He thought a few might have come inside the building. Out of the corner of his eye

Mendez caught a glimmer of light, as it got closer it separated in two. It's a pair of headlights, rolling recon slowly down the street toward the Town Hall. For the first time in an hour Mendez thinks he might make it out of here alive.

The truck garners the attention of some of the mob. They start yelling; "take it, take it, take it", as the truck rolled closer. The truck cut its head lights. The street went pitch black the only light cane from the three or four torches held by the mob. The truck came to a full stop maybe fifteen feet from the mob on the steps, Mendez smiled, he knows what coming. This is a classic maneuver by the Special Ops Command. He doesn't want to miss the show but he needs to be cognizant of the noise in the building below him. It wouldn't do to have the extraction team at hand and be killed because he was too busy laughing at the hell about to rain down on these bastards who killed his partner.

There is a flutter of movement in the darkness as six Marines rise up from the Dark Lady's bed and proceed to mow the fuckers down with six more *grandfathered-in* AK-47s. The ones who try to escape to the right or left are met by two more teams. Reluctantly Mendez pulls his eyes away from the bloodbath taking place on the steps of the quaint Town Hall, realizing there's gunfire below him on the second floor. He thinks prone is his best option unless they see him before he kills them. He's hoping the roofs parapet will afford him an element of shadow for cover. Mendez holds his breath... and the door blows off it's hinges. Nick and four more marines step out on the roof. From the shadows Nick hears, "I recognize the work of *grandfathered-in C4* when I see it."

Outside Mendez sees he underestimated the size of the mob; it was closer to forty. The Marine who took the bag of rifles from him asks if there is anything else they should recover. Mendez tells them where the radio and generator are. The others are gathering the weapons from the dead. Nick asks about Parker. He sends Freddy and his team with Mendez to the motel to retrieve Parker's body. As the SUV leaves, Nick signals the men, they're out of there. Nick tells the other SUV to cover Freddy's 6 while the rest of the convoy heads home.

When they're about ten minutes out from the Qs gates, Nick radios Reno to wake Andy and the Doc. They have no dead but three wounded. Two leg wounds and a shoulder. Then signs off.

Charlie looked over and saw blood seeping out from under Nick's vest onto Dark Lady's seat. "You dumb bastard. The Lady isn't going to like this. The truck's not going to be too happy with you either." The Dark Lady surged forward as her speedometer rises to 85.

Nick says "You're really pushing it on this winding country road."

"How about I do the driving and you sit there and try not to bleed to death?" Charlie radios Reno "Tell *her* we're going to need AB negative blood. The chest wound is Nick."

chapter 14
RIDERS ON THE STORM

"There's death on the road
The Lady steps up
to shoulder the load"

9:45 pm EDT, October 1,
Tennessee Righteous Hideout
Holly Springs, North Carolina

Ash and Micky hunted around in the
dark for Tucker's traps. They checked all
the traps they could find. Mick said this
was stupid crashing around in the dark.
They agreed to go out at first light to
reset the traps they'd found and to
collect what they'd missed in the dark.
They went back with a coon and two more
rabbits. Sally Anne was still on the
porch when they returned. Mick set about
dressing the animals on the back porch
while Ash went to tell Sally Anne what
they had found. Ash listened to her
doubts about Colter and told her he
didn't trust Colter as far as he could
spit. He was going to scout around down
near the road for any sign of the four of
them. Sally agreed Colter needed
watching. Since arriving at the farm,
they'd been keeping back from the front

of the property so as to not attract attention to them being there. Ash said he'd be careful.

Sally Anne went back to daydreaming about her life back in Tennessee. She was sure all the trouble that had happened to them and the whole country were somehow caused by all the people the Tennessee Righteous hated. Life had been good in her ranch house in the suburbs. Her kids went to a good Christian Baptist school with kids whose parents thought like her and James. She missed her air getting her hair done, her conditioner, and driving around in her big diesel king cab pickup that took two spaces to park at the Piggly Wiggly. Oh how she missed her microwave and prepackaged meals. No dishes to wash just toss the Styrofoam plates and plastic cups in the trash. Here the garbage had to be buried. At home James just put it all in a burn barrel. And she really missed soda, they drank it by the liter.

A sound in the bushes brought her back to the present. It might be a rat, she'd seen one in the barn. It had been three and a half hours since Colter and them left. They'd have been back by now if they was comin'. Her food problem was solved for the moment. Ash and Mick did okay tonight. She still needed a car to get her kids back to her mamma's. The life in another state she and James had talked about was a whole lot different

than this life on the run, a woman alone
with two kids and now the world's gone to
hell in a hand basket. Maybe Ash and Mick
would help her get home cause of the
kids. Ash came running up the the
driveway lookin' behind him as he ran.
He'd seen a convoy of SUVs, jeeps and
pickups, they was headed towards Holly
Springs. They didn't look like regular
cops more like a government black ops
team. He didn't try to follow cause they
were going the other way. He went about a
mile in the direction Colter and the
other three had gone, he didn't see any
sign of Colter or the other men. He was
just climbing out the ditch on the edge
of the drive when that convoy came back.
The front truck was blowin' down the
road. He thought the driver might have
seen him but he got undercover before the
other trucks and the jeeps came by. He
was just roundin' the turn in the
driveway when two more SUVs went past. He
didn't think they saw him, he was too far
up the drive.

Sally Anne figured this was a good
time to talk about moving on and needing
a car to do it. She told him she needed
to get back to her mamma's she could not
spend the winter in this place with her
kids. Ash agreed the FBI might not be
looking for her. Maybe they weren't
looking for him or Mick either. Ash
thought they should go up to Virginia and
leave her at the Tennessee border. She
could get word to her mamma through a

friend he had with a HAM radio there. When she got home she could check and see if they were wanted and get word back to them. Colter and the others had not returned, after her talk with Ash she went up to bed feeling things were going to work out now that she had a plan. She forgot the part about planning for the worst.

9:45 pm EDT, October 1,
Devil's Fork Gap
Smokey Mountains, Tennessee

It had been a busy day for the girls. They had put up twenty-two quarts of meat and meat meals. Dan was bringing up a load from the freezer for them when he found a package of steaks. Dan told the guys he was going to cook steak and potatoes on the grill, giving the girls a break after their day slaving over the stove. Billy had wrapped the fridge and the freeze as his wife suggested. When they weren't on the radio they did plug the fridge in and made blocks of ice. Billy even split some wood down to a size Betty Lou could pick up with one hand and put them in their bedroom wood basket. Frank set up a DC powered fan to blow the heat from the kitchen to the other rooms. When Dan was preparing the steaks, there was a wistful moment for everyone. Pauline had packaged the meats in meal sized portions, there were eight steaks. Pauline lightened the mood by taking Rory and Cindy's steaks and slicing them up for steak and eggs in the morning.

After dinner Dan and Billy brought up more jugs of water for the bathrooms. Frank got on the radio. He managed to contact a few more of his friends. The news was being passed across the country and it was pretty grim. North Carolina had thousands dead from the planes, fires, and the coastal flooding. All the refugees in Charlotte died by fire. The ones sent to Camp Lejeune drowned when a 30' high rogue wave hit the camp. New England was just as bad. The states were losing feet of shore by the day. Matters were made worse by torrential rains. In the southwest no news came from west of Arizona.

S   till no word on DC. No one knew if there was anyone left to search for the president. There was an unconfirmed rumor that NORAD was safe. Tennessee was being run by the Army troops that had been stationed there for the processing centers. They were running out of food for the Army, the refugees stranded there and the people of the state. The biggest question was what to do with the inmates in the fourteen state, one federal and over thirty county jails and prisons. The inmates were on one meal a day and confined to their cells. There were hundreds of deaths from cellmates fighting over food. There was a rumor that those who had not yet been convicted were to be let out along with those convicted of nonviolent crimes like DUI's and failure to pay child support. It wouldn't solve the statewide food shortage but it would reduce the number of bodies the dwindling number of guards had to control. After Frank had shared the news with the others, Pauline said they all needed to take a moment to say a prayer of thanks that they were so well off when so many had nothing. Afterwards she announced they would all be fine. They had Jesus on their side, food in the pantry and plenty of guns to keep it and them safe. In the afternoon Dan took the path to check on Harvey and Barbra. They were rather well. Nothing had changed for them. Their solar system was working fine. They had known about the EMP coming and disconnected it. It was just another day in Shangri La. Harvey picked some tomatoes from the greenhouse for Dan to take back. They had gone nicely with the steak and potatoes.

9:45 pm EDT, October 1, Damascus, Virginia

Ann and Rory finished moving the last of the tools in and went upstairs. They found the women in the kitchen laughing and and cooking. Cindy said, "Hey guys great job on the shutters. Babe, I have two amazing things to show you. Okay, one I'll tell you about but you can't see it until tomorrow... there's a Willys under a tarp behind the garage. Like mine! Can you fucking believe it?"

Rory shot her a look for her language. Laughing Beth said, "Its okay Rory, Ann and I swear." to Cindy she said "Girl you didn't tell me you had one."

"That's how I knew what it was before I lifted the tarp higher. I had to sell mine to buy into the compound. I see that look in your eye Rory, not tonight. Come in the sitting room - there's something equally amazing."

Rory looked in the boxes. "Holy shit, where was this?"

"In the garage it belonged to Beth's father. Don't kick the little box it's full of tubes for the set."

Ann looked at her wife and smiled. "Beth honey I forgot your dad had a HAM radio. Now we can find out what the fuck is going on out there."

Ann and Rory wouldn't come to the table to eat they were so engrossed in cleaning and testing the equipment. Cindy brought them plates so they could eat while they worked. In the kitchen Beth opened the second bottle of wine while Cindy cleared up.

Beth was leaning against the door jam into her second glass of wine, watching Rory and Ann on the floor. She leaned over to Cindy and said "Look at them they're like long lost school buddies. If I didn't know my wife better I might be jealous!"

They both laughed that laugh that says, 'say this wine *is* good', all the way up the stairs where they went to check if the wood stoves in the two bedrooms need stoking. Beth had moved Cindy and Rory to a bigger room with a wood stove at the front of the house. Now they had heat and ears at two sides of the house.

Back in the kitchen, Beth and Cindy put together a binder where they could list their resources so they would know how much they had of everything. There was even a barter list that included not only items they had found in the garage but their skills. They had team 'Rory Ann' who could build or fix just about anything. Cindy's medical training could become rather valuable. Beth made quilts out of old clothing. People were going to need more blankets with no heat. Even if they heated with wood, save a log put another blanket on the bed. In the morning they would tackle the basement. Rory had said he was going to add crossbars to the basement door to keep their stocks and tools safe. They had sectioned off an area for food storage and cobbled together shelving and racks. Then they would inventory all the food at the Inn and the supplies Rory and Cindy had brought. Cindy's guess, just from what she'd seen, they could make it through the winter if they were careful.

Beth told her she still had some veggies under a tunnel in the back yard. Cindy added another section for seeds and growing supplies. She also wanted to pot what she could and bring them inside. One of the bedrooms had large south facing windows. Beth said they could move the furniture out and turn it into a growing room. There was a small woodstove in there too. Oh, and she had a two foot lemon tree a guest had sent her last spring as a thank you for a wonderful stay. That could go in there too. Ann had come in for a glass of water. She liked the idea. She said "We can add mirrors to the other walls in the room. When the sun hits it will give light to the other side of the plants. Rory and I can build easels for them so we get the angle right."

Rory almost had the radio ready. He said they should keep track of the information that came in where, when and who. Maybe set a schedule for when certain people would be on. The ideas rolled into the creation of a 'situation room' for themselves. They gathered items from everywhere. The mention of maps and pencils sent them back to a stack of boxes in the garage marked DAD. After two hours the scavenger hunt took its toll. Rory said they would try out the radio in the morning after breakfast. No one protested. They were all tired from an afternoon of heavy physical labor. Tired but pleased with themselves they all hit the sack.

9:52 pm EDT, October 1,
Dancing Goats Farm
Moon Mountain, North Carolina

The guard had closed and bolted the gates after the last two vehicles had left. Reno checked on the vanguard to make sure they had taken up their posts. They had. After all the shit that had happened already today, every soldier was at their peak performance. Reno returned to the veranda. Gianna was curled up in one of the big wicker chairs. He looked at her and was about to ask her if she needed anything before he went down to check on Tiny but instead he said, *"What are you wearing?"*

Gianna stood up and looked at herself. "I flew out of bed the second the alarm went off. After the shit earlier today I didn't know what was wrong. The foremost thought in my mind was to get here and find out. Some part of my brain realized it probably would be better if I didn't arrive here naked. So I grabbed 'things' as I ran. This is a silk camisole I snatched off the bed, this the flannel shirt I found draped over the banister. When I got to the door I realized I'd lost the bottoms to the cammi on the stairs so I grabbed for the yoga pants on the back of the couch. I was at the east portal when found out I had Victorian French knickers *not* yoga pants and I wasn't going back. Then I got cold sitting here, so I took Nick's leather off the hook inside to complete this unique ensemble."

Reno couldn't hold back the laughter any more. "It's *unique* I'll give you that." and continued to laugh.

"Shut the fuck up Reno." she snapped. "21 of my men left here on a dangerous mission, frankly I don't care *what* I'm wearing or if I'm wearing *anything* at all!"

Trying to stifle his laughter he said, "I'm going to monitor the radio with Tiny. You and your *unique* outfit might be warmer downstairs with us."

Reno had sent Tiny upstairs to make coffee a minute before Nick's message came through. Reno looked over at Gianna, she had her annoyed face on. "Really? It's not like he's being charged by the frigging word. A little more information would have been nice, *Nick*." She was ringing Andy when Charlie's message came through. Reno watched all the color drain out of her face, then she ran for the stairs.

"*Wait*! Don't you want to be here

328

when he pulls in? I'll go to the
infirmary."

"No! *I* have to go. I'm the '*her*'
Charlie's talking about. It's my blood
Nick needs. Sadie too, get Sadie there,
we don't know how much blood he's lost.
Why didn't that asshole tell me it was
him?"

Tiny came thundering down the
stairs. "What the hell happened? She
nearly knocked me down flying out the
door."

"The Boss is coming in with a chest
wound. Three wounded total. Get the barn
open-now!" Reno ordered the Q gates wide
opened with six men outside and six
inside. He sent another six to light a
path to the infirmary with flares. He
informed the sergeant inside the farm.
One minute out Charlie picked up the
radio. "Reno, I'm coming in hot, the barn
better be open cause I'm driving through
if it's not."

"It's open go on through. They're
ready for him. The Lady is at the
infirmary waiting for him." The second
Tiny was back Reno flew up the stairs.
Thirty seconds later Dark Lady slid
through the gates. Reno jumped on the
running board as Charlie slowed to enter
the barn. Once they were clear the barn,
Reno could see the infirmary is lit up, a
hive of activity inside and outside,

there are three gurneys standing by out front.

Tiny comes through Reno's Catsear. "Two on the way."

"Send them through, then lock it down. Wait, how many convoy vehicles still out?"

"Two SUVs coming with Mendez and Parker's body."

"Send Mendez and Parker through, then lock it down."

Reno jumped off before the truck came to a stop. He got Nick under the arm and on to a gurney where Andy and the Doc took over. As they wheeled him through, Nick sees his kaleidoscope of butterflies are already in the waiting room. In the exam room Andy turned Nick's head to get the oxygen mask on him. He sees Gianna in the corner with a tube attached to one arm. It takes a few seconds to figure out what she's wearing, when he does, he starts laughing, much to Andy's dismay. Two minutes later they're telling him to count backwards. All he can think of is *her* in his leather and a pair of French lace knickers. The woman was *nothing* if not entertaining. He went under smiling.

One of the nurses came out to tell Gianna the bullet went through. He's lost almost a pint of blood. Doc just wants the one pint for right now, but don't go far in case he needs a second one. Sadie sats in the chair next to her mother and said

"Just hook me up babe and take it now so you have it. We don't want to take chances with Nick's life over a pint of blood. I've got this, mamma. You go check on the others. Andy knows to keep him sedated after they're finished sewing him up or he'll be up bossing people ten minutes after surgery." The aid put a band-aid on Gianna's arm. Gianna kissed her daughter on the forehead and left to check on the two wounded and let Reno know what was happening with Nick so he could tell the men.

Gianna gave Reno an update and went looking for the wounded. Antonio has a graze but DJ took one in the thigh. Satisfied they would be okay Gianna stepped outside. She needed to breath the cool night air to calm her. What she saw was anything but calming. "Reno, *WHO is that*?" she asked pointing at Mendez.

"That's Agent Mendez."

"What is a fucking FBI agent doing in here... in my sanctuary... *my secret village*?"

Reno suddenly wished he'd been the one who'd been shot. "We had to bring his dead partner in."

"Reno, I don't have a problem with the partner, He's dead! What is the live Fed doing in here? Why isn't he in the Q? You do remember what Q stands for? It's The QUARANTINE AREA. The place we keep people who should never know about *this* place. Is he hurt? I don't see any blood. Even if he was, we have nurses who could go to him. Why isn't he in a room in the farmhouse? I understand the need to risk MY men to rescue a fellow Marine. What I don't understand is WHAT THE FUCK he's doing INSIDE my FUCKING FARM!! Get him out of here NOW!" She started to walk away but came back. "And FYI *You* are now at the top of the shit list. *You* sailed right over Nick to the top of the list. Nick's number two and *you're* in first place on my shit list. Now go!"

The overly animated conversation between Gianna and Reno caught the attention of Freddy and Mendez. Mendez asked, "What's going on over there? Who's the woman?"

"That would be the owner. If I had to guess, I'd say she caught sight of you and he's getting his head handed to him."

They watched as a rigid Reno approached. "Agent Mendez, The Lady has asked me to get you settled into a room in the Farmhouse."

"I'm still kind of keyed up, thought

I'd have a look around at you're set up.
How big is this place?"

Through his teeth Reno explained,
"It's not actually a request."

Over confident perhaps from his
resent brush with death Rick said "Just
let me have a word with her. I'd like to
meet her. I'm sure she' like to meet me."
Freddy started chortling.

His patients gone Reno put firmly
his hand on the agent's shoulder. "You
know all the shit you went through
tonight? That'll seem like a walk in the
park compared to a conversation with her
right now. Come on, you can have the room
across from Nick's."

Mendez turned to Freddy with an 'Is
he kidding?' look. Freddy answered it.
"That's if you live through it. That
woman took out six armed men this morning
because they wouldn't go away when she
asked them to. You *do not* want to
question her orders." As they walk away,
Freddy couldn't resist busting Reno's
balls. "Hey Reno, how's your ass? From
here it looks a little chewed." Reno
flipped him off and kept walking. Freddy
watched Gianna come back out of the
infirmary and get in a cart. She drove
right past Reno and the Agent to the east
portal, parked it, then went through.

Gianna found Charlie in the barn

with the guard that stayed behind. Mikey
was busy removing Nick's blood from the
truck seat. Through the driver's door she
says, "Mikey, make sure you leave baking
soda on it when you're done." Before he
can answer she added, "Honey, I know you
know what you're doing. Just cut me a
little slack to be a bossy micro-managing
asshole tonight, okay?"

Mikey looked up. "I understand,
Ma'am, we're all worried about the Boss
too." The others gather around for news
on Nick, DJ and Antonio. When she's done
she asked Charlie if he has a few
minutes for her.

Inside the house they find Reno
coming down the stairs. As she passed
Reno she said "Reno see that your 'guest'
has food and I'm sure he could use a shot
or two." Mendez was on the landing
outside his room. He smirked thinking
'Not quite the bitch I thought she was'.

In the kitchen Gianna poured herself
a brandy. Over her shoulder she asked,
"Charlie, brandy or whiskey?"

Charley dropped exhausted to a
chair. "Whiskey ma'am please."

Gianna placed both glasses on the
table and then both bottles. She sighed,
and rolled her neck. The first a sip
burned down her throat. "Charlie, it's
been a fuck of a day. What the hell

happened out there? How did Nick get shot? Is society breaking down already?"

He leaned back in his chair and matched her sigh. "Ma'am I believe that is an understatement!" He took another swig of whiskey then he began. "Mendez had maybe four or five minutes left when we got there. Nick figured Mendez would go to the top of the last place he called from. I rolled down the center of Main Street while two teams flanked the building. At the first shot, Nick and his team breached the back door. Gabe said they took out twelve to reach the agent on the roof. It was maybe six minutes start to finish. Six bloody minutes. Lee said Nick got hit in a skirmish on the second floor. On the ride back, Mendez told Freddy he'd been dozing in the Town Hall when they attacked. He killed eight with the rifle Nick dropped off today. Guess he had to fight his way to the motel. He found Parker dead along with a dozen or so employees. He got back to the Town Hall, called, and waited for us."

"How many did we leave dead?"

Charley didn't like the set of her jaw. She'd been through too much tonight already. But he knew better than to keep any of the details from her. "Looked like close to 40. Seems like the townspeople just turned into a rabid mob. Freddy said the mob had killed everyone they came across. People running away who been shot

335

in the back, were dead all over the motel parking lot and streets." Charlie banged back the last in his glass and reached for the bottle. "We took out around 40 but the mob killed upwards of 50 before we got there."

Mendez appeared at the kitchen door. Gianna looked him up and down twice and asked "Did you need something?"

Mendez thought, How did she make those four simple words sound so menacing? "I was looking for Reno ma'am."

"I imagine he's seeing to his wounded men. I'll let him know you're looking for him. You can wait for him on the veranda." Then she turned her face back to Charlie.

Mendez took his dismissal and retreated out the front door. As he left he heard her say, "That's all we need Charlie. Fucking feral bands of assholes wandering the countryside... you know we're going to have to start burning the bodies."

Reno was coming around the farmhouse when he heard the back door slam. Charlie stepped on to the veranda as Reno cleared the steps. Mendez looked up at Charlie and shook his head. "I see what you mean about her. That look she gave me almost froze my balls off."

Charlie and Reno took a chair on either side of Mendez. Reno said, "She gets really upset when any of us gets hurt. Her blood sugar's probably low, she had to give blood for Nick."

Charlie snickered. "Yeah, that's what it is, her blood sugar, not that Nick has a hole in him. Reno, what's up with the outfit? Yeah, it's sexy but an odd choice considering..." Reno told them the story about the unique outfit laughing the whole way through.

Charlie said "I'm gonna check with the guys on duty inside to see if any of them saw the Lady racing bare assed across the yard. Oh Reno, The Lady wants the twenty-five who went out to sleep now. She said, until she, *and she emphasized the she,* says otherwise, half the guard and half the regulars are on at all times, twelve hour shifts. So you better make that happen. Cause you don't want her any more pissed at you than she already is."

Mendez asked "Why do you call her the Lady?

Dead serious, Reno said "Cause Nick told us to. Only he can use her first name."

"That's kind of fucking Medieval."

Charlie slapped him on the shoulder.

"There's a lot of that here on Dancing Goats Farm." As he went down the steps he added *"Welcome to the Matriarchy!"*

In the barn, Charlie found there was a new problem. The trap Nick had set to lure in any leftover snot-zis had worked. Four of those bastards had tried to break into the zone, where the LeSabre had been parked as bait. Three were dead, the fourth wounded in the leg. They were bringing him in now. He called Reno. "Becky found a rat in the trap. She's bringing it in. Oh, and there's three more bags of trash to go out."

Reno ran his fingers through his hair and exhaled. "Will this fuck of a day ever end?"

Gianna stopped by the infirmary to check on the three men. Antonio was back with the guard already. DJ tried for a release but Andy shut him down.

Gianna looked in on Nick, he was still sedated. She brushed his hair off his forehead. He felt a little warm. Maybe 99.4 she guessed. She smiled, "Nicholas, you scared the shit out of me. When you're awake we're going to have a conversation about your lack of words when reporting a shooting! Then the fact that you failed to tell me it was *you* bleeding to death. Grateful he was alive her tone softened. "Tough guy, if you only knew how helpless you look right now. I do like having you totally submissive for a change. It's a shame you look so vulnerable. I really was looking forward to telling you how pissed I am with you. Nicholas, don't you ever fucking do this to me again." She smoothed his covers and left. Nick was hanging in a drug induced fog but he heard every word she'd spoken. When Andy came in to check his IV she found him still out with a smile on his face.

Becky pushed Colter through the barn door. Reno took in the swastika tattoos. He knew by the set of his jaw this one wouldn't speak without some *encouragement*. Reno stepped closer matching the mans hateful gaze with one of his own. "Freddy where did you say that driveway was you saw a guy running up?"

"Back at that abandoned farm about three miles out."

Reno watched the vein in Colter's pulse faster when Freddy mentioned the abandoned farm. Reno stepped back grinning. "Freddy, take a few of the boys and see if Colter has any more friends there we haven't shot yet. How many are we up to now? Hmmm the six idiots who tried to climb the fence, the six idiots in those fucking stupid uniforms the Lady blew up, two the sisters shot and the three tonight... Seventeen dirty nazis dead. Sweet. Becky, kick this filth down in the hole."

On the way back to the veranda Charlie asks, "How?"

Reno said, "The dipshit had his name tattooed on his forearm."

Back on the veranda they found Mendez still wire and awake. Charlie asked, "Want a beer?"

Mendez said "Yes, thanks. Reno not now, but in the morning, I need you to look at the files that brought Parker and me here. We were after the members of a white supremacist group, the Tennessee Righteous. Most of them got away when we raided their farm. And a psycho killer named Axel Jones. The leader of the Tennessee Righteous has Hitler tattooed on his neck."

Reno said, "They were pretty much a pile of parts by the time I got there, but we have the footage from both cameras. I can tell you from watching it you can stop looking for the leader. The Lady took his head off with her tank."

Mendez's shock was very apparent by the way his eyes nearly popped out of their sockets. *That woman has a fucking tank? Holy Shit!"*

Reno smiled. "Yep, Sweet Audrey."

chapter 15
DREAM ON

*"What's gone is gone
But denial lives on
Things change... again"*

**4:00 am EDT, October 2,
Damascus, Virginia**

Rory sat at the table in the 'HAM
Shack' he and the ladies had cobbled
together. A whiteboard with markers sat
on an easel to the right. Last night Beth
had unearthed a box of her father's paper
maps. They stood alphabetized in a make-
shift file box at the end of the table.
While searching for the supplies Beth had
pointed out how precious paper had
suddenly become. Cindy said they would
definitely add writing supplies to the
binder. Another of DAD's boxes yielded a
cache of what looked like 100 pencils of
every length and DAD's ancient metal
crank sharpener. Cindy said it had been
screwed to the corner of his desk.

Ann picked it up, *yah of course the
screws were taped to the bottom*, she'd
packed it. "Hey Babe I owe you an
apology. I busted your chops on keeping

341

this stuff. Now these are a very hot commodity."

The sharpener now sat screwed to the corner of the table in honor of DAD who made this set-up possible. Rory absentmindedly twirled the handle. He felt they had made a lot of progress in one day but there was a laundry list yet to do to make the property secure. A group of rowdy teens banging the front gate is what had woken him. They moved on after a few minutes. A phrase from the mysterious email was running through his head. "*the sheepel, consumed by their fear, will become like rabid dogs.*" At the time he though it was hyperbole, now, not so much. He switched on the radio searching for anyone who might have information on the state of the country. He over the next hour he made contact with other HAM operators in Georgia, New Hampshire, and Kentucky. The news was really bad. He noted all the pertinent information on the chart Cindy had made and attached to a clipboard.

By 5:30 am he could hear the women in the kitchen making coffee and hopefully breakfast. Cindy came in and set a mug on the desk. She kissed him on the top of his head. "You are just the best. None of us was looking forward to starting a fire in a chilly kitchen. Ann said she was beginning to see the perks of having a man about the house. How do you want your eggs babe?"

342

Rory put his arm around her hips. "So it's my caveman skills that earn me breakfast! Over easy would be great. I've contacted a few people. They painted a shitty picture of what's happening out there. Come on I'll fill you ladies in while you make that well earned breakfast." When Rory hung out with the guys at the compound he'd slip into using certain southern verbiage like y'all and girls, but it faded once he was away from them.

In the kitchen he was greeted with a pair of thank yous for the fire. Over fresh eggs and grits he delivered the dark and unsettling news. Cindy guided the conversation toward more productive topics. He and Cindy learned the women had a pair of bunnies and five chickens out back beyond the hooped garden. Rory suggested they move the animals in at night. Ann said the roof of the back porch was the deck off their bedroom. They could build a small coop to transfer the four hens and rooster at night. Also, they should move the chicken run to the area near the back porch, where they could keep a closer eye on them. Beth said the bunnies could have a hutch in the garden room they were making. Rory suggested after breakfast they go out and really look at the yard to find their vulnerable spots. While the white picket fence was charming, it offered zero protection from anyone wanting to break into the house. The house itself was solid brick and he had confidence in the way he and Ann had recessed the shutters into the window frames, but he'd rather try to keep them from getting that close. And the garage needed reinforcing. His truck would be high on the list of things to steal.

6:00 am EDT, October 2,
Devil's Fork Gap
Smokey Mountains, Tennessee

Their friends at the compound were sitting around the table having breakfast and talking about the same things. Dan had talked to a lot of people last night after everyone else had gone to sleep. He was deeply disturbed by the reports of violence in the cities and towns. He'd talked to a guy around 1:00 am over in Mount Airy, North Carolina. He said something really bad happened in a small town south of them. A handful of townsfolk had pulled into Mount Airy around midnight. They say a mob had run through the town killing everybody. Just as the mob was talking about burning the Town Hall, a bunch of men came in and shot them all. They rescued an FBI agent that was holed up there. Folks thought it was a military team cause they were dressed in black and were very efficient the way they killed just the bad guys. The agent left with them. One agent was killed at a motel. They took his body too. There was a lot of argument about

344

who 'they' were. Had they been sent by
the government? Cause the story going
around was there isn't one.

Tracy said, "Wasn't Mendez the one
who talked to us after the murders?"

Pauline said, "Tracy I do believe
y'all are right. He was the sweet one who
liked my chocolate cake. What was the
other one's name?"

Dan answered his wife's question.
"It was Parker. I had forgotten about
them, so much shit has happened since
then. Other guys said that kinda mob
violence was breaking out everywhere.
Talked to the guy in Greensboro, North
Carolina too, he said he had to shoot two
men that were trying to break down his
front door. Said he has two new peep
holes cause he shot them right through
the door. Said the bodies were still out
on the front steps. He was too afraid
he'd be attacked trying to move them. One
guy said just leave them as a warning to
others. A woman down in Frog Pond added
that the Army had taken over the town.
Sheriff Willis didn't have much say any
more."

Frank worried, "Shit, that means we
might be safe from mobs, but who's gonna
keep us safe from the Army."

Billy offered hi well meaning if not
well founded assurances. "We are Frank.

Y'all know this is what we planned for. We have to get that list we all made done. One of the girls needs to be watchin' the cameras while we're outside so she can warn us if she see anybody comin'".

They all agreed things had reached the point where Billy was starting to make sense. The girls took turns sitting watch while the other two replaced empty water jugs and replenished the inside wood stacks. The men worked on the back fence. Their daily routine and worries had changed a hell of a lot in the last eleven days.

**6:00 am EDT, October 2,
High Above the Earth**

The astronauts on the International Space Station watched the changes on their home planet - they would most likely never set foot on again. They were amazed and horrified at how quickly the land masses were becoming smaller and whole islands vanished beneath the rising oceans. Greenland was becoming more green, Antarctica more brown. A haze of smoke hid most of the Middle East from view.

**6:00 am EDT, October 2,
Holly Springs, North Carolina**

The townspeople's had already begun to clean up the dead bodies scattered all

346

across their once charming small town.
All but a few of the faces of the dead
were known to them. Among the bodies
lying around the Town Hall were several
who were not locals. It was decided they
would bury them in a mass grave, for all
the pain and death they had brought to
their town. They were not deserving the
respect of a good Christian burial.

Many townsfolk simply sat on porches
and steps of their empty shops, overcome
with despair. Who would bring them food
and heat? The FBI agents were gone. One
of the staff that was hiding in the motel
kitchen during the attack said afterwards
the other agent and scary men in black
with very big guns had come and taken the
dead agent's body. She didn't come out
for fear they'd take her too. There were
several suicides and murder suicides that
day. Holly Spring was one of the first
towns to be abandoned that day but by no
means the the last.

6:00 am EDT, October 2,
Dancing Goats Farm
Moon Mountain, North Carolina

Andy opened the door to Nick's room.
She was not happy but neither was she
surprised to find the bed empty. She
should have given him a larger dose to
keep his ass in the bed. This was not the
first time she had to treat Nick or the
first time he'd walked out too soon.
She'd send one of the male nurses he

couldn't bully to check his stitches. He was impervious to the the female nurses' charms. He usually sent them away in tears.

Mendez was making a pot of coffee when Nick walked in. "Hey, it lives. Guessing this isn't a doctor approved discharge since you're standing here with no shirt or shoes in a pair of hospital greens that look a bit too tight."

"Good morning to you too. Save me a cup of that, I'm going to change."

Nick returned in a pair of jeans and a flannel shirt. He couldn't get his normal T shirt on with both sides of his shoulder stitched up. He poured a mug of coffee and joined Mendez at the table. "How'd you sleep?"

"Like the dead. This is a very nice setup you have for yourself here. The rest of the world has gone to hell and here we sit with fresh brewed coffee, there's even a basket of warm muffins. All this and you would have left me out there? Greed is not a nice trait in a Marine."

Nick gave him a dirty look. "How about a thank you instead of bitching like a little girl?"

Reno and Charlie came through the door. "Whoa, the Boss is in the house.

348

Andy been by to bitch at you yet? Mendez find everything okay?"

"Yes, Reno thanks for the four finger shot last night. The whiskey put me right out."

Reno poured himself a cup and joined them at the table. Charlie had already take his favorite chair at the end of the table. "Don't thank me, it's the Lady's booze and she told me to give it to you. Guess you owe her a couple a thanks now."

Charlie shook his head. "I'd wait as long as I could if I was you. She was pretty frosty with you last night. How did you put it... oh yeah, her look like to freeze you're balls off." Charlie and Reno start laughing at the Agent's discomfort.

Mendez saw Nick's grin. "Nick, what the hell are you smiling about? You weren't even here."

Trying not to laugh Nick said, "So, you got to meet the Ice Queen. Don't take it too personally. We've all had the experience before. Guessing she was pissed because I brought you here."

Charlie busted out laughing while describing the ass chewing Reno got for letting Mendez onto the farm.

Nick laughed. "Reno, I'd stay out of

her way for a day or two. She's not going to forgive that one for long while."

Charlie asked, "Mendez, why don't you show us that file you mentioned last night?"

While Mendez went to retrieve the file. Charlie and Reno filled Nick in on everything that had happened since he'd been shot. Reno held off sending anyone to the abandoned farm until he talked to Nick. Nick told him to wait until they saw what Mendez had. Mendez dropped a two inch thick folder on the table and sifted through it to find the photos. Reno picked out Hale, Ethan, Bubba and Big John right off.

Charlie asked, "Damn, how many times did you watch that recording?"

Smirking Reno said, "A... few dozen. The sisters taking out the first two was a thing of beauty. You would have thought they were a trained strike team the way the three of them moved in unison. Lizzy slid the Glocks into their hands like a pro. The fact that they knew she had them to give, is a mystery I can't figure out. I checked the footage from the front camera, Lizzy never says a word. Sadie's little sidestep to correct her stance is so fucking smooth. I can't quite make out everything Violet says to make the guy with the gun on the girl turn but I'm pretty sure she calls him a twat-waffle.

350

Fucking Sadie, as the guy turns she says 'Yes please' then puts one in his heart. At the same instant Violet nails the other bastard between the eyes. They're really hot to watch in action. If you want to see the *Ice Queen*, watch the Lady's face when she tells Tiny to fire. Now *that'll freeze your balls off!* She doesn't bat an eye as she blows six men to scraps. A second later she was firing off orders like Nick."

Mendez looked at Nick. He answered his friend's unasked questions. "What can I say, I trained the sisters well. The Lady was already a bad ass when I found her." The back door banged open. Nick thought 'Speak her name and she appears'.

Gianna stepped into the kitchen. Reno thought the temperature dropped ten degrees from the icy stare. She pointed toward the front door. "*You three out.*" She once they're gone Nick feels to brunt of her rage. Her voice is raspy as she leans over the table. "Nicholas, in case you haven't noticed the world is coming down around our ears. I'm a little fucking busy trying to keep it from crushing us. For some God forsaken reason you seem to feel *Right Now, Right Fucking Now* is the time to make my life a living broiling hell!" Her palm hits the table so hard the coffee cups jump. Nick is expressionless as he watches her tirade. "Clearly you've forgotten what *I* had to do yesterday morning because you were off visiting your little *friend.* Then the *whole fucking farm* had to suffer through your temper tantrum. As if YOU had been the one who had to kill the bad guys. As if *that* wasn't enough shit for me to deal with. You leave me *again* and take *my* men, *my* equipment and *my* ammunition on a dangerous rescue mission for the same dam *friend* you left me for in the earlier... without asking or without even telling me you were going! If the fucking bat phone hadn't gone off would you even have woken me when you came back bleeding to death? Now, I have Antonio on light duty, DJ will be down for a week at least. Then there's you... The man in charge of keeping us safe... almost dies." She was shaking with rage.

Nick suddenly realized what was at the heart of this explosion... 'She thought I was going to die".

"You don't even have the-the-oh I don't know! You won't even stay in the *God damn infirmary!*" Spun around looking around for something to throw.

Nick was out of the chair at her back, as her fingers closed around the French press. He circled her waist with his arm and his hand closed firmly around hers holding it still. He whispered in her ear "Breath Gia... close your eyes and just breath... everything is alright. I'm not dead. I'm right here. I've got you." He held her until her breathing slowed. When she released the pot he guided her to a chair. "SIT and keep breathing." He should have realized the events of yesterday have struck at the heart of her abandonment issues. He really should have spoken to her before he left, coming back shot only exacerbated the situation. He also should have gone to see her first when he left the infirmary. She probably went there when she got up. Finding him gone is what sent her over the edge. Nick sat across from her and took her hands and looked in her eyes. There are tears threatening that she is fighting back. "I'm sorry I wasn't here for you. Gia I'm sorry I frightened you." Someone started to open the front door, Nick bellowed, "NOT NOW". If anyone sees her like this she *will kill* him. No one is allowed to see Gia vulnerable but him. No one can get away with calling her Gia but him. They sit while she reels in her temper and gets her emotions under control.

When she was calmer he got up and poured himself another cup of coffee. "I'm glad you didn't throw this at me, Mendez makes a mean cup of coffee it'd be a sin to waste it." Sitting he sees there's a smile she's fighting. "So, I hear you scared the shit out of my *friend* and tore into Reno, you *did* have a busy night. But... was there a costume party I didn't get invited to?"

This time she did throw something.

One of the muffins hits him in the chest the crumbs fall into his coffee. "Fuck you Lorenzini."

Knowing it will irritate her, he ignores the muffin. "I was wondering, do I get my leather back or is it now a permanent part last nights new fashion statement?"

The treat of tears gone she narrows her eyes. Dripping sarcasm she bated him back. "Just for that smart ass remark I'm keeping it. You'll have to buy a new one... Oh... wait... the world has gone to hell and the stores are all trashed. Poor Nicky will have to go without his jacket. Didn't Reno tell you about me running bare assed through the farm last night - he knows what happened... with my outfit."

Nick made a mental note to knock Reno on his ass for forgetting to include that tidbit in he report. He knew she was thinking she'd won this round... not by a long shot woman, "Gia I think you should know... the last thing on my mind, when they put me under knowing I might never wake up... was the image of you in my leather jacket and those very sexy French Knickers. Gianna would have died a happy man."

She leaned back, crossed her arms. "Keep it up *Nick*. I'm going to stab you in your fucking stitches with that spoon." Nicks reply was thwarted by a knock at the front door. Gianna leaned her chair back to see who it was. "Come on Charlie. The storm has passed."

Charlie walked in and looked at Nick with crumbs stuck in his chest hair , muffin still all down his shirt. He looked at Gianna. "You should have called me, I would've brought you a rock. That's a waste of a good muffin. Next time call me." Knowing there would definitely be a next time... their disagreements were just part of life on the farm.

Nick was pissed at the interruption. "What is it you want Charlie, beside offering to arm people who want to assault me?"

Gianna narrowed her eyes at Nick. "Don't start picking on *Charlie* now just because you lost!"

Nick raised an eyebrow, "They always take your side. I think that means they're more afraid of you than they are of me."

Gianna laughed. "As they should be. They're not fools like someone else I know."

Charlie shook his head at the two of them. "While I'd love to stand here and see who wins this battle of repartee, I have a pressing issue in the barn that needs addressing. Nick, you know that rat Reno told you about, well it's dead and its stinking up the barn."

Nick and Gianna stood in unison and headed to the barn. Charlie and Gianna were walking ahead of Nick. Charlie leaned toward Gianna. "Ma'am I do believe you were winning in there."

"That's because you're a smart man Charlie."

Reno and Mendez hid from the Gianna storm downstairs in the com room going over the footage of the snot-zi take-down. Mendez was amused by the sisters' name for the group. Parker would have liked it to. *Damn, he was a good partner.* Rick was going to miss him. With the help of the footage Mendez found all the Tennessee Righteous he was looking for. He's very happy to see Axel's face in the crowd that Gianna tanked. He didn't like the thought of that bastard out in this world with no one to stop him. He could mark the case as closed, not that there was an FBI office to report it to. They couldn't hear what was being said in the kitchen, just loud muffled shouting and banging. Mendez asked Reno if they were a couple.

Reno said "Yeah, a couple of maniacs."

"I got that, but are they sleeping

together?"

Reno shrugged. "Nobody knows for sure either way. *Nobody* has the balls to ask either one of them. Last night I thought I knew. She went white as a ghost when Charlie said Nick was shot and needed blood, but then she didn't hang around while he was in surgery. Now he's sitting there with a hole in his chest and she's up there throwing a bitch of a fit. So nope, don't know. They do fight like a married couple. Some times I'm sure they're flirting, then... I just can't say for sure. Even Charlie doesn't know. He's been with them almost since the beginning. What I do know, is Nick has killed and will again to keep her safe, but that goes both ways. If he'd been trapped last night, she would have led the team to rescue him. If they'd killed him she would've taken Audrey and blown the town off the map. They are unbelievably loyal to each other." Reno heard them leave. "I'd say it's safe to go up now."

Gianna and Nick found Reno and Mendez in the kitchen when they return. Gianna started to turn and leave, Nick firmly grasped her upper arm, and squeezes it so she stops resisting. " Rick, this is the Lady of the house. Ma'am this is Agent Rick Mendez also known as Sergeant Mendez of the United States Marine Corps. Why don't we sit so you two can get to know each other. Reno, make more coffee. I think the Lady could use a cup." Nick pulled out her chair for her. When she was seated he whispered in her ear, "We need to settle this, there's a war outside our gates. It won't do to have one in here too."

Gianna pushed Nick away. "*Fine.*" She gave him one of her 'shut the fuck up' looks "Do you prefer to be called Sergeant, Agent or Mendez?"

"Ma'am, I prefer Rick."

Gianna gave him one of her 'don't even thing about fucking with me' looks."Well then *Rick* it is." Nick shot Mendez a look that said, 'don't fuck with her'.

Reno suddenly gets the feeling the storm is still winding down. He's thinking about leaving when Nick says "Take a seat Reno." To Gianna Nick, "*Ma'am*, as we discussed earlier, I have failed to fully explain Agent Mendez's situation. He and his partner were stranded in Holly Springs when the EMP hit. They had no firepower to speak of, remedying that situation was the purpose of my *unfortunately timed* trip yesterday. I don't remember if I told you that Rick and I did a tour together."

Reno knew Nick was doing this to irritate her, he just couldn't figure out why he was pulling the cat's tail.

continued, "As it turns out, the men you killed, with *your tank*, are the men Rick and his partner were looking for."

Gianna held up an index finger signaling Nick to stop talking. "Reno would you be a dear and pass me that spoon so I can stab Nick with it?" She turned to Nick, *"As we discussed earlier*... now, are you going to stop, or do you want me to stab you? Front or back stitches, you choose, can't decide which would be more painful?" She spied a spoon next to Mendez and snatched it up.

Nick grabbed her wrist and removed the spoon from her fingers with his other hand. He leaned almost nose to nose with her. "OK, no throwing or stabbing, you win... *But... it could have been the last image...*" She punched him in his shoulder before he could utter another word.

Gianna turn to Mendez who was sitting there with his mouth open. "Close your mouth *Rick*. I hit the side of his shoulder the front stitches are fine. More importantly, we've kept this place a secret for a decade. *No one* comes in here I haven't vetted. *I don't care if you have Semper Fi tattooed across your ass!* Everyone has to be approved by me. Reno knows that or at lest I *thought* he did." Reno was looking at Nick's grip on her wrist. He's starting to leave a mark.

Gianna looked up at Nick, "Do you want to go another round tough guy?" Nick stopped squeezing but kept his hand there. She turned back to Mendez. "That should explain my attitude toward you. That and Nick wasn't here and *I* had to kill all the bad guys it's just all the things..." She took a breath and let it out slowly. "So what is it *you* want from me?" Mendez was taken back by the question. An hour ago he thought he wanted to stay but now...

At his hesitation she asked, "*Rick*, have I explained it sufficiently? Do you understand you *will* follow every order I give you, yes or no?"

Mendez looked at Nick. He couldn't tell if he's smiling or just in pain? 'What the fuck, why not. What better option do I have?' "Yes ma'am."

"You'll have to fill out some forms with Tiny. Forget about saying no. Only two people here haven't filled them out and that includes my daughters and nieces."

"Who are the two?"

"That's a stupid question... hopefully your last. Nick and myself. Reno, is the scheduling as I asked?" Reno nodded yes. "Good then take the trash out, and let me know what they find at the farm house. I want to annex that in

360

the next few days. Chain link fencing will do. Oh and get Mendez to Tiny. After he's finished have the sergeant get him set up in the barracks." The Mendez problem situation hopefully resolved she turned to Nick. "You can keep checking my pulse while we walk." Nick smiled. "What? Did you think, I didn't know what you were doing? Come on GI, you me go infirmary. Your stitches are bleeding in the back. I'll even let you tell Andy I punched you and made you bleed so she doesn't yell at you. Mendez, close your mouth. I saw the blood on the back of his shirt when we were in the barn. I am the *Queen of Cunts* but generally, not to Nick." At the door she yelled to Reno, "Reno, explain the Hotel California clause to him."

Reno grinned, "She forgot to mention you can check out any time you like...But..."

chapter 16
MURDER BY NUMBER

*"No big thing,
we just took them out
one, two, three."*

7:30 am EDT, October 2,
Dancing Goats Farm
Moon Mountain, North Carolina

Nick wasn't ready to let *things* drop. "So you were just going to let me bleed to death at the kitchen table? You know, when I saw you in those knickers I thought, the Ice Queen might have retired. My leather, that lace around you knees, well... the thoughts running"

She stopped and pulled him around to face her. Inches from his face she hissed, "Stop it. Just fucking stop it. Everything is a big fucking joke to you. Why are you're such an asshole? I should never have snatched up those stupid clothes as I ran out of the house. I should have just arrived there naked! I'm sure whoever was on guard here last night caught me running bare assed across the yard. Now I'll have to deal with that! I never should have gone at all. I should

362

have stayed in my nice warm bed. Clearly I should not given a fucking that you were running off to get yourself killed! From now on I'm going to be more like you. Not give a shit and treat everything like a big fucking joke." With that Gianna stormed off.

Across the yard both pairs of sisters were coming from breakfast and caught the heated exchange. Sadie said, "Holy shit, look at mom and Nick."

Alexandra said "If he kisses her, we'll know. Do either of you two know?"

Violet said, "Ahhh... really don't want to discuss my mother's sex life."

Sadie said, "I don't know if they are having sex."

Amber finished what she was chewing. "She told me they're not."

Alexandra turned to her sister. "She told you? You asked Auntie if she was sleeping with Nick? No shit."

"Yes, I did. I wanted to know if I should hook Nick up with someone so I asked her."

Vylet threw her hands up. "I'm leaving. I'm not standing here listening to you two. It's gross."

363

Sadie asks, "What did she say?"

"She said they had agreed it would
be best if they didn't. BUT they enjoy
the game so definitely do not hook him up
with anyone."

Having gotten her answer Sadie ran
off to catch up with her sister.
Alexandra said, "So it's a mind fuck they
have going on... *cool*."

Nick knows he's gone too far again.
'What the fuck am I doing?' Lately he
finds himself pushing her right to the
edge on everything. She's gone off
obviously he'd hurt her. He should go
after her and fix this, but the blood is
drying. The shirt is sticking to the
stitches. Because he doesn't know why
he's behaving this way he chooses the
infirmary over Gia.

Inside the infirmary Andy read him
the riot act. It hurts like hell when she
peeled the shirt and the dressing off.
She has to add a few more stitches. She
tried to give him a local for the pain;
he says no. She tells him it's going to
hurt. "Yes I know,just get it over with."

10:00 am EDT, October 2,
Devil's Fork Gap
Smokey Mountains, Tennessee

Betty Lou was sitting in front of
the monitors when she saw a group of

people coming up the driveway. She grabbed the radio. "Billy, Dan, Frank, can any of y'all hear me? There are people comin' up the drive." She ran to find Pauline and Tracy repeating the message into the radio as she searched Tracy has gone off with the men into the woods for another tree. Pauline heard Betty Lou's radio call. Pauline grabbed her rifle and handed one to Betty Lou. She told her to go back to the monitor and report what they are doing. Betty Lou catches sight of the monitor. "Pauline, they're bangin' on the gate1"

Pauline pressed the talk button on the intercom to the gate. "Y'all best get back down the way ya came. There's nothin' here for y'all now git!"

One of them pressed the talk button. Pauline can hear them talking among themselves. "It's just a woman. Go around front I'll keep her busy. How does this thing work?"

Pauline said, "Just a woman with 26 medals for sharp shooting since I was a girl. I will shoot you."

Betty Lou says "Three are comin' around to the front."

Pauline slid the glass door open quietly and stepped out on to the balcony. She can hear them talking. They spotted the generator. One is helping the

other one over the wall. Then he reached
down and pulled the other two up. As they
jump down inside the yard. Pauline fired
a warning shot at their feet. Betty Lou
came running.

The three men started laughing. "She
totally missed us." Two pulled out hand
guns.

Before they can raise them Pauline
hits the closest one in the chest, before
he hits the ground the second one takes
one in the head. The third one put his
hands up and got on his knees. Pauline
lowered her rifle. Betty Lou sees
movement out of the corner of her eye.
She turned to see the forth one standing
on the wall taking aim at Pauline's back.
Then there's a shot and he fell backward.
Pauline spun around to see Betty Lou with
her rifle still pointing to where the guy
had been standing. Pauline gently raises
the barrel of the gun up and backed Betty
Lou into the kitchen. "Turn it loose,
Betty, I'll take it. Y'all sit. The shots
will bring them runnin'." Pauline stood
the rifles in the corner checking the
safeties are on. She turned back to her
friend. "Girl y'all just saved my life. I
had no idea y'all could shoot so well."

"Me neather. I don't even remember
liftin' the rifle just seein' him in the
sight and squeezin' the trigger like
y'all taught me."

She can hear the others pounding up the stairs. Pauline watched the last intruder scrambling over the wall. 'Good riddance' she thinks. Pauline tells them all to calm down, that everything is just fine. Well *not everything;* there are three dead men in the yard. Then she told them how Betty Lou saved her life. When she got to the end everyone was staring at Betty Lou.

Betty Lou stood up, she says kinda cocky like, "No big thing, we just took them out one, two, three."

12:00 pm EDT, October 2, Damascus, Virginia

Beth and Cindy made great progress in the basement. The shelves with the food were neat and labeled. Cindy put a clipboard there to check off what was removed to make keeping track easier. Then they organized the tool section. Rory put up three crossbars across the door just to be safe. Ann put up a new run for the chickens off the back porch. They found Ann had stashed four 2'x 4'x 12's in the rafters. They turned them into crossbars for the garage bay doors. Then they screwed the bay doors closed on the inside and put a padlock on the side entrance. After lunch they planned to reinforce the door. On the front porch Ann had drilled a hole through the brick to run the power cord through from the generator. They would have to wheel it in

367

and out when they used it but it was the best they could do for now.

Rory had give a lot of thought on how to secure the front line. The property was about an acre. The sides and back had chain link fencing. When they bought the place, Beth thought it was ugly so they had stockade fencing put up along the inside perimeter. It looked better and gave their guests privacy if they wanted to sunbath. It was the 80' of 4' high picket fence that troubled Rory. He needed a barricade. Over lunch they talked about the danger of having the generator outside after dark. It was decided to make their radio time for a half hour after lunch every day. As Rory wheeled the generator onto the porch he saw a group of five ragged people moving down the street. As he watched them he realized across the street there was scrub pine and brambles growing a mile in each direction. It wouldn't be fun work but he didn't see another option. He'd talk to Ann later while they worked on the door.

They gathered in the front room to hear the news. Beth and Ann snuggled on the love seat. Cindy curled up in the overstuffed chintz arm chair. Rory talked to some of the same people he had spoken with in the morning. The news was getting more grim. Small pockets of people were banding together and metering out justice as they saw fit. A group in Vermont had

executed six people they suspected of
looting. Similar stories came in from
around the country. One guy was talking
about two women in the mountains of
Tennessee who had just killed three armed
men that broke into their compound. This
perked up Rory and Cindy's ears. Rory
didn't use the radio much at the compound
so he didn't know Frank's call letters.
The guy told Rory what the letters were
and what frequency he'd talked to Frank
on. Frank was relieved to hear Rory's
voice and even happier to learn they were
safe. Rory filled Frank in on their new
friends in Damascus. Cindy laughed her
ass off when she heard about Betty Lou.
She told Frank, "Tell Betty Lou I said
'You go Girl'." They agreed to check in
every day at 1:00 pm and signed off.
While they worked on the afternoon
chores, each wondered when they'd have to
shoot someone.

5:00 pm EDT, October 2,
Dancing Goats Farm
Moon Mountain, North Carolina

After the blow up outside the
infirmary Gianna made it clear to Charlie
she was in charge until further notice.
Charlie called Gianna to let her know the
men were back with a report on the old
farm. Rather than take her normal route
through the house, walked around it. She
did not want speak to Nick or even see
him. She didn't have time for his crap.
She had to keep her head in both jobs

369

now.

From his bedroom window Nick watched
her make her way to the barn. He had gone
by her house after Andy stitched him up.
The door was locked. If she didn't want
to deal with people she hung a 'The Queen
wishes not to be disturbed' sign on the
doorknob. This did not bode well for
their relationship. In ten years her door
had never been locked to him. She'd told
him to get the fuck out at least twice
but never had she locked the door. Of all
times for them not be speaking this was
the worst. Reno hadn't gotten the
Gianna's in charge memo. He'd given Nick
the report on what they'd found at the
old farm first. Nick told him to make the
report to her since she'd sent him. Nick
watched to see how she'd deal with this
clusterfuck without him before he offered
to help. Evidently Reno wasn't the only
one who hadn't gotten the memo.

Lined up against the wall were two
men, a woman and two children. They taken
from the old farm house. They were filthy
and refused to speak to Charlie or Reno.
Reno told Gianna he'd found nazi shit
scattered about one bedroom in the house.
Gianna sent Gabe to find Mendez. She
called Violet, she needed her to come and
take the children to the Q's farmhouse.
While she waited, Reno told her about the
property and the house and barn. It would
need hundreds of feet of fencing they
could no longer buy. Gianna told him they

would get back to this after she dealt with the prisoners.

Sadie arrived with her sister. Gabe and Mendez were right behind them. The children didn't want to go with the sisters. Gianna walked up to Sally Anne and looked her up and down. "Your children are filthy. They need food and a warm bath and clean clothing. I don't give a shit what their mother's political views are, they're children who need to be cared for. If you love your children you should tell them to go and eat. These are my daughters. *I* would do whatever it took keep them fed and warm. What the fuck is more important to you, your ideology or you children? I give you my word woman to woman they will not be harmed or questioned except for do you want peanut butter & jelly or ham and cheese. It would be nice if we had a first name so we don't have to call them child."

Sally Anne looked at the two women. Lord knew her babies needed food and cleaning. "Jimmy and May, you go with the ladies, they're gonna give you food and let you wash up. Maybe get you some clean clothes. Go on now, mind them."

Gianna added as they left, "Violet, call Simon and have him make up soup and bread for five I'll send Gabe for it. Sadie find them clothes, thank you ladies." After the children were out of earshot Gianna turned back to the adults. "I don't wage war against children, but make no mistake, you come after what's mine or my people and I will give you a war. Reno, free her hands and get her a chair." Gianna walked over to where Mendez was waiting. "Are any of these people in your folder?" His eyebrow went up at the mention of his FBI file. Gianna leaned in, her voice went raspy. "Learn now, there is fuck little that happens on these thousand acres I don't know about. I'm waiting?..."

"I don't have photos on all of Tennessee Righteous members. She may be the wife of one of the men we picked up in the raid. Without a name I can't tell you if we're looking for her. Same goes for the two men."

Becky entered the barn and handed Gianna three driver licenses. "Found these when we search the men. Hers was in a purse in the house ma'am." Gianna handed them to Mendez.

Begrudgingly Mendez said, "She's James Blaylock's wife. We busted him driving the truck loaded with guns and drugs. I don't know what kind of law there is in Tennessee now but my guess is the Army is in charge. Not seeing him getting out any time soon. I got nothing on her or the other two."

"Reno, will a full tank of gas in

the Le Sabre get them to Tennessee? And will that car make it there?"

"Yes ma'am, a tank should do it and the car is in good shape. Might want to check the oil."

"Make it happen. Reno put five gallons in the trunk. I don't want a woman and two kids stuck on the side of the road."

From his perch Nick watched Gabe cross the yard with the food.

"Cut them loose so they can eat." Gianna walked back to Mendez. "Do you have your credentials with you and something with the FBI letterhead and maybe the seal?"

"I'm sure I have all of that. Why?"

Gianna ignored his question. "Charlie, take the agent to get the things I've asked for. Take the items to Adrian. I'll call him with instructions."

Mendez went all FBI Agent and in the wrong tone of voice said, "I'm not going to just hand over my..."

Gianna cut his protest off in mid sentence. "I don't *need* your bullshit. Nor do I *need* your paperwork. It's just faster to copy documents than it is to forge them from scratch. A few hours ago

373

you agreed to follow my orders. Now the first one I give you is met with refusal? I thought Marines were men of their word." She narrowed her eyes and got in his face. "You can give me your papers so I can send these people back to where they came from or... Reno give me your side arm. Or you can take this and put a bullet in each of their heads while they eat their soup. Your call, *Rick*."

Mendez stared into her eyes, they cold and give nothing away. He knew he didn't want to shoot 3 people. "I'll get them." Gianna handed Reno his gun. She saw the question in Reno's eyes. "He made the right choice. If he'd made the wrong one I would have shot him."

Nick studied the look on Mendez's face. Evidently he's not happy with what transpired in the barn. Nick considered she might be taking her displeasure with him out on Mendez, but why call him there at all?

"Reno, they're not going to like what I have to say. Please be ready if they take it badly." Gianna walked back to the prisoners. "I have spoken to FBI Agent Mendez. He tells me he knows of no warrants out on any of you. I do not want you people in my state. I have several options open to me. I can have my men shoot you and dump your bodies with those of the assholes who showed up here in SS uniforms and stupidly attacked us. Or I could put you in my jail and keep you there until you die. Or, and this is the option you really should take, I will give you the Le Sabre with a tank of gas and send you back to Tennessee. My men will escort you north of Mount Airy to the state line. I will give you documents from the FBI giving you passage to Tennessee. If you are ever stupid enough to come back to this state, you will be shot on sight. Reno, what were the names of the assholes I blew up?"

"I believe Bubba, Hale, Ethan, Axel, the one last night was Colter ma'am, but we shot him. Do you want me to get the rest of the names?"

"No, I think those will do. What's it going to be Sally Anne?"

Sally Anne looked her captor. She may be wrong to trust her but for her babies she had to. "My children and I accept your offer."

"What do you two have to say?" Ash said yes ma'am. Mick wasn't so smart. He snarled a nasty string of insults, he'd clearly learned from Hale, at Gianna and her multi-racial men. Gianna smiled, "Sergeant Jackson put that dog down." The last thing Mick saw was the brilliant white smile on Sergeant Jackson's very black face. To Sally Anne and Ash she said "That should make it crystal clear that I'm not fucking around. Cross me and you'll end up like him." She turned to Reno, "Give them each a blanket, let them get some sleep. Becky, when the car is ready load their shit in the trunk."

"Ma'am we found a 38 special in her purse along with several rifles in the house."

"Show them the rifles. Which one is yours?" They each pointed. "They can have them back at the border. A woman needs to be able to defend her children." On her way out of the barn she said "Sergeant Jackson, get that garbage out of our barn."

"With pleasure ma'am, and thank you ma'am."

Nick heard the shot. This not being out of the loop was starting to really piss him off. He watched her walk toward the house. He moved to the hall to try to find out what she's up to. All he caught are bits of the conversation.

"Violet, where are the children?"

"We're in here, mother."

Gianna smiles at the frightened children. "Oh my, what lovely clean children. Have my girls been treating you well? I see they found you some chocolate cake and ice cream. Your mom had something to eat and she's resting. As soon as you're ready you may go back to her. You're going on a road trip back to Tennessee. Violet, please go to the kitchen and make a to-go supper for two children and two adults. Make sure there's milk in there for them. Now I have to see Adrian about forging some FBI documents. Crap, I have to talk to Reno again. I'll go down and call Adrian."

In the com room she called the Shack. "Adrian, did you get the package from Charlie? Bit of a change - Mick won't be joining them. Just something that will get them home to Tennessee. Put Mendez's name on it. How long will it take? I do love when you read my mind. Have Ferret bring them over to the Q kitchen when they're done. Thank you darling."

Sadie met her at the top of the stairs. "They're ready to see their mom. I'll clean up in here and head back and give Vy a hand. By kids, have a good trip."

Gianna walked the children back to the barn. Nick's shoulder was throbbing, adding to his frustration of not being involved. 'What are you up to woman? Forging FBI documents? No wonder Mendez didn't look happy. Since when do we feed prisoners Simon's food? Where the hell are you taking them?' Nick watched Becky bring the Le Sabre around to the barn. Charlie crosses the yard. 'I'm not cut

out to be a voyeur. How pissed could she
be if I show up to her party uninvited?'
Nick decides against finding out.
Another thirty minutes passed then Ferret
crossed to the barn. 'What the hell?...'
Minutes tick by, his irritation continued
to grow. 'What the fuck are you up to
woman?' He watched Gianna put the
children in the car, Sally and Ash
follow. Sadie ran across the yard with a
bag she put in the back seat. At 8:00 pm
Pepe pulled out the gate; the Le Sabre
followed and Dark Lady brought up the
rear. Sadie and Ferret cross the yard and
disappeared around the house. Another
fifteen minutes crawl by. At last Gianna
and Charlie leave the barn she goes
around the house.

Inside the farmhouse Charlie yelled,
"Boss you up?"

Nick walked into the kitchen. "Yes
I'm up! Who could sleep with all that
shit going on out there? What the fuck
happened out there? Who got shot? Where
are they going? What the hell is she up
to?"

Charlie pretended to be looking at
something on the floor. It would not do
for him to be laughing at the Boss in his
state of mind. "The Lady sent me in here
to give you a full report. Do you want me
to answer your questions first or give it
to you in the order it happened?"

10:00 pm EDT, October 2, Damascus, Virginia

Rory was lying in bed thinking about his barrier. Cindy had just drifted off when he heard voices in the yard. Rory jumped out of bed jolting Cindy awake. "Babe, there's someone on the property go get Ann tell her to bring her shotgun. Rory raced down the stairs rifle in hand. With the porch windows boarded he can't see how many there are. It sounded like four or five. He can hear the women coming down the stairs. He whispers, "Ann, I'm going out the kitchen. You go out the front door. Just don't shoot me when I come chasing them down the drive." Outside Rory wonders, 'Why didn't I put shoes on?' He worked his way around to the side of the house. There are five of them trying to pry open the garage door. 'Not my truck you fuckers.' He shoots the one farthest away in the back. The other four turn and one pulls a gun. Roy shoots him in the leg and he goes down. The other three start running. Ann is at the edge of the porch when she sees one of them stop running, turn and fire at Rory. He's so close to her the twelve gauge takes half of his arm off. "That's what you get for try to rob us!" She turned and fired at the last two as they jump over the fence. One of them got hung up on the fence for a few seconds. He was screaming, "Help me, my balls are caught!" He fells the other would-be

379

robber helped him run.

When the gunshots stopped Cindy flew around the house looking for Rory. She found him still standing and rubbing his arm. "Rory are you hit? Let me see."

Beth came up behind them with a flashlight. "Here Cindy."

Cindy ripped his shirt "It's literally a scratch. Oh thank God."

"Where is my wife? Ann?"

Out of the darkness she hears, "I'm fine. Just went down to the fence to see if he'd left his balls hanging there. Thought I'd hang then on the gate with a warning sign. But he took them with him. Too bad."

The one shot in the back is dead. Cindy looked at the one with the leg wound "Leave him, you hit the femoral artery. He'll bleed out shortly. Don't waste the bullet. Would one of you shut the other one up please." Rory obliges his girl.

Ann scanned the yard. "Hopefully the two that got away will warn people about coming here. All in all I'd say three out of five isn't a bad night's work."

10:00 pm EDT, October 2,
Dancing Goats Farm

Moon Mountain, North Carolina

Gianna was running as fast as her legs can carry her. She slams through the farmhouse and out the front door. Nick had been dozing when the crashing of doors and pounding of feet across the old wooden floor wakes him with a start. He pushed the intercom to downstairs. "What the hell is going on?"

"The escort was ambushed-they're trying to outrun them. They're taking heavy fire." Nick ran downstairs to the veranda. Gianna was standing barefoot in the center of the yard shouting orders. The gates open. Men tooks up a positions on the far side of the road. She shouts to open the barn in case there are wounded. Nick watches her take the tower steps two at a time. She takes the Glock from the spotter in the tower. Carmichael is in the hay loft. Twenty regulars flood the yard. They can hear semi-automatic bursts from down the road. Thirty seconds later Pepé slid through the gate and stopped in front of the veranda. The Dark Lady is right behind. She plows through the barn to the infirmary. The men in the ditch begin firing at the attackers. They hit the driver who flips their truck. The six survivors are yanked from the road. They're marched in to the yard and made to kneel.

Gianna walked up the line of prisoners. "Whose idea was it to attack my men?" One of the prisoners says something Nick can't hear. Gianna turned, walked back to him, and put a bullet in his head. "Cowards, all of you. And very very stupid. Anyone who comes after my people comes after me. You're not worth wasting my ammunition on. Kill them all... *with their own guns.*"

The shots ring out behind her, she walks up to Freddy and hands him the gun she took from the spotter. Nick can see the blood spatter across her nightgown. Nick runs back upstairs for shoes and a shirt - he should be out there for her. From upstairs he sees her talking to Charlie. As Nick is turning from the window he realizes there is a person standing across the road in the shadows. No one on the ground sees him. The figure takes aim at Gianna's back, Nick fumbles with the window, as he gets it opened the figure's head explodes. From the hay loft Carmichael says, "I got your 6 ma'am."

Without missing a step Gianna replies, "I know you do, babe. Okay let's get that truck upright and inside. Let's lock this down NOW. We may have attracted attention. Q this place up." She and Charlie walk into the house. "I'm going to see the four in the infirmary. Four more men down. Charlie, this fucking shit has to stop. Close this down fast Charlie. Send Reno to me there. I want to know what happened tonight." Nick started down the stairs, he can see the blood spatter is also on her hand and arm. She either doesn't see him or doesn't *want* to. She walks out the back door.

Charlie does see him. "You picked a hell of a time to be out of action Boss." Charlie looked toward the back door and shook his head. "I hope that fucking FBI agent was worth it. *This* isn't her job. It was never supposed be her job. Her defending the front gate wasn't part of the plan Nick!" Charlie left to make the Lady's orders happen before he said something he couldn't take back.

chapter 17
BOHEMIAN RHAPSODY

*"A word about killing men
and liking it...
We find the rumors are true"*

**1:00 am EDT, October 3,
Damascus, Virginia**

On the balcony outside their bedroom Ann inhaled the cool night air as she contemplates the events that brought her here. She killed a man tonight and liked it. She had savored the taste of vengeance as she and Rory dragged the bodies of the three intruders behind the garage. Now, hours removed, she rolled it across her tongue again. Yes, it still thrilled her. She had wondered what they meant when they said the sweet taste of revenge. Now she knew. She questioned whether it had always been there buried deep below the layers of civility. She thought she should at least consider the morality of the act and then perhaps her new moral guidelines, which seem to have revised themselves with no conscious effort on her part.

The world had disintegrated and it's former moral code was now grossly out of step with the current state of the world. Ya, she was going with that. There was no need for hours of self-examination or self-flagellation. The world had changed and if she and Beth were to survive, she needed to change too. What wouldn't she do for the woman she loved? Now, she knew the answer with absolute certainty: not a fucking thing.

She must remember to thank Rory and Cindy for coming into their lives. Without their knowledge she and Beth would not have the grasp they now had on their ability to survive. Without them, she would not have learned just how sweet the taste of revenge could be.

3:00 am EDT, October 3,
Devil's Fork Gap
Smokey Mountains, Tennessee

Betty Lou had enjoyed all the attention yesterday. For the first time she felt like a valued member of the household. She had never known the thrill of her husband beaming with pride at being her husband. It certainly made a difference in bed tonight. 'Who knew killing a man could make you so sexy? Maybe she should have shot someone sooner. Whatever was happening to her? Good Christian woman such as herself would never have harbored such a thought before yesterday.' She needed to talk to

Pauline about this today.

Pauline didn't seem ruffled by the fact that she killed two men. She had taken it with a sense of pride when Frank had hugged and kissed her calling her his little sharp shootin' honey. She had watched through the window as the men dragged the bodies out to the woods. She did not feel sorry for them in the least. Simply glad they wouldn't be stinking up the yard. Tracy had told her she didn't know how Betty found the nerve. Tracy didn't know if she could take a person's life. Betty Lou told her shootin' a mans' gun out of his hand was a real tricky shot. She better learn to be a better shot if she just wanted to wound her attacker. Otherwise she'd be the one who got dead.

6:30 am EDT, October 3,
Dancing Goats Farm
Moon Mountain, North Carolina

Charlie wondered how long this feud between the Nick and the Lady was going to go on. There had been one time they didn't speak directly for a month. But that was more like another form of the game they'd been playing, as long as he'd been here. Sometimes it got a little rough but it simmered down after a day or two. This was different. They would always drop the pretense if a situation threatened the farm or it's people. The world was pounding at our door. The Lady had to do some hard shit the last few days. Things that were not her job. What made this place work was that she and Nick were an unstoppable team. She'd stepped up and done what had to be done. No matter how last night ended, she'd made the right call. *'We don't wage war on children'*.

Last night had cost her. He'd seen it in her eyes as she handed the gun to Freddy. It had to be done. The men needed to know she could do what she asked them to do. Now they would follow her anywhere. 'If this thing between her and Nick went bad she could and would lead them, but at what cost to her?' He didn't know what had happened so he couldn't offer advice. She had shut down in the yard. He had asked her if she was okay and she snapped at him. "Why wouldn't I be okay? A job had to be done and I did it. Keep your mind on the job Charles!" Nick wasn't any better. He was beyond speaking about it. He let Charlie know the topic was not open for discussion. At her back door Charlie could hear *"Bohemian Rhapsody"* blasting. He let himself in because she was right there with her back to him and couldn't hear him banging.

She saw Charlie out of the corner of her eye and reached for the music remote. "Good morning Charlie, how are the men this morning? Do we have a damage report on equipment and the buildings? I've been down to the infirmary already. Everyone is doing as well as can be expected. It breaks my heart to know my orders put them there." She paused then hit the counter with her fist. "Well no more. Fuck everyone else my people come first screw the rest of humanity. Coffee, honey?"

"Yes, ma'am, I could use a second cup." It was worse than he thought. One or two more days like yesterday and she was going to slip over the edge and turn into Nick. He wasn't going to watch that happen without as least trying to reach one or both of them first. Charlie gave her the answers to her questions. He added a few things he felt she needed to know. Then they got around to the farm they found the nazis at.

"Let's hold off on that for now. My thinking was to make it a safe house for people who show up at the gate. Last night showed me I need to rethink my sappy attitude. They are where they are because they failed to take responsibly for their own lives. Devoting our time and resources to making a place for them is tantamount to big government coddling. Things are going to change here in the farm too. As for that place, lets run razor wire from it to the zone fencing. Hang signs every hundred feet that say **trespassers are shot.** Mark the trees and posts with the purple paint. Put a chain link cage around the house. Hang the signs on the cage too. It will give us a buffer on that section of the zone. Have patrol check the house every day. Put a chain across its drive. Anything else?"

Charlie thought... *here goes*. "Ma'am that about covers the business end of things. Just want to say you've done a fine job of stepping up. Can't think how any of it could have been done better. I don't think you have to shoulder so much anymore. Nick is really on the mend this morning."

"Thank you for you kind assessment. You know I have always valued your council. As for your Boss, I'm sure when the Captain feels he's up to it he'll return to his duties. Charlie, I think this worked nicely this morning. Would you mind bringing me the reports from now on? It was refreshing to talk about business without all the confrontation."

"That works for me, ma'am. I'll get things moving on that property." The second he closed the door he could hear the words to the song blaring through the house again. 'Fuck, she may have already gone over the edge. Keeping her from the edge was Nick's job. He needed to get off his ass and fix this now. Nobody wanted a 'Nick' running the Farm.'

7:30 am EDT,

Charlie went by the infirmary to check on everyone. Becky had had taken one in the vest that broke two ribs and another in her calf. Charlie found her in good spirits drinking an herbal fruit smoothie Alexandra had made for her. The Huntress was there packing Becky's wound in an herbal poultice. "Morning ladies, Alexandra, how is our girl doing?"

"She's doing well. The comfrey is healing this nicely. Oh Charlie, you said you want to hunt deer. I need to cull two bucks from the herd. As soon as Becky can stand we're going out. You in?"

"Deer hunting with two beautiful women, what could be better? Let me know when."

After making the rounds Charlie ran into Nick getting chewed out by Andy as she checked his wound. "Hey Boss."

Interrupting Andy's tirade Nick asked, "How are *things* this morning?"

"Chilly, real fucking chilly. Think we should rename the building to Snow Castle where the Ice Queen lives."

Nick's head snapped around at this. He moved the dressing and Andy threw Charlie out. "Nick you do realize you would heal faster if A you took my advice and rested and B stop constantly undoing my work!"

8:30 am EDT,

Nick stomped across the yard. In the barn he found two of the farm girls flirting with the men. "What the fuck is going on? This is not a social club. You ladies get yourselves back to the farm. Don't let me find you in here again. And you idiots get this place clean. It looks like a third world outpost. And keep your romantic conquest to the other side of the wall. There's a fucking war out there and last night it nearly breached our gates... AGAIN. Your sloppy work nearly got the Lady killed. The only one who was doing their job properly was Carmichael." Nick stormed back to the house.

Above the ruckus Carmichael was asleep in his bunk. The sound of his name woke him. "What did I do now?"

Lee said, "Go back to sleep. The Boss just said you were the only one doing your job last night." He did go back to sleep with a smile.

Gianna was in the greenhouse talking to Amber and Dawn about production when the two girls Nick had banished came in. One was crying. Gianna wasn't in the best of moods. "What is all this sniveling about?"

"We went to see our boyfriends and that asshole Nick screamed at us and told

391

us never to go to the barn again."

Gianna turned to face them. "Asshole? Are you talking about the man who's job it is to keep the hell that's outside these walls from coming in here and destroying your cushy life? The asshole here is you- both of you. You have no fucking business beyond the east portal. How fucking dare you ignore my orders? You two report to the infirmary and get a good look at the people who nearly sacrificed their lives last night to keep your sorry useless asses safe. You break that rule again and I will put you both out. Do you understand me? I put a Glock to a man's head last night and blew his brains all over me keeping you ungraceful fucks safe. GO!"

Gianna called the infirmary. "Andy I just sent you a pair stupid ungrateful twats. I want them on every shit job you have. Make some up if you have to. Make sure they get a good look at the damage from last night. They are your slaves until I say otherwise. If their parents want to bitch tell them they can do it from outside the walls."

Amber knew her Aunt well. Last night had affected her deeply. "Auntie are you okay?"

"No, but I will be."

"Did you get the blood off your

nightgown?" Amber had seen her Aunt running across the yard in her silk night dress and wrap. Then they heard the fighting.

"No I threw it out."

"I'll clean it. I know it's one of your fave's. We've covered everything here. Why don't you take a nap. I know you, you didn't sleep after that shit." Amber squeezed her Aunt's hand as Gianna left.

Dawn watched Gianna leave. "You know she won't rest. You go take care of the nightgown. I'll handle things here."

9:00 am EDT,

Freddy walked in the back door of the Q farmhouse with a basket of fresh tomatoes. Mendez was sitting at the table like he owned the place. "Mendez what are you doing here?"

"Just relaxing and having coffee. Why what's it to you?"

"Regulars stay on the farm unless otherwise ordered. This place is for the vanguard. So finish you coffee and get your ass back there."

"I don't think you know who I am."

Freddy put the basket down hard

making the asshole's mug jump. "I know exactly who you are. Your the man the Lady said to bunk in the barracks. You have no fucking business lounging around here drinking our coffee."

Nick stepped into the room with Charlie Nick, "Freddy what's up your ass?"

"The Lady made him a regular. Rules say he stays on the other side of the wall. The Lady is on a rampage about following the rules. She just shredded two of the farm girls in the greenhouse for coming over here. She sent them to Andy for all the shit work she could give them and if their parents bitch they can do it outside the wall. So if she walks in here and sees him here, she may shoot him. She's got her scary voice on. You know, the one where you believe she's gonna reach in you chest and rip your heart out while it's still beating." At that moment as if on que, Gianna's voice came over Freddy's radio. "I fuckin told you. Yes ma'am."

Are you back at the Q?"

"Yes ma'am."

"Is that lazy fuck Mendez there? Theo is trying to find him to give him his work assignment."

"Yes ma'am, I just walked in. He's

sitting here drinking coffee."

Through her teeth she rasps. "Send the fuck through the portal now!"

Mendez looked at Nick. Before the Boss got himself in any deeper, Charlie said, "Don't look at Nick. It's her farm, we live here because the Lady lets us. That was a direct order from her. Get your ass out that door." Mendez left slamming the door behind him. Charlie turned to Nick. "Nick, before you say anything we have to talk. You don't know what's going on." Nick looked at the two of them and walked out the back door.

At the portal he could hear a go-cart stop. Then Gianna, "Mendez! I don't know you, I don't like you, and I sure as shit don't trust you. You were forced down my throat by Lorenzini. You will follow my rules. Do you understand me? And if you and Lorenzini don't like it, you both know where the fucking front gate is." Nick listened to her drive away. It felt like there was a vice tightening around his heart. *This* has been his home for ten years. *She's* been his home for ten years. He thought he'd die defending them. Is this his doing? Did he just push her to the edge and let her fall? He'd promised Gia, he'd always be there to pull her back. Nick walked back into the kitchen. Freddy and Charlie asked what happened and he told them what she said. Nick turned to Charlie, "I guess we better have that conversation. What is it I don't know?" Freddy took his cue and left.

10:30 am EDT,

Theo saw Gianna coming and cringed. He still had nothing on Sean and now, no way but the HAM radio to try to find anything. She'd stopped asking but he can see the question in her eyes.

"Theo, I found that stupid fuck Mendez. He was over in the Q. I left him by the portal. Put him to work, no soft guard duty for him. Make sure who he's working with watches him. I don't trust him. And fuck Nick for forcing him on me."

Theo though it best not to voice an opinion either way. "Let's sit and I can give you the news. We are in wonderful shape on production and harvesting. Stephen says we have enough feed to get us through to May or June. Simon has finished with the pork. Oh my God the bacon is amazing. Amber and Dawn are producing so much food we have caners working four days a week. Unfortunately the infirmary is doing a big business but Andy says she hasn't scratched the surface on the surplus yet.

"You want the gossip now? Dawn has been seeing Freddy. That's why there's always fresh produce in the Q these days.

You remember that was a problem for awhile. I think Alexandra has something going on but she won't tell. Ch the only thing Andy seems to be going through at a higher rate are condoms. She says near death situations make humans want to procreate; thank God they're just having good sex."

Gianna had been listening with her head back and eyes closed. Now she opened one eye and asked, "Theo, how are you so sure the sex is good?"

"I don't really, I just wanted to see if you were paying attention."

Gianna cracked up. "You're such an idiot. Enough with the Mary Poppins number what's the bad news. I know there's nothing about Sean so just skip to the second item."

"Well there's not much for the tech people so I've utilized them in other areas. They're on three hour shifts so that frees them up. Two of them are my personal office slaves because, while the world may have come to an end, office work hasn't. Have I told you lately how exhausting it is being your brain?"

"Not today dear."

"As for legal, let's just hope they never bring law and order back and make it retroactive. Cause then, *You'll* be going to jail. I'm fairly certain I can get the girls off on self defense. Your gun was just too big. Oh, never thought I'd hear those words coming out of my mouth. Anyway, bringing a tank to a gun fight, would be the definition of overkill."

"I see you have your Grand Poobah hat on today. Have 'Fred and Barney' called a meeting of the 'Loyal Order of Water Buffaloes' or is there another reason you're walking around the office in a fur hat with horns?"

"There was an ugly rumor going around this morning, that you were less than your normal sweet self. I didn't believe it, but in the event I was mistaken, which as you know I almost never am, I thought it would afford me some protection in the event... that the ugly rumor was true."

Gianna sat up, "The ugly rumor is true my dear, I'm so happy you got a chance to wear your hat."

11:30 am EDT,

Nick was sitting on the veranda, boots on the rail, halfway through a bottle of Jack Daniels, mulling over what Charlie had to say. It was a lot. Most of it had crossed Nick's mind but he'd shoved it aside.

He'd fallen for the front she shows the world. He'd missed the signs that were right there. Charlie was right, Gianna always steps up, whatever the task, even when she knows what it will cost her. The perfect paradise they'd created was in grave danger and she was afraid she wouldn't be able to protect it, and the people in it. Even the Amazon Queen has moments of doubt. She was afraid of failing them and it.

He asked himself, not for the first time, 'So why have I been so antagonistic to her? I had just seen her on the verge of tears.' Charlie shed some light on that. She had gone to the infirmary and found the bed empty. She thought Nick had died during the night. A nurse told Charlie, all the blood drained out of her face. Even after she told Gianna, Nick walked out, she was still shaking. 'What do I want from her? Why did I keep jabbing her with the outfit? I wanted her to know I wasn't joking... I would have died happy with that image of her in my head. I want from her what I'm not willing to give.'

Nick poured himself another four fingers of ol'Jack. His internal dialog switched to external. "Well, I'm glad I got to the bottom of that. Now, how the fuck do I fix what I broke? I'm drunker than I thought or is she really walking to the barn dressed in her *Sarah Connor* outfit? Got to be an hallucination, she's

got aviators on. She hates those they get
caught in her hair.

Where was I... oh yah, got to fix
what I broke. An apology, right... but in
what form? I'm sorry probably isn't going
to cut it. I said that at the table. Then
I was an asshole. I can't give her a
reason cause we're *not* going to open that
Pandora's box right now. The whole world
is a fucking Pandora's box right now.
Where is Reno going in Pepé? This is
fucked up. *Sarah Connor* is sitting in
Pepé with Reno."

"Boss... *Nick*, do you know you're
talking out loud... to yourself?"

"Hey Charlie, what did you say?"

"I said you're drunk on your ass,
talking out loud to yourself! *AND* that's
not *Sarah Connor* or an *hallucination*!
It's the Lady going out on recon. I
thought you were going to fix this...
instead you're sitting here getting
drunk. That woman leaving the gate is
what I wanted you to prevent. The guys
don't get it. After last night they think
she can do anything."

Charlie's words were starting to get
through to Nick. "Shit! Charlie, get me a
vehicle now!"

"No way you're driving anything. You
can't even stand without holding onto the

railing. I'm not taking you cause she left me in charge. I'm not letting any of the men see you drunk chasing after her. Did you think about anything we talked about before you got shit faced? Sit down before you fall of the veranda. Drunk people aren't suppose to fall off verandas. Porches are for drunks to fall off of." Charlie got Nick back in the chair. He went to move the bottle away but thought better of it. If Nick has one or two more he'll fall asleep and not try to go and find her. "So did you think about it or is this a pity drunk?"

"The term is pity party not pity drunk. *And yes I did.* I got to the underlying cause of of my behavior. And I was working on what type of apology would work when *Sarah Connor Gianna* walked by. Then you came in or out."

"Did you think about telling her the truth, as in the underlying cause?"

"No, can't do that. Can't go there... right now... with *her*. There's too much at stake here on the farm. Instead of irritating me and offering people rocks to hit me with, why don't you help me think of an apology?"

"That was yesterday."

"What was yesterday?"

"The rock. I offered to give her a

rock to hit you with yesterday."

"Charlie, why would you do that on any day?"

"Wish I had given her the rock. Then whatever you did to upset her when you left here wouldn't have happened."

"Ya know Charlie, I wish you had too."

"Do you want another drink?"

"NO, I want to be able to walk when *Gianna Connor* gets back."

"What's the underlying cause?"

"An agreement we made years ago. I want her to break her side of it but I don't think I want to break my side of it."

"That's fucked up. I don't even understand what you're talking about and I know it's fucked up."

"It is fucked up. That's why I can't tell her what *the underlying cause* is. So we're back to the apology."

Having worn out the subject of the underlying cause, they both fell silent pondering the apology. Nick's head was starting to clear enough to understand how fucked up he got. "Hey Charlie would

you make me some coffee?" Charlie went to
make the coffee thinking they all might
be better off if Nick was passed out when
the Lady got back but since that ship has
sailed he might as well sober him up.

12:30 pm EDT,

    After the third cup Nick went to
take a piss. He had just stepped back
onto the veranda when they heard the
shots. Charlie jumped up - he counting
three... then Reno's semi-automatic...
then a Glock fires one two three four
then a fifth. Nick and Charlie were
opening the gates. The guard are taking
their positions... the sound of a truck
breaking free of the bush... tires on the
pavement... Pepé is hauling ass... as
Reno slides through the gate a body rolls
off the hood.

    Getting out of the truck Reno shouts
"My radio was hit."

    Gianna got out the other side
shouting, "Burn that mother fucker... he
shot me." By the time Nick got around the
truck she was holding on the roll-bar
standing on one leg with blood running
down the other. His heart was pounding in
his chest Nick ripped the pant leg to
check the wound. It'd gone though her
outer thigh... it's just a flesh wound.
Standing he pulled her to his chest then
picked her up and headed for the
Infirmary. Charlie radioed Andy.

403

Her arms around his neck, her faced pressed against his shoulder, he's sure she could the fear raging through his veins. He rasps "You're a fucking *exasperating woman!*"

"Put me down you fool! You shouldn't be carrying me you'll rip your stitches."

"Quiet woman. I know where I can get more."

Inside the infirmary Nick set her on the gurney. He's trying to assess how much blood she's lost. Andy tells the nurse to cut Gianna pants off her. "OH No you don't! These are my fave!" Gianna slid off the gurney and started to unbutton, she glanced over her shoulder at the faces crowding in the doorway. "This is not a fucking peep show! Clear the fucking room." Everyone backed out but a nurse, Andy, Doc and Nick.

Andy was shaking her head NO. Nick's on the floor slipping the pants over her foot getting blood all over his hands. He stood lifting her on to the gurney and pulled the other leg free. "Andy she's all yours. If she gets up again call me, I'll come and hold her down."

Gianna grabbed his arm and pulled him to her, she can smell the fear pulsing off him, she whispered in his ear. "Now you know how it feels." Then she pushed him away. "Get you stitches looked at NOW."

1:30 pm EDT

Forty-five minutes later, leg stitched, dressed and wrapped, Gianna is ready to leave. "Where are my pants?"

The nurse said "Nick took them."

"Ahggggg He's such an asshole."

Alexandra rushed in "I saw him leave with them Auntie I ran and got you these from your house.

"Thanks babe. All right. Everybody stop fussing. This was a walk in the park after giving birth."

Andy says, "That local's going to wear off what do you want for pain?"

"That would be why the Goddess gave us Vodka. Thank you honey and thanks for not cutting my pants."

Andy shook her head. "Don't thank me, that was all Nick. If he hadn't gotten them off you so fast I would have cut them."

Gianna turned to find all four sister cousins looking at her. "Stop... all he did was take my pants off. You're all so bad."

Sadie put her arm around her mother to help Gianna to the cart. She says "Yeah mom, *he just took your pants off,* but you've been going commando for years."

"Smart ass, just get me to the cart. I need to get back over there."

Sadie and Gianna round the corner of the Q house to find Nick in front of Pepé yelling at the men. They go a few more steps and stop. Gianna yelled across the yard "Hey, Lorenzini, Where the fuck did you go with my pants?" Nick turned to look at her. Everyone else was looking at Nick. Then so only Sadie can hear, "Gotcha asshole. He'll have quite a few uncomfortable moments explaining that one to the men."

On the veranda a smiling Charlie says to Reno, "And... they're back."

Reno asks, "Yeah but why the hell did he take her pants?"

Chapter 18
SHE WON'T GET FOOLED AGAIN

"Not to be argumentative, but... No."

4:40 pm EDT, October 3,
Dancing Goats Farm
Moon Mountain, North Carolina

Theo was having a moment of quiet after a day of dealing with the insane behavior of too many people. 'Now that 'Mom & Dad' have stopped fighting, things should start running smoother. It's a shame mom had to get shot to end the bickering, but since she's not too damaged it was worth it, to have peace in the kingdom again. Maybe she'll give Nick back his job and stop all this gun play. The snot-zi thing, well that had to be done. But this new thing of hers... running around having people killed, shooting people in the head... this has to stop. Maybe the leg will slow her down.

Gianna limped into the Q kitchen. Charlie, Reno, and Nick were seated around the table. They look up at her entrance and a wicked grin spreads across Nick's face. She looked him in the eye, raises one eyebrow, and said, "Don't even think about it. If hear the words 'hop or along' out of your mouth I'll be wearing your huevos for earrings."

Nick got up still grinning and pulled out a chair for her. He helped her navigate watching her face tighten as she sits. She doesn't take pain meds because they make her sick. He knows too well how much effort it just took not to make a sound when she sat. He leaned down to her ear and whispered, "Nice to see you too."

Before anyone else can speak "Let's skip all the how are you's and get right to business, but first, thank you for your efforts on my behalf. Reno, that was some amazing driving to get me back here, thank you. And not to be forgotten let's have a round of applause for, right off the cover of a romances novel - Nick, for sweeping me off my feet and saving my fave pants from Andy and her wicked scissors." Reno and Charlie are loving it, they start clapping and hooting.

Still grinning, Nick shakes his head. The scene had been anything but romantic. His heart had been pounding from the second she uttered the words 'he shot me'. The blood was causing a drag on the frigging pants. He was trying not to cause her any more pain, his fingers kept losing their grip cause they were covered

in her blood. It felt like an eternity,
in reality it took him maybe fifteen
seconds to get her ass back on the table.
When he'd picked her up he could feel she
was shuddering from the pain. It may well
be his record time for getting a woman's
pants off but romantic it wasn't. And her
parting comment... yeah he now knew what
he had put her through.'

Later, Reno told him the guy had
come at her from the side and caught her
in the leg, then he jumped up on the hood
and tried to shoot her from above. She
was ready and pumped five rounds into him
before he fell on the hood. When he heard
this Nick had gone and dumped the bastard
in a burn barrel, rolled it outside the
gate and torched him.

The guard were looking at him
questioningly when he came back inside. A
few of their faces showed worry. Nick
shrugged it off by saying "The Lady said
burn the motherfucker, so I did. Let it
be a warning to any other asshole who
thinks he wants to shoot her."

Nick realized his thoughts had
wandered. 'What did she want with that
farm?'

"Charlie what's happened with the farm?
Have we made any progress?"

"The cage is up, the post painted,
and the signs hung. It'll take a another

day to run the razor wire."

"What is the purpose of this?" Nick asked.

"It's changed since it first came up. At first I thought we should have a safe house for people we won't let in. Then all this shit happened now I've got my head on straight, fuck them. They should have been doing what we have for the last ten years. Maybe not on the scale we have but something. I've listened to their whiney ass... *it's too hard*, for years. Or *I don't have the time*... bullshit. All they had was time. Oh, another thing, I want to make sure the men are not going to crumble when some mother and child comes crying at the gate. Anyone you think might, should not be on the gate. We've taken that farm as a buffer. Those snot-zi fucks attacked us from there. The two that rammed the gate in the zone, one of them was Ethan. He's the one Violet shot. Then the double attack - on the zone fence and the morons I took out with Audrey, and then the group with Colter. Who knows if the three we got out of the house wouldn't have tried again. So now it's ours."

Nick doesn't like her hardened tone but it makes sense strategically. Nick says, "It would be helpful if we could find more fencing. Charlie, have the recons keep an eye out for places we can pick some up. We really need to make a run to town to find out what's going on. See what they have for a government and law enforcement. It can't be much with the attacks and gun fights going unnoticed. You shot off a tank and no one came to check. I'll make a run tomorrow."

Gianna looked over at him. "Nick, please wait another day. Give your shoulder one more day to heal. Let Alexandra put some herbs on it this evening."

Nick was about to say no, when her words echoed in his head. "You're probably right, another day wouldn't hurt. I did strain it when I *had* to carry you."

Gianna slapped the table. "What were the first words I ever said to you? '*I could have handled it myself*' remember? You didn't *have* to carry me - you're just a show off."

Charlie banged his hand on the table. "Come on, you kids were playing so nice don't start that shit. I have work to do. Where the hell is Freddy? He keeps vanishing."

Gianna said, "I bet you'll find him down by the greenhouses. Theo told me Freddy and Dawn are a thing."

Reno got up too. "I need to check over Pepé. I was pretty hard on him."

With the room to themselves Nick asked, "How bad is the pain?"

"I think a very very very very a lot, about covers it. I should go find a very tall vodka."

"Gia, stay, there are a few more things I'd like to cover. I have some Rain up here I keep for you and because you're a lightweight who can't drink straight booze, we have pomegranate juice." Nick made her a drink and placed it in front of her. "We need to address the Mendez thing. If you really want him gone I'll send him on his way. I think it's foolish to evict a trained soldier, but it's your call. You want to tell me what the problem is with him?"

Gianna thought about it for a minute. "Mostly bad timing. It's been a rough week. First I had to kill the snot-zis, you got shot and had just gone into surgery, DJ and Antonio were hurt and I looked up and saw a stranger in our nest and a Fed no less. My bad attitude snowballed from there. You know what a cunt I am when things don't go my way."

"Ya, *I know*. 'Be reasonable do it my way and nobody gets hurt' is your rule around here."

"Then, the first thing I tell him to do he gives me shit. I know the FBI has

412

rules but the FBI is gone, at least right now. He needs to get his head around the fact that you and I are the Law here. If I say give me your papers, you hand them over. You don't go FBI cocky on me. I was a heartbeat away from changing his lodgings to H&G.

I was in the middle of a fucking difficult situation and he balks at an order in front of the men *and* the prisoners. It was a hellish situation. If I shot them, then what would we have done with the kids? Are we going to start shooting children because their parents might attack us? I did enjoy the look on that dickheads face when Jackson stepped up to shoot him. His worst nightmare, being shot by a black man. Now *that* was justice."

Nick studied her as she spoke looking for signs of damage from the situation he left her to deal with.

"I believed I'd made the right choice right up to the moment when I realized the people I'd sent out were being shot at. I should have found another way to deal with them."

There it was, the guilt that comes when someone is injured or dies following your order. She had her hands over her face rubbing her temples. He took one hand down. "Look at me, I would have made the same call. There is nothing wrong

413

with the way you handled it. The only thing I would have done differently would have been to send a third vehicle. But I have twenty-six years of combat experience, you don't. *And* if I hadn't been such a fucking asshole I would have been in there with you. Everything would have gone the same way. It may have gone better without me because you connected with the woman in a way I couldn't. Our people got shot not because of your choices but because the world has become a war zone. No matter what I say to you, you'll still feel badly about the injured. I always do, it's part of what makes you a good leader."

She pulled her hand away and adjusted her hair clip. "You're right it doesn't really help the guilt. Thank you. Nick, I really do like those pants. Would you like to tell me where they went? I've had them as long as I've had you."

Smiling he told her, "I sent them to be cleaned and mended. I was a little rough when I ripped them to see how bad the wound was."

"Thank you."

"For ripping them or having them fixed?"

"Both."

"You made a very good point about

the men on the gate. I'm going to interview each of them over the next few days. Starting now, I will resume full command of the men. You can take that off your list. No more reconing with the guys for you, Lady."

"Not to be argumentative, but, no. You're not going to put Gianna back in the box. *As previously discussed* I know, I could have made a very good serial killer. A *Dexter*... not all the slicing, just putting bad dogs down. Here's my chance. I see that stubborn set of your jaw Nicholas. It's your own fault. You never should have let me loose. Now sweet cheeks you can train me and take me with you or I'll just go it alone."

Nick brought his fist down on the table nearly upsetting her drink. "*You are, without a doubt, the most exasperating woman to ever have walked the earth!*" He could see by the set of her jaw he was never going to win this one. "Fine, but you're going to have to learn how to shoot the big guns. You can't go out there with just a hand gun." She started to speak, "Don't... this morning you were lucky. Do you understand you were a split second from being dead? You shot him five times because you were angry and frightened. You'll learn to fight calm and cool or you'll be cooling your ass on the farm. Oh, I burned the guy who shot you as you asked."

"I know, thank you. Nice touch leaving the barrel out front."

5:30 pm EDT,

Nick noticed at the relaxed way she's leaning on her elbow holding up her chin. "Yep, that drink is have a very relaxing effect on you. If I weren't a romance novel hero, I'd say you're drunk lady. Let's get you in the cart. I'll drive you home. You need to stay off that leg."

"Oh, you mean, I have to baby it, like you've been doing with your shoulder?"

He getting her out of the chair... between the leg and the five ounces of vodka he gave her, she almost went down. "This is not going to work." He put her over his shoulder and carried her out to the cart.

"Nick-o-las, this seems to be becoming a habit. Noooot shur how I feel about this."

He set her on the seat. "I'd say by the way you're slurring your words, you're feeling just fine." He backed up and heads for the manor house.

"You have your serious face on. What are you thinking about?"

416

"I'm thinking about what I might want you to agree to while you're in such an *amiable* state of mind... Such as, not going out on runs with guns."

She laughed at him. "Nope... I'm not *that* drunk. Be a lamb and help me up the stairs and *not* like I'm a sack of feed. People will start talking."

"They're always talking about us, and some of it isn't very nice." He grabbed her around the waist and got her up the stairs. "The couch or up stairs?" She pointed to the couch. "There's an ugly rumor that you shredded two farm girls and offered to evict their families."

"It's true. All the ugly rumors are true. They called you an asshole. That privilege is mine alone."

"Is there anything you want before I leave?"

"Another drink would be lovely darling." While he's making it she says. "Nicholas, I'm really very happy you're not dead."

He put the drink in front of her. "I'm sure. Who'd make your drinks for you?... Me too." He brushed her hair out of her eyes and left.

On his way back to the Q he passed

Freddy and Dawn. *Guess they are a thing.
Theo is the All Seeing Eye around here.*
He pulled up to the Shack to check in
with Adrian and Ferret to see if there's
any news about Sean. He hasn't forgotten
his promise to her. Adrian and Ferret
caught Nick up on the rumors and facts on
the world outside their gates. People are
leaving rural areas seeking protection in
the cities from gangs and wholesale
violence rampant in the countryside.

The ocean waters are still rising.
For six months prior to the earth
changes, the twin scourges of red tides
and Cyanobacteria had plagued Florida.
Now with Florida under water, the blue-
green algae blooms that had tainted
Florida's lakes, canals and rivers has
spread to every fresh water source across
the entire southeast. The ocean tides are
all red. People are not only running from
the rising water, they have to move even
farther inland to avoid the toxic stench
of the millions of dead marine animals
piling up on the new coastlines. Hundreds
of humans have died from contact with the
water. The lack of food has driven some
to try to harvest the dead fish. The
absence of medical aid has left them
dying from vomiting, diarrhea and
pneumonia. Raleigh is two miles from the
shore.

There is no Federal government in
DC. A few places are claiming they're it
but they have no way to communicate or

418

regroup the military. The few states that are functioning have closed their borders.

Canada is not letting anyone in. The **Mexican government** has fallen. Volcanic eruptions, earthquakes, and rising water have taken every country south of Mexico. There is no longer a land bridge between North and South America.

In Europe tornadoes of rotating columns of fire have caused a wave of destruction. The winds caused power line towers to collapse, uprooted trees, removed bark from some, and consumed 1,500 structures in one town.

Sweden's Kebnekaise mountain, has lost it's glacier causing water shortages.

6:00 pm EDT,

Leaving the Shack Nick sees people heading to the Hall for dinner. Tyler and Amber are swinging Angelena between them. Nick pulled a U turn. 'A meal with people would be a nice change. Normal families gathering for dinner. Laughter, no talk of war and killing, simply enjoying each others' company.' Tyler and Amber wave him over to their table. Crossing the room he wondered if these people knew how lucky they were? He and Tyler started in right away discussing the grid.

419

Amber said she'd get Nick a plate. She returned with a porter house, black and rare. Simon had seen him come in and prepared it for him, for getting Queeny to the infirmary so quickly. Angelena told Uncle Nicky it was good to be the queen. He answered he imagined it was. The sisters joined them as Amber asked about her Aunt. Nick said when he'd left her she was feeling no pain. The steak was excellent but the company was better. It seemed almost everyone stopped by the table to thank him for Gianna, keeping them safe, or for not getting killed. He spent a few minutes with Mendez. He told him he'd spoken to Gianna and the two of them should start over. Mendez agreed he was beginning to see why she fought so hard to keep this place a secret. Nick thought the redhead he was having dinner with helped too. Driving back he saw the sisters going in to check on their mother. 'It had been her vision and between them, they had built an amazing place. Life was really fucking good here. He'd find a way to keep it safe or die trying.'

7:00 pm EDT,

Charlie and Reno were on the veranda when Nick got back. Reno said he made chili - it's on the stove if Nick wants a bowl. "Thanks, Simon made me a perfect steak. I had dinner with the family. I haven't done that in far too long. Amber is a pisser. Sadie is just fucking funny.

And tonight I learned from Angelena *'It's good to be the queen'*."

Charlie asked,"Speaking of the queen how is her leg?"

"When I left her at 5:30 she was feeling no pain."

"Don't tell me you finally killed her with your fighting?"

"NO, we had a very civilized conversation after you left. She was in pain so I made her a drink. Then she wasn't in any condition to get herself home. I took her home, made her another drink, so she'd stay there. She was alive when I left her. Then I went to talk to Adrian. I saw Tyler and Amber so I had dinner with them. Anything else you want to know about my day?"

"Yeah, Did you settle the Mendez situation with her?"

"I think we worked through it. Saw Mendez at the Hall; he's willing to start over and she'll give him a shot. The only thing that was an issue is the Lady is going to be training to go out on raids. She likes killing bad guys."

Charlie nearly jumped out of his chair. "We're suppose to keep her safe in here. What the hell are you thinking?"

"My options were, I train her and take her out or she'll go out on her own. Either of you want to be the one to tell her she can't leave? I managed one condition. She has to be able to use the big guns. If that's all, I'm going to see what going on downstairs."

7:43 pm EDT,

Carmichael radioed in from the loft... "We have a small herd of civilians moving up the road. They're approaching the gate. Antonio was on light duty in the command room. He reached for the button to alert Gianna.

Nick warned him, "Touch that button and I will break your arm. Let her sleep. If it's a problem *I* will tell her." Outside Reno was already going up the tower steps. Charlie was in the entrance of the barn with a few of the guard. Nick climbed the tower steps two at a time. Outside the gate there was a ragged bunch of 14 men, 5 women, 3 kids. The leader was banging on the gate begging to be let in. Nick yelled, "We won't open the gate. Go away we have nothing for you. I have my own family to think about."

"But my wife and child are hungry you can't turn us away it's not Christian."

Nick scoffed. "We're not Christian and yes I'm turning you away. *Your* family is not *my* problem."

The leader begins yelling,
"Bastard, devil worshipers! Take it
down!" The mob began to beat on the gate
trying in vane to take it down.

These people present no danger.
They're more of a annoyance. Nick is
irritated at their intrusion into what
had been a perfectly enjoyable evening.
"Hold your fire. Hopefully they'll
leave." Off to the left one of them is
climbing a tree to hoping to jump to the
wall. His annoyance escalated to pissed.
"You have ten seconds before I start
shooting." To Reno he says, "Wing the
asshole in the tree." The man fell
screaming. Some of the crowd ran, some
just move back from the gate. The leader
pulled out a hand gun and was trying to
see where Nick is.

Now he's fucking aggravated.
"Carmichael." the man fell dead. "Who
else wants to die?" The rest ran off into
the night. "Reno, leave the body there,
we'll deal with it in the morning. I am
going to try and get some sleep. *Do not*
wake her unless I say so. She's had
enough the last three days."

8:32 pm EDT,

Nick's head hit the pillow, sure
he'd sleep like the dead. But sleep
eludes him. He hasn't had this much shit

happen in one day since his last tour. In his head the days events keep playing in a loop. It keeps getting stuck on the words 'he shot me'. He really should open that box and see what's inside, but not tonight.

An hour later the faces of the family at dinner hover in his mind; Angelena calling him Uncle Nicky, Sadie entertaining him with her colorful rendition of the morning's events, Amber making sure he was properly fed, this was the family he never thought he'd have. He's surprised at how important they are to him now. He drifted asleep wondering why it never occurred to him before tonight.

10:45 pm EDT,

Ferret was in the shack skimming through the channels when she heard a word that made her double back. Yes, the guy is saying *ZOMBIES*. This has got to be a joke. She listened for a half hour. At least four people in the conversation were talking about zombie attacks in their towns. She picked up the radio and called the command room. Antonio answered; she tells him what channel and asks him to listen and then call her back. She doesn't know the town. Her ingrained Hackers caution doesn't want them to know she's there unless she has to.

At 11:00 pm Antonio and Reno called her back. The town is Flat Rock. They don't think it's a joke but they don't believe in zombies either. Reno says they will keep checking the area. They'll let her know if they find out anything, and she should do the same.

This is too fucking freaky. She calls Adrian. Ten minutes later all of Python house has piled into the room listening to the crazy shit. At 1:00 am JonJon asked if they should tell Theo. Sammy says, "*Right*, wake the Grand Poobah and tell him there are zombies a few miles away... be my guest. I'm not doing it." JonJon joined in the conversation with the HAM operators. He gave his location as Mount Airy, then started asking questions the group in the room were feeding him.

By 4:00 am they have a collection of insane stories and Antonio called back with confirmation it's not a joke. He heard a police car transmission, the cop was calling in a case of zombies. They shot one guy five times and he kept getting back up - they had to shoot him in the head to stop him. The cops were called because the guy was in the street eating a dog alive. Reno says send someone over with a copy of the stories they've collected.

4:55 am EDT, October 4,
Dancing Goats Farm

425

Moon Mountain, North Carolina

With trepidation Reno knocked on Nick's door. "Come." When Reno's head appeared a slightly annoyed Nick said, "Reno, I don't dream very often and this one was really hot, so this better be dam good."

"Sorry Nick, I don't know how to tell you this, there are reports of zombies in a town fives miles away."

Nick sat up and rubbed the sleep from his eyes. "I'm going to need coffee for this one."

"Just made a fresh pot. I figured you'd want several for this shit. I'll down in the kitchen."

While Nick is sliding into his Jeans, Reno was pouring coffee, and the Zombie Maker rolled his Spyder to a stop in the sleepy town of Moon Mountain, North Carolina.

Reno set the mugs on the table thinking, that must have been one hell of a dream cause he was sure Nick was going to punch him when he woke him for a zombie attack, instead he'd just asked for coffee?

Nick picked up the mug, inhaled half the cup, set it down, sat down, and said "What the fuck is a zombie attack?"

Reno started with Ferret's call and ended with the last cop call about a woman eating a cat, on her front stoop, naked. When the cops tried to stop her she tried to bite them, they tased her but she still kept coming, they shot her, she got back up, so they shot her in the head.

Nick rubbed his hands over his face. *"This is unfucking unbelievable."*

Reno sat back and asked "Now do we wake her up?"

The brisk morning air jolted Nick another few degrees awake. He needed to figure out what this zombie shit was. He couldn't seem to stay focused. The dream kept drifting to the front of his thoughts. Out loud he said, "This is what happens when you get more than six hours sleep. You start dreaming!... thoughts of running your hand up silken thighs keeps you from concentrating on your job!"

He found Gianna asleep on the couch where he'd left her. She looked so quiet. He savored the silence for a moment. The quiet would be gone the second he told her of the zombies. Softly he called her name. She woke up swinging. When she saw it was Nick she relaxed and rubbed the sleep from her eyes and asked "What time is it?"

"It's almost 5:30."

Sitting up she said, "By that very 'Nick's Not Happy' look on your face I'm guessing it's not good news. What fresh hell has the morning brought us? Wait I need coffee and something for my head and leg first."

Nick helped her to stand and went to make her coffee. She returned as he was placing the cups on the counter. "Well that was fun, trying to not pee on my bandage. I don't suppose you had that problem when you got shot last year."

Nick laughed "No, but now we have matching scars."

Holding her head Gianna said, "This may come as a surprise Nicholas, but matching bullet scars was not something I was looking forward to sharing with you. Crap, I don't know which hurts worse, my head or my leg. Who knew the apocalypse would be so fucking exhausting *and* eventful?"

Nick took a bottle of Excedrin out of the cabinet and put two in her hand. She smiled gratefully and gulped them down with the coffee Nick handed her. "Okay, I'm medicated, what is it today?" Nick took a breath, held it, exhaled slowly then explained the... fresh hell du jour.